THIS
BRUTAL
HOUSE

ALSO BY NIVEN GOVINDEN

We Are The New Romantics
Graffiti My Soul
Black Bread White Beer
All the Days and Nights

THIS
BRUTAL
HOUSE

NIVEN
GOVINDEN

dialogue
books

DIALOGUE BOOKS

First published in Great Britain in 2019 by Dialogue Books

10 9 8 7 6 5 4 3 2

A CIP catalogue record for this book
is available from the British Library.

HB ISBN 978-0-349-70070-0

Typeset in Berling by M Rules
Printed and bound in Great Britain by
Clays Ltd, Elcograf S.p.A.

Papers used by Dialogue Books are from well-managed forests
and other responsible sources.

Dialogue Books
An imprint of
Little, Brown Book Group
Carmelite House
50 Victoria Embankment
London EC4Y 0DZ

An Hachette UK Company
www.hachette.co.uk

www.littlebrown.co.uk

CONTENTS

And no one stands up
Our silence stands up for us

Ilya Kaminsky

Witness the dark night of the soul in
individual saints

Flannery O'Connor

Voguing came from shade

Willi Ninja

INTO GREAT SILENCE

1.

We had Church here: on the steps of City Hall, waiting for answers they were reluctant to give. Power in silence over voice. Communion in holding hands; our flesh raw from molten candle wax; a chain unbroken. We had been taught from infancy that with pain comes purpose – comfort too, but prayer could rarely provide this once our children began to disappear. Our actions were fearful but emboldened, understanding in those first days that this had to happen now: our presence; a physical mass of our discontent. That as elders and mothers to these children, it was our duty to organise, to bring the candles and the people; to stand on those steps whilst they sweated inside City Hall and formulated their response. For as long as it took, we would wait.

We had a Church: a banqueting hall above a Korean supermarket, long neglected and dependent on our dollar. We worshipped in the parts of town that were still open to us; where we could not serve as reminders to various bigots of how nature could warp and deform. For all the progress our people made, however best we served them, loyal to our name and our origins, we were disapproved of, and unwelcome in our family neighbourhoods. We had to forget ourselves, regress, if we wanted to make a life there; which we could not do. We – men; older than the children who flocked around us, drawn to the vogue balls we created, the family we promised – became Mothers because we no longer had mothers of our own. We were drawn together by the air of absence that framed us; sadness matching sadness, unspoken but acknowledged. Within this space we created our Church, where joy and fierceness could reside; but also something beyond that: a higher consciousness to reach.

We stood on the steps of City Hall, reaching higher.

2.

It is our lawful right to protest. They cannot tell us otherwise. We are entitled to our rage, and to use this anger. It underlies our efforts to draw the community into the square where City Hall lies, making it clear to the children that we feel as they do; that we are bone tired from having to be strong, ashamed of our failings as protectors, and sick from the violence which we cannot escape. Mostly we are tired. It lines our faces and dampens our movement. We would lie down and hide were it not for this anger, which needles and keeps us awake; which sends us to the all-night printer to create leaflets; sets our feet across every nightclub, bathhouse and cruising joint to distribute them. We walk along cinema aisles, and across seats, where members of our Houses are giving out hand-jobs and the like to cover the rent. We remain in the era of community and brotherhood, whereby the children would turn down a trick once they understood why it was important to join our cause. Their obedience gave us strength; their docility as each followed the other on to the street and towards the square made our cheeks flush; how persuasion could be successfully deployed. The complainers were those whose needs went beyond mere remuneration: sex occupying a destroyed space that could never be filled. Still, this was anger that we could harness, so long as they too complied.

We were capable of leading armies in more progressive times; how the country could have utilised our talents were the culture a more compassionate one and we were not so afraid. If military success can stem from luck over judgement, benevolence from the unknown over what is planned; our contribution would have carried heft. Pride of America in our bearing; what can be read in our eyes. Instead, we must channel it here: two hundred strong at City Hall's steps, and unmoving. From a long-held wish to command, we lead, clearing blocks step by step; an even pace held until the stragglers at the back fall into sync. We will not leave this place until we are heard, until there is satisfaction. Children who disappear cannot return. We know this. But we need the fact of their disappearances to matter; for those agencies in charge to listen and act. How it should not only be lost pageant queens whose faces grace the back of milk cartons but girls who are trapped inside the bodies of boys; those who break out of their incarceration by wearing make-up; boys who like boys; kids who come from nothing; children who are yet to understand the true creature they are, something beyond their origins. We are asking for our concerns to be taken seriously; for their lives to be investigated if there is hope, honoured if there is not. We need another to share our burden for we are at the point of crumbling; unbelieved and unheard.

Children disappeared from us for years. We lost Sherry, TyTy and Diamonds. We lost groups of banjee boys who were our nexus. T-girls with airs, desiring a greater life than we could provide. We could embroider quilts to cover this nation twice over, with the names of those we loved: those young people in our care who went out and did not return.

They will not hear us outside City Hall, for we say nothing; our bearing and gestures urge the children not to speak. We wish those inside to fear the silent minority; the weight of what is unsaid conjoining, growing, as planets slowly take their form over millennia through the accumulation of rocks and dust. We are the dark matter that rises above the front doors and threatens to consume them. They should fear as we now fear; jump through hoops if it gives them the relief they crave and the answers we need. Only silence, the promise of silence can deliver this. Slogans and missiles mean nothing, for society has built them to deflect such attacks; nuisance flies to be swatted away. Now that our previous attempts have failed – using their methods; their agency: bureaucracy and all the playacting involved there – this approach is the only way.

We reached our position through trial and error; wasted years adhering to the official channels of complaint; registering our dissent through community action and the ballot box. Years of putting faith into the power of statistics at the ballot box; how power could be swayed by tipping the balance in marginal precincts; our energy focused on the campaign trail, believing that it was in our power to inform and persuade. When that failed, we attempted direct action – we recognised that we did not have decades to regroup, politically, nor did we have the taste for it; patronised and belittled, forced into a ghetto they viewed as essential to our enlightenment – taking to the streets in the spirit of our community-organising and activist forebears; an arsenal of placards and loudspeakers, baseball bats and rocks. Their thinking was that we would fear the rows of turned-out riot police, military in their bearing, but as threatening as country barn-dancers; that tear gas would contain us, when we had lived with nightclub smoke machines most of our adult lives, and learned how to see past the mist. We were pissed and no longer afraid.

We finally had use for the bodies we had spent so long starving and pumping. We learned the power of our physical strength. All that we had shied away from as children we discovered now: how far a rock could be thrown by a single hand; the furthest we could run when chased; the speed at which our blood glucose was assimilated after physical exertion; the power of our voices; the solidity of our fists. Battles on our neighbourhood street corners; blood spilling on the steps of our markets and dry-cleaners. We took pleasure in learning that a punch landing correctly upon soft flesh is a tangible result; one that cannot be discounted as an ineligible vote by righteous town hall staff, or lost in City administration paperwork, lodged among stacks of other investigations. We understood how fear could be successfully employed to our ends if we remained consistent in both our actions and our number. That we were not the weaker party in these episodes; our knowledge of the streets, our physical prowess, and the force of our anger propelled us further than we would have otherwise dared.

We found success through rioting, making our dissatisfaction known. Effecting prolonged change was harder still. We were not prepared. What we had not factored on was how our spirit would be weakened by a sustained assault on our home streets; how it was impossible to switch off; smoke and blood trailing our movements; the imprint of a gloved fist sending us to sleep atop our battlefields. (The owner of the dry-cleaner's beaten by the police, mistaking him for one of us, but not the 'us' they were thinking of.) Our voice was strong but there was nothing healthy in our attitude, often ready to turn on each other rather than concede a slight against the opposing side. Long after the police lines dispersed and our long-cherished complaints were addressed, we remained ghoul-like in our ghettos, fighting our shadows. Only through prayer did we remember ourselves and our capabilities.

Through our formative years, prayer was all we had. Devotion of the Projects and Inner Cities. We experienced periods of intense belief when the saviour's light filled us and we felt it our duty to spread the message. Our work was our future; immeasurable riches that came from piousness and doing well. We seldom reflect on these times, inextricably linked as they are to the desire to please our parents; how obedience was expected in both church and home. That through prayer and ritual we were burying other desires; withholding the part of ourselves we were not yet able to share. Our questioning and later cynicism mostly occurred during this break: a domestic schism followed by a religious one. For the support found in certain quarters – a priest or family member who could readily accept our deviancy in private – we were forced to abandon our belief once we too had been cast aside. What light was had was then of our own making and could no longer be divined. For decades it remained so, as we became more fully ourselves. The gap widening as we moved further away from our families, who saw what we had become but lacked the bravery to support it. Our knowledge and adherence to all holy ritual fading into memory.

But in the same way that a flavour or scent can transport you back to childhood – a sip of warm milk flavoured with honey or the charred edge of a fried egg – so too can the peel of downtown church bells. Sunday-morning bells calling us to church. Once we opened our ears to them their summons was loud and resolute. They marked the start and end of each day. Their clear ring echoed the hollowness of our internal lives. We were happy mostly, but rudderless. Vogue balls were our cornerstone but they did not explain why we often felt alone in the days following. Something of the light returned once we accepted that faith needed to play a part in our lives. That's not to say that we would return to blind worship – far from it – but more an understanding that our own church could be founded from the core principles that had kept us straight in youth. The Apostles started from the same point zero. We would follow.

We allowed ourselves to be guided by the Church; tentatively attending Sunday services in sympathetic neighbourhoods, visits that were both a refresher course and an exercise in nostalgia. The Father's tone soothed and terrified, taking the briefest glance at us before preaching at length on sin. Afterwards he was welcoming and kind, offering us tea and introductions to various groups within the congregation. Knowing not to outstay our welcome, we shied away from church hospitality, though something in his manner and the particular quality of light there brought us back over successive weeks. Thick shafts of light emanating from beyond the stained glass; hitting the side of our faces as we knelt, and seeming to cleanse our imperfections. It was not His approval we were seeking, we realised, but our own.

The children indulged us, though suspicious of our conversions. One eccentricity among many. We expected no generation below us to follow our practice of worship. How could we, when we too had traversed a free-flowing discovery of what the city offered during our youth? Of places, and lovers; our bodies, and the sanctuary of the vogue balls; what freedom could mean. This we could not deny them. The children had their own points of faith, which we accepted though barely understood. When one of their own went missing, there was a sporadic turn to prayer, but they had no faith in its power or validity. Penance evaporating into the air, the moment the words left their lips; empty of intent; useless. They may as well have prayed to ice cream. Easier to curse Jesus and all the saints for a loss of protection that was not wanted in the first place. It was left to us alone – the house mothers – to follow a more structured path, for only through this would we arrive at answers.

When your child goes missing you will move heaven and earth to find them. You have the strength to rip buildings from their foundations; such is your determination to restore all that is precious. You will ask all the questions that need asking; implore every agency you can find. You fight the darkness that descends, any obstacle that limits your strength. True blackness only occurs when the second child goes missing, then a third. Any last methodology you cling to, the agencies you pursue becomes redundant. The chase that filled your days, from which trickled scant drops to nourish those seeds of hope you had protectively buried, is halted. After the fourth child has disappeared, you look to save yourselves and others around you; searching for an explanation and a space that goes beyond prayer.

Through silence we acknowledge our pain and are able to name what we feel. It near breaks us to contain the enormity of it, but somehow silence gives us strength. City Hall sees this in our faces and manner. It is why they are unable to turn us away. They recognise how our sadness could flood the city, with no rain or water cannon to wash it away; how we embed its fabric. We shall not engage. We will verbalise no demands. They will study the notes we leave and they will learn. They will acknowledge the size of our number, the physical weight of our presence, and understand their need to act on our behalf. Nothing will happen otherwise. We shall sit at their door and remain present, leaving them no option but to watch from their windows and wait for us to go away.

3.

On our first night we made the decision that we would sleep on the steps of City Hall. For all the effort it took to gather the children – the energy spent in explaining what we would do, and how – the beauty of seeing our mass pooled on those sandstone steps unravelled us; a trickle of an idea leading to a dark reservoir of unknown fathoms made it impossible to pack up and leave once we fell into deeper night.

'Now you're getting crazy.'

Teddy's voice in our ears; the man we most relied on to help us organise; once one of our legendary children, still one of ours, but more than a decade past what the role allowed. At the balls, there were children, upcoming legends, and mother legends. He was forever upcoming, not interested in taking our role, only working as our legislator, improving what was already there. He allowed us the luxury to fall back upon our status as elders, taking care of our day-to-day business and leaving us to indulge our ideas. Now working for the City itself, in a minor role, of which we were still so proud, he was the rod that beat the children's asses to keep them in line.

'You want to keep this up. Seriously?'

Our movement, the justice we were seeking, could not keep office hours. That was unthinkable. Consciousness beats twenty-four hours a day. We would stay there to show that our belief did not waver, even while we slept, even when there was no one to watch us. This pain, this thought, was ingrained.

We were not prepared for an enforced stay, barely dressed for the day, never mind night, but it felt like the right thing; the only course to take. Once evening turned to night, still illuminated, because we were in the heart of the city, free now of gawkers and the noisiest of news folks, the police themselves growing tired and moving back into the shadow of their vehicles where sleep beckoned, we took our repose. We each lay across a step, our heads resting against shoes and whatever extraneous clothing we'd thought to bring. The children were left to decide whether they would join us. We did not explain. We simply grew tired and prepared for sleep.

Our expectations were met once the children saw us settled and left, promising to return at some point the next day (no mention of the morning; only a cursory acknowledgement of supplies needed). Belief could not be forced, only acted upon. They were not yet at that stage, having too much other energy to expend. They needed to drink and fuck their sense of unease away. Both the situation and our manner felt alien to them, and in their fright they strove to shake off these talismans: of age; our odour; and the hypnotism that led them to follow.

We could not be dismissed as nuts for we were lodged deep in their hearts for all we had done for them up until now: the protection we had given; battles fought. We were the strength and common sense they lacked. We were their home; the cornerstone from which they moved forward. The day's events had unsettled them, seeing how we were so comfortable in our silence and our firmness of purpose; for the first time seen as something other than parents who fed and clothed them, and coached them for the balls. They were frightened of how quickly they had followed us to City Hall; that they could be led so easily without full knowledge of what was ahead. It was not combat they feared as such, more their commitment to silence, fearing they could not live a life without voice. Later they would align, but for now, they ran. Kept running until exhaustion took hold.

'This is what you want to do? This is your plan, huh?'

We were now six: five house mothers, shielded by Teddy. He too was sent away once it became clear that his heart was not in it, self-conscious and vulnerable once the others had dispersed. Protection was a blessing that could wait another day. We were never safer than on these steps. From where we had come from, the barren monoliths from which each vogue house was founded – a spark that ushered us out of the Stone Age; a series of blind leaps into an energy we could only describe as kinship; the work we had undertaken on ourselves – City Hall was riches. The pleasure was in knowing that there was nowhere to hide.

Never had we made our intent more known as we did lying on the steps; understanding the tableau in our formation: actors performing at the Colosseum; revolutionaries at the gate. We feared no trouble. We had each other for comfort and the police guardianship from the distance of their cars. It was clear that we would not be moved, even by stealth. They did not yet have the appetite for it, preferring that we left of our own accord. Neither did they groom us towards any particular behaviour: several officers bidding us good night; a round of coffee handed over a barricade. They had no stomach for what we were, but still respected the art; from a city that seemingly had the protest ground out of it, up we sprang, naive, hopeful, silent.

We loosened our belts; stretched and massaged our muscles to relax. Each looked at the other, a circle of assent, agreeing that our position would hold for the next day, and the one after. We prayed for the children who have disappeared and for strength of mind. For as much as we appeared outwardly sure, we were fraught with uncertainty at every step. Only our unity held us together: the collective history of house mothers propping up the weak and undecided. Still, we made it a day and a night, which cannot be taken away – even by ourselves. We slept in short, deep bursts, worn by the exertions of the day, learning to find grooves within the sandstone steps where we could meld. Knowing from the first that our beds would be made here – there was no other place we could rest without leaving the square – we took the hard shock of the ground without complaint, understanding that comfort would only come with familiarity. So it was true of prayer as it was here.

4.

What we overhear in our sleep: two cops as they circle
the square.

'They ain't serious, these people. First drop of rain, they'll
disappear. Others come equipped. Prepare like they was in
the army, with their boxes and flags. Loudspeakers and they
noise. These men got nothing. Their shawls and their fancy
walks. Relying on jack else.'

'Not their brains, that's for sure.'

'Amen, brother. Don't know what they were thinking
walking up in here. What plan they got? We all got people
we lost. All have sadness we don't talk about. That's part of
life. And they wanna react about this way? Speak to lawyers,
the DA. Europe's the place if you want to pull off this rev-
olutionary shit, with your beret and your daily letters. We
got no time for this here.'

'How do they find the time, these men? They have obligations elsewhere, right? Work and families.'

'This is their family, the young people who cluster around
them. This dancing is their work.'

'These five pushing fifty and they still call dancing their work.'

'Look at their clothes. Suggests that they've not had
work awhile. You have nowhere to go, then routine counts
for nothing.'

'Rules for us and rules for them. My ma taught me that
self-respect came from work. Yours too, I bet.'

'I heard they could perform magic tricks. That's what they were saying out by the news truck. Fire-eating or some shit.'

'Bullshit. They turn tricks, that's what they got. Try that here and the cuffs'll go on them so damn fast, they'll think they're having an out-of-body experience.'

'You're willing it to happen, brah.'

'Houdini shit, right there. I'm tellin' you.'

'No one's making trade here. For real. They got no interests besides sitting on those steps with the noisy kids around. They get those kids damn quiet when they sittin', though. These look like they've never shut their mouths in their lives. Bunch of ragamuffins. And now they sittin' all quiet, like they listenin' to a conversation. 'Cept there's no words.'

'None. They wanna swap places with a dumb mute for forty-eight hours. See how they like it then.'

'Maybe that's what the magic is. How they get these street rats to shut the fuck up.'

'Brainwashing is what it is. How old are these guys, anyway?'

'Forty? Fifty? Old enough to know better.'

'They will know better before this is over, brah. I guarantee it.'

'Those wigs they wear.'

'Not all of 'em.'

'Cheap, hooker wigs. Six feet tall with a blonde bob

hanging lopsided. Looking like deranged mannequins when
the sun fades on the steps.'

'Leave them be.'

'Ghetto scarecrows keeping everyone away from
City Hall.'

'Some imagination you got. You're wasted in the
squad car.'

''Cept they've forgotten how easy it is go up in flames.
How little it takes.'

5.

We dream of the children we failed; those we could not
keep. Our motherhood comes from an imperfect place
where good intentions and inaction lies. Those who accuse
us of being lazy and self-serving have good reason; finding
petulance when we are not listened to and cannot have our
way. We can be destructive if we are not acknowledged
as pack leaders; how we may serve but do not follow. We
expect mandatory attendance at our table and a nominal
contribution made. Through paying their share the children
find respect, something which may have been in deficit in
their previous families. We take care of those in trouble but
do not tolerate freeloading or disrespect.

Mostly we chose to nurture; reaching the age where it
meant something to bring forward the next generation of
children; to educate and pass on all that we had learned, all

we had not been told. We had no property or other assets, nor family lining up to claim them even if we did. The balls, what could be achieved there, the life you could make for yourself, was all that could be left behind, and we were selfish in our need to see it continue. We thought of village women telling stories to the young; how fairy tales opened the mind. What we had was something akin to their legends: how magic could be conjured from the dark.

We would ask the children if they were hungry, that was the first thing; knowing that they would find it easier to trust if their bellies were full; if they were made to feel welcome at the table. Simple things that they would take to be important. We were no chefs, but there was always a pot on the stove. A pot of meat stewing and a carton of cigarettes. Even later, when they learned to despise us, it was still the basic things that they would return for. There was nearly always food on the table at the balls: plastic salad bowls filled with popcorn, plantain chips, and the regular kind. One of the older Mothers, no longer with us, would bring tamales, as taught by her mother in a Mexican church kitchen. Another brought a pot of jambalaya, which stayed warm half the night in its Mississippi clay pot. They would eye the liquor being passed from one mouth to another, but even with the most strident requests, this was denied. They were too young. They had yet to earn it. For the times when there was no food in the house, we encouraged them to gorge with their eyes: the gowns, of course, and the sequence of lights flashing from the DJ box; the drama of each walk, and the unpopularity of the vogue caller's final word. Countries could be won or lost on the battles that erupted here: a fur coat deemed too feminine for use in an executive realness walk; a stumbling colt far from ready for their first time in drags. They saw everything, same as happened in their homes. What they chose to take from it was up to them. For those who had been kicked out of their home for their desires, we offered shelter; those whose employment barely gave them enough to get by, curtailing their potential in the balls, we took in. Any child who had the temerity to approach us in the street or at battles, whose hunger for what we served went beyond a passing interest, was adopted. A battalion of dancers training for war. A drag army waiting to conquer. For this we expected obedience, and loyalty; and even when both were tested, we still opened our homes.

As parents we had no other choice. It would be easy to group these children as having been rejected all their lives, but it wasn't so. Many had siblings they helped to raise; grounded in responsibility; men of the house who could be trusted to take care of things. They were wanted at home; needed until they failed to live up to expectations of manhood. Most were loved, even if they were seldom heard.

Our table was an opinionated one – we said our piece about every muthafucka we came across – but we listened when it came to the children, for this was the way to keep them. We did not agree with everything that came out of their mouths, but we allowed them a voice; something greater than painting a face or walking in heels. The most significant luxury we could provide was a space for the children to express, something that went beyond the balls; that started in the home. Clothes could be stolen, and food scavenged; but this could not be replicated elsewhere.

The first time the children sat at the dinner table wearing a pair of heels like it was nothing was the prize. How they could be relaxed and talk banalities, all the time swinging their legs under the chair. The same for those whose truth was something less opaque than heels and jewellery, but still worlds away from the street; eccentricities that could never have taken place in their neighbourhoods; the way the hand would rest at the base of their throat; laughter that was free of burden; eyes unafraid to roam to others of the same sex. They could be sixteen or twenty-five, all experienced that first moment when they softened in the midst of the rabble we catered for.

For these times we gave thanks for the environment we shared. We did not draw attention to the change in each child for they could speak for themselves when they were ready. So long as we were able to provide safety and a place at our table, we were sure of the good we could do. How great things could come from the smallest contribution. There was no self-congratulation in this, only an understanding that the best example we could give was by living well; that a space for prayer could coexist alongside more physical and material expressions: pushing femme or banjee realness through competing in vogue balls; finding love. The pride felt around a swelling dinner table. This was all of our doing: vogue houses and their growing families; each looking out for the other.

Our apartments were filled with music. This too gave us life, pushing sofas aside for dance-offs after dinner. Rows over whether hip hop could be more radical than house. We acted like regular families too, squabbling and holding grudges; being held to account over charges of favouritism – unfounded – by those who felt that they were not being listened to. Early on we accepted that we could not be all things to all children; that there would be disappointment and resentment for all the problems we could not fix: childhood anger that would not subside; jealousy of those easy personalities to whom many would radiate towards.

In these unexplained rages, we saw our ignorant, unformed selves, figuring out our lessons in haphazard bouts of learning: chancing upon a co-worker or trick who would take kindly to us until we messed up. How we had also been too stubborn or lost to accept help when it was sincerely offered, instead looking for inconsistencies to destroy any goodness we found. That it would take years until we learned to find stillness, and the true ability to listen.

The answer we gave to the most troubled children was never the right ones to their ears; never the words they wanted to hear: to wait their turn as the food was being passed around; to allow others to talk equally, and not pick fights with those they did not agree with. Where we were guilty was in those instances of quieting those children before their negative behaviour infected the others.

'If the meal is not to your liking, cook the next one. We're all equal here.'

'Our choice is to love each other. It's why we started the balls.'

Though we did not demonise, we nevertheless employed tricks to mute and discredit their claims. These children were wary, wanting to believe that this was a place of safety, but they had been tricked before. They would never relax entirely in our presence, hiding within the scrum so as to blend; positioning them to the nearest exit when they were not.

To test the sincerity of what we were offering meant testing us: insults and complaints; defensive nastiness we would not accept from the others. In retrospect we were colder than we needed to be once we saw that our efforts were in vain; our patience spent from trying to calm agitated personalities that could not be contained.

'Cold from the hate outside, isn't it?'

'This bed or the street. Take your choice.'

Our minds were cast back to when we played the black sheep in our own families; often forced into that role without understanding why. Now we repeated the cycle – for the same reason as our parents – to stop every apple rotting, not realising that it was these neglected children who would be the first to disappear.

6.

On the second day we waited for Teddy and the children to return; a test of our patience and strength. What had appeared achievable in darkness was negated by morning. We felt dwarfed by City Hall in daylight; exposed with no army to back us. Weaklings scattered across the steps, asking to be displaced; the strength of police numbers becoming apparent in our sobriety. We felt protected as we slept; now their irritation was more keenly felt. Backs sore from sleeping in squad cars; feet swelling from regulation shoes pulled tightly. They wanted to be anywhere but here, not quite willing themselves to be at crime scenes though painfully aware that babysitting was not what they had signed up for. Consequently their hatred for what their job had become was directed at us. We're here as the result of crime, we wanted to say. Your failure to take crime seriously got us to this place. Children disappeared from the streets because their lives were lesser than yours. Our history of pleas to the authorities included accusations of this nature, wild and emotive in their wording, at the stage when we had no feelings left to spare. We were less impulsive in the open letters penned to the more civic-leaning newspapers, though remained strident in our retelling of events. In both cases we spoke into a vacuum: a modicum of attention given but no concrete action taken. Our children continued to vanish. Now we are past words.

They shall know our names; memorise these faces. Sherry,
TyTy and Diamonds. All the others, whose names we could
embroider onto quilts to cover this nation twice over. Even
without photographs or other details, they shall dream as we
dream: underscored by a meaty, substantial fear that snakes
through fattened guts and settles in the marrow. They shall
think of their own children and grandchildren and quake for
their safety; insides rotting with worry, and unable to live
their lives, weighed down by the omnipresent threat of what
might happen to their young if they too strayed to our side.
They will learn the names of ours.

Alone we shrink back into ourselves, at a loss until the
children arrive. In fleeting moments we thought of our
domestic affairs, the comfort that awaited us were we to
venture home; drawing the curtains for welcome shade;
the company of the radio; finishing food in the ice box
that would soon be spoiled. Our apartments remained our
trusted place to hide; sacred for the sanctuary it offered; the
numerous times we have retreated to heal. Still, we accepted
that our homes would elude us infinitely for we had no idea
of when we would return. It took something big for us to
leave behind our domesticity. For the legends told of how
our personalities could eclipse planets when we ruled the
balls; how we finessed into higher versions of ourselves; the
perfection that could be found in figurative sculpture, now
transplanted and coming to life under lights; our jibes that
crackled with more electricity than a Hollywood writing

team could dream of; we remained domestic animals, never happier than within our four walls.

This is what we would sacrifice for the children's safety; to make it clear to all that we would no longer hide. We would each have moments of private complaint, when our bitterness would spill into the atmosphere of the square; how we were being forced into this corner because no other muthafucka was strong enough to sit on these steps; how there was no strength to be found. The ability to sit quietly in your home should be as revered as a walk to slay all runway walks. It is as refined; as considered, but carries greater weight. If we could have channelled our action simply by sitting quietly in our homes we would have done so. To challenge the legitimacy of institutions by staying in our favourite chairs; showing how we mean business in do-rags and slippers. This has always been our fight: to be seen over what is unseen; the inequality of truth.

When Teddy arrives, he is prepared. Food and water, plastic chairs and blankets to make our wait a comfortable one. He's given thought to our night and wishes to make amends for his parting tone, impatient and incredulous. The children too are still cagey regarding how long they will stay, but making a show of their presence nonetheless. None of the apparatus is familiar to us and we do not question its origin; our bodies aching too much to establish their provenance – most likely chosen at speed from displays outside hardware stores and Goodwill en route to the square, resulting in chairs of differing colours and heights. Selfishness makes us blind this way. We will forgive anything if it gets us to the end.

Those children who have brought placards into the square are sent away or persuaded to destroy their contraptions, as a reminder that our message is one without words. We do not wish to plant slogans into the minds of those inside City Hall. They must come up with an explanation wholly by themselves, outlining every detail and probability beyond what they think we need to hear. Our silence and mass is what shall drive action. Puns and questionable drawing only detracts from our message.

The children who arrived straight after Teddy were those with most to lose: jobs held by a shoestring, relationships pulled threadbare by their devotion to the House; simple acts that humbled us as we struggled to shift the cold from our bones. For all their attention, however, Teddy remained the most frequent visitor to our apartments, whether he was wanted or otherwise; his habit of checking in and being present without ever knowing if he was needed; always thorough and attentive: taking note of our spirits and raising them if required, stocking the refrigerator and making sure the most urgent bills were paid.

How had it happened that the children we once sheltered we now increasingly relied upon? Though age had progressed, we were years from infirmity. We were capable! Yet, we needed this help; both cursed and depended upon it; younger hands to make light work, to clear the confusion of modern administration, of phone trees and form filling. Teddy, with better penmanship and turn of phrase, who could reply to the electric company and the rent control board in the language they wanted rather than the guttural tongue by which we were raised. We were not short of money – still dirt poor, but able to scrabble enough nickels and dimes to enable the illusion of freedom. It was not a question of buying help, more learning the need to acquiesce; how every struggle did not need to be taken alone; that it was OK to be looked after when we had tended to so many.

So as these children arrived we crumbled, falling into a pathetic routine of neediness and complaint, swiftly grabbing their food with a grateful hand; eyes rolling inside the back of our heads to negate the efforts of the police line; shading their previous kindness. We regressed into familiar behaviour; self-pitying obsessions that competed with the need to lead our cause, though we were aware that this did not play out well in sunlight. We played out until it became ugly to us; a scab picked and picked again; stubborn nappy curls twisted straight. The children were disappointed that we could be babyfied so easily, wanting to see something other than our old tricks. We had surprised them with our hardiness by staying the night – in their talk amongst themselves admitting that they had no longer thought us capable.

As they walked the flight of steps leading out of the subway they expected to turn the corner and find an empty square, with no evidence of our hostelry bar the discarded litter that would soon be cleared; our effort as invisible and impotent as all they had seen before. (Only history revealed the times when we had the power to change things; changes in the law and community relations; achievements we could not make up. How they wished to see that beast rise again: magnificent and principled; not always educated in the ways of the fight, but naturally equipped to attack at the right moment.) They were expecting to follow the trail of our sour odour back to our apartments where we would be raging at our treatment and neglect by their hand. They would watch as our anger flared then faded, with the same intensity and regularity as a disco light; our rants as reliable, predictable as those elders they had run from.

Only, we had not left the square. We were still here. Still silent. Nourished by the warm food and the efforts of their attention, our bodies slowly responded to the role that was expected of us. We rose off our bony asses and stood straight, acting the part. We had lasted the night. We had handed over today's letter of instruction to Teddy. Everything would come to us if we remained focused and did not retreat into the interior. Our weaknesses only served to detract from the progress we had made. We could not salvage that which could not be repaired, but answers were possible via this action. Sin was in ignoring the call.

The children told us to remember ourselves. That we were bad-ass muthafuckas; the ones who got them down here; that it was our presence that had the Po-Po dancing in line. How they did not entirely understand our logic but knew that we crazy bitches meant business. Something in this voodoo we were casting around warned these bastards to keep their distance; that we were on fire with our magic.

But they were the ones acting oddly, not ourselves. They hid behind the bravado of their observations, using a jocular tone we seldom heard from their mouths on the street or even at their most relaxed, at the balls. We assumed it was a manner they adopted at work to blend in and be liked, seeing how they were stealing glances at the police for reassurance as much as from ourselves. There was volume in their speech but most were unable to look us in the eye, instead surveying those workers navigating around us to enter City Hall, the news folks kept behind a cordon having been instructed not to engage with us directly, and the police who remained unmoving at the front of their vehicles.

Later we would succeed in bringing the entire square to a halt, but we were still days away from that paralysis. For now, life teemed around us. We were a curiosity and a possible public safety risk, nothing more than that. Our action was a brief water-cooler discussion, raised for laughs and a chance to deflect their own anxieties, and even then was limited to our age and our clothes. The high-ups were sweating in their rabbit-hutch offices, of that we were certain, but the lower ranks of the administration remained blissfully unaware, taking us for fools; hobos in all but name lining up to detail our grudges, agony by agony. We would become immortalised as unemployed rabble-rousers for many weeks before they learned the truth and were forced to question their loyalty. For now, we were humiliated from the safety of their work stations.

'I have to put in some time, but I'll be back. Keep those blankets on and behave yourselves.'

Teddy sat with us for an hour before returning to his job at City Hall – not in a role that could help us, but something in his presence gave legitimacy to our place here. If asked by those inside, he could speak our names and make it clear that we were not hostile.

His hand rested atop our heads before leaving us; the warmth and care that flowed from his palm. We were being indulged, same as those times at our table when it was obvious that he wished to be elsewhere; out in the park or studying at his desk; or like the less industrious children, sleeping; feeling the breath of a new lover on their backs, and wanting no other responsibility outside of that moment.

They had dragged weight most of their lives; just for one day they wished to be carefree; for the spirit of the balls to carry through into their everyday lives. And though we tried to facilitate this as much as we could, we were no shields. We could not protect them from ugliness: bottles thrown from passing cars as they walked in full drags en route to the balls; bigotry in the workplace; faggotry from bitter children in competing houses. For every paradise there comes a payback. The balls were heaven as we divined; a right we would give our last breath for. We were not atoning on these steps, we were making a proclamation: that we had a right to be happy and to live freely. Everyone who watched us in the square needed to understand that our lives mattered.

We looked at the donuts the police were stuffing into their mouths, of the same variety that were offered to us last night. The most egalitarian food of our nation was ours as well as theirs. We could each buy a donut and stand on a street corner to eat it, but if one of us disappeared on leaving that street corner – the wrong us – there would be no investigation as to why. How truly donuts represented the interests of our nation and its priorities, and how the worth of our lives could turn on a dime.

Company came and departed in waves; even the most attentive of the children unwilling to stay with us entirely alone until they were sure of our motives; afraid of looking foolish, and wanting to avoid unnecessary jail time if the police became restless. The cause was all well and good so long as others could shop for their groceries and ensure their shifts weren't stolen by opportunists. They had no confidence in either. Nevertheless, our number swelled past one hundred during the ebb and flow of the afternoon; some staying for the duration, others for less than twenty minutes, that being the most their attention could afford. Those who brought more food than was needed, and music, were sent away, reminding others that this was no picnic we'd organised. We were not looking for indigestion or entertainment, only to sit quietly; our intent moving by osmosis through brick and stone, ever closer to those inside who needed to hear it. Previously a day in the park with this number would have been a dream; to eat and argue, roller-blade, with breaks for hook-ups in more clandestine areas, while others got softly woozy on blunts and malt liquor. We could not let the children discern our enjoyment, but even in these reduced circumstances their company brought us pleasure. Every moment.

7.

We no longer use words because they are a defunct currency. What we say carries no value in this world; pennies rolled along the street that fall into the gutter; representing the ugliness of small currency that cannot be acknowledged. We no longer wish to contribute to the noise, deafened by the hollow talk that comes from the mouths of others. We are so used to hearing 'no', 'unfortunately' and 'unable', that these words have stopped making sense, becoming nothing more than a series of coos and grunts to wave us away. They have used 'no', 'unfortunately' and 'unable' as pacifiers, shushing us the way a nanny calms an agitated baby. We are unwanted noise, not to be seen or heard. There is more language – and honesty – in a punch to our faces than the babble with which we're addressed.

Those we wish to hear from do not have the guts to show their colours in so visceral a way. They fear how we would see the truth in their eyes. The weight remains with us; our domain. We are tired of how quick we are to still say 'please'; not simply the weakness of its ring, but how simple it makes us sound. Even at our most hostile we are unable to stop saying 'please', because we know it only takes one person to recognise our courtesy and our desperation and investigate our claims. It only takes one person to look closely, really study our faces to see how these events have eaten us away.

Before the children – when we were children ourselves – we were still wounded, but remained hopeful of repair. We had not reached the shoreline of disappointment, preferring to believe that paradise lay beyond the sea. Running the balls changed our lives, gave us a power we didn't know we had. How we would run up the avenues in full drags clutching our trophies and stop traffic. We cared not for fools and naysayers: those we could barely see for we were running too far ahead. We threw insults into the wind as we ran, feeling the breeze blow up our gowns as we sprinted along Broadway; laughing at how far they receded into the distance as we followed yellow cab tail-lights into morning; how little our enemies meant.

'Kiss my dust, muthafuckas. See how we're running this town. Watch this green as it passes through our hands. Kiss the fucking couture, darling. Kneel and kiss the hem.'

The children should've had the same freedom. Better:

greater freedoms. They should've fed from our achievements and taken the city for their own. Instead, we watch them struggle to find their place. We turn and they disappear.

We have run out of words; the combination of words to explain how our families have been decimated. We have run the course of terms to describe how a boy can disappear from the street because he wore a dress on the street to pay the rent, or left the wrong subway stop at the wrong time of night. How it was no longer possible to spend an afternoon alone at the pier; how harder still to make conversation with strangers.

When the City Hall guard walks down the steps to address us at the end of his shift and starts with 'unfortunately', he cannot be surprised by our failure to verbally respond. He doesn't know the children's story, how well they spoke; that they would speak to anyone who was friendly and showed respect, once they understood that friendliness was not the enemy if you had confidence and power over it. That if the children were guilty of anything, it was most likely their easy turn of phrase that helped them to disappear: trying to hold their own against hoods insulting them on the street but having no back-up; trusting co-workers or johns whose friendliness hid something uglier, relaxing at a kind word, happy and unsuspecting.

Those situations had presented themselves to us over the years, but somehow we found a way out each time; thinking on our feet of how best to outmanoeuvre company when it flipped into trouble; sometimes not even thinking at all – the nervous system taking over, adrenalin powering our most basic need to get the fuck out of danger, kicking the glass out of a bathroom or car window; plying men with drink until they passed out; remembering that our physical frame did not always equate with how we gender identified, making it possible to punch your way out of trouble in a cocktail dress or kimono. The body took over when our minds failed. Over the years we have ground ourselves to dust thinking of the lost children and their skewed reflexes: how a misjudged step in the wrong situation could lead to their vanishing; creeping out of a hotel room more heavy-footed than they intended, waking their oppressor; the failure to power a run.

We cannot express to the guard that in memory of the children and their gregariousness, we don't speak, for everything we would say falls flat from our mouths. Once again we are reduced to five as we bed down for the night and he looks at us sadly, though more for the threadbare Goodwill blankets we have been left with, than the loss of our speech. He is yet to understand.

8.

We pray by the clock; four calls during the day when we take the vow of silence anew. What started through a rout of defiance slowly becomes our cornerstone, something that we cling to. It is the time we give to reflect, strengthening any lapse in our observance. We are not perfect; always known for our loose mouths, chasing argument for the sake of having the last word; attention-seekers and predators, all, if it meant that we were heard. Our quarterly call draws a line under our misjudgement: periods of excitement or anger when we forget ourselves. It absolves us of guilt, serving to remind that each period after prayer is a fresh start; that the strength of our belief comes before any prior history or knowledge. One quarter at a time. Progress, self-containment, is all we can hope for.

Our possessions are minimal but over three days we have accrued a collection which turns us from individuals to base camp. It is not our business to ask the children where the sleeping bags came from, still tightly rolled in their clear cellophane, of the same midnight hue underneath to avoid any argument. The blankets remain part of our accoutrements; by day we drape, re-drape, and huddle under two or three, taking comfort in how the untreated wool irritates our skin; each scratch a reminder to remain still; how silence comes from posture, what is withheld in movement as well as voice.

To the naked eye, those squinting at us from the subway entrance, a distance of a block and a half, we represent something far more organised than we actually are. There is no machinery in place to erect a village overnight, as some of the news folks are saying, as for the most part, the children still leave us to sleep alone. The makeshift city they talk of does not exist. Cities were built on more than sleeping bags and nylon windbreakers. What we have has developed piecemeal, some determined, some unplanned. We sleep in a camp of found objects – junk from the sidewalk and other treasures. There is nothing here that we own; all will be left behind.

When the donut-bearing policemen start leaving a tray of coffee on the steps each morning we understand the journey ahead of us; how everyone has accepted before us that this will be a long haul. The sly comments first made when we took our turn for bathroom breaks at the burger joint across the street have ceased.

'Calling it a night, sister?'

'Early bird special at the disco?'

'These queens, man. All talk and no action. Ready to pack up their eyelashes the moment the weather turns.'

The police are not cowed or deferential by any means, but they are self-conscious of the bravado that came to them under the safety of darkness; the discredit it gave to their badge; how they can no longer be disrespectful to faces that grow more familiar by the day. We stop fearing the opportune destruction of our set-up and removal of our things, as witnessed in the sporadic attacks on the homeless around our neighbourhood – something we were prepared for, and kept us from deep sleep.

It also crosses our mind that the coffee could be laced with laxatives or something more harmful for their own amusement, tricks we have fallen for in our youth, but see nothing of this on their faces, merely a benign neighbourliness. Our place within the square has been accepted. Inside City Hall they will claim that a space to protest has been designated; their approval, their timescale, but it is us who have twisted their hand. They understand that we are entrenched, ready to dig deeper if needed, until we reach the building's foundations; further if we have to, into hell, where the city's ghosts remain tormented and ready to be set free.

The ugliness of our congregation on the square is a mere reflection of what would come should we be moved. From our pop-up chairs we hold our conference, the children resting at our feet. If laws could only be assessed and decided in this manner, all the better for our country. Judgments would weigh on the side of fairness if the wind could roll through those airless courtrooms and brush aside the prejudice of the state. We would govern from these steps, if allowed. Already we create our own rules: sending folks away, those attempting to join us out of curiosity or a sense of mischief; empathy on some faces, novelty on others.

We recognise our foolishness in turning back supporters to our cause, particularly those whose standing would add heft to our presence: community leaders, musicians and prominent liberal lawyers, drawn here by street talk, and what they read on the news. How our ride would be a more comfortable one with other voices to speak for and defend us; enabling us to stand as noble figureheads, bruised yet divine, whilst they rolled up their sleeves and fought dirty.

But we still bear scars from previous times when we placed our faith in representatives, only to have our voice erased; losing out to competing agendas, lawyers or editors blinded by a bigger catch during the investigative process, rendering our needs benign. Most often we were betrayed for career gain, a promotion or raise from haunted employers; the offer of becoming firm partner used to silence trouble-makers, making us understand that those who loudly claim to have mettle are often the first to be broken. If others wish to join once we receive the answers we are waiting for, they shall be made welcome. For now we rely only on ourselves and the children; to disallow all guilt for our perceived self-ishness. We own our selfishness. We will not apologise for our actions.

We walk the steps to City Hall's door several times, for the exercise as much as the threat it conveys: a trail of five blanket-clad figures rising and falling; a caterpillar feasting upon secrets. Our dance takes us three steps shy of the guard but he does not engage, either choosing not to recognise us through the throng of children who surround us, or no longer having the humour to play along before an audience. Our respect informs the distance we keep, important as it is to keep friends rather than antagonise.

We have not gathered for frivolous means: street perform-ers out to pocket loose change. Still, we are disappointed not to be humoured, for to see the levity in our games would be to accept us beyond our unofficial tenancy of the square;

beyond our silence. We are not yet seen as city neighbours and so he remains wary, his eyes focusing on the distance ahead rather than the olive branch we offer.

Several times he turns his back to the door, willing to be called inside, wondering how is it that he alone has been left to deal with the city's mess; colluding with all that he does not believe. A man can be driven to hate when there is no respite to his frustrations. This we understand. When every door is closed, locked in by your oppressors, hate is all there is to kick against. He will crack before we finally leave the square – kicking against us – but not of our making; each of us a product of what City Hall devises. The police also, will raise arms and fight.

We are desert rats seeking shelter from conflict. The City deems us rodents, guarded by the armies of the night, where neighbourhood officers become corporals; desk sergeants, now men of a more noble rank. When did our police force augment into a military mindset, after funds allowed purchase of the first armour-plated SUV, or the second? When the small tank was rolled in circles outside the precinct yard? Is our roughshod settlement protected by the vehicles that surround us, or are we at risk from them?

Even through our fear we are reminded of the frontier origins from which our country was founded, wagons encircling camp; how this could represent both comfort and danger at the turn of a dime. Our softness, fast enclosed by rubber and steel, becomes evident; a trail of vehicles blocking our path to the sidewalk, and preventing a clear view of the street. Sealing us from the world, and from those prying eyes who do not share our intent. Separating us from those sympathetic night birds, inspired and ready to follow.

9.

So many children taken from us – oh, the ways we could marks their names! – but these were the first. We had Diamonds who disappeared. We had TyTy who disappeared. We had Sherry, who was safe, but could no longer communicate with us, needing the freedom on another coast to start afresh without those who knew her joins. We were hurt but we understood. A child who says she's going out for a milkshake after the club and then disappears for years, only to be found by Teddy alive and well in the far country, leaves you wounded and betrayed in a way that you have no right to be. We did not bear this child but still we feel her absence; something now missing within ourselves.

We have to be reminded of the rules; how those who enter our homes are free. If the shelter we provide, the family we offer, cannot meet their needs, who are we to judge? It took us years to find our place. As much as we wish to accelerate the process for the young, to avoid the misery that haunted us until we had confidence in our meter, you cannot trap those too wounded or spirited into remaining. All we can do is pray for their safety, and hope that they find solace in people who can give what they need.

'Remember this,' says Teddy. 'Think of Sherry leaving of her own volition, before you camp out on those steps. You're protesting against her freedom, in a way; making it a demonstration against your lack of say in whether she stayed or left. Sherry could be representative. This is what you're afraid of.'

It takes time in some cases, but we are always aware of who is in the most need; the kids who have passed their adolescence without emotional underpinning; how the tiniest motions of stability on our part stops them from drowning. Teddy's dependence on us was never a vocal one, more physical, reassured by an open front door and the solidity of our presence.

The children never returned to empty homes; somehow we made it possible to be the first voice that greeted them as they turned the latch key. It came through a consciousness of effort; with more patience than we knew we had, forgetting ourselves and our obsessions to ensure a state of constancy they may have otherwise lacked.

Sherry, skinny as a starved cat with an attitude to match, needed a more vociferous reassurance than Teddy. A girl who was never told as a boy that he was good, had goodness in him, needs to hear it as she becomes her true self; not just the stuff about being pretty, a lipstick shade popping off her skin tone, the lustre of her hair now that it reached her shoulders, but that she was all right; that she had qualities beyond her looks that earned her a seat at the table; how she had intelligence, and something to offer the world other than her skinny body if only she could believe it too. But as a victim of home war, still suffering its repercussions, she was incredulous, looking to pick holes in our every affirmation.

'You're only saying that about my hair because I used your shampoo. I'll go back to being a scarecrow tomorrow.'

'Stop telling me I'm kind. No one wants kindness outside. Kindness will not help you cut the bitch who steals your last dime.'

'Starving me with your rotten-ass food. Broken back from the shitty mattress you give me to sleep in. Some shelter you're giving.'

Our job is to soften; untangle all that knots her insides. Douse the fires that threaten her future if left to burn without intervention. We never had a plan with the children, we simply reacted to what we saw; actions that would have benefited our younger selves if we too had felt the weight of a guiding hand. There could be no judgement because we were still knotted ourselves despite all we had learned and the space we'd created. We could still find ourselves in places of frustration and despair, unrecognised and unheard, our light swallowed into a fathomless dark. It was the children's voices that brought us to heel; that if you were needed by others, you were in some way healing yourself.

When Sherry screams outside our window late at night, choosing bars she is too young for over food at our table, we take all that we have learned, opening the door to welcome her, rather than striking her face and throwing her belongings from the top floor. We throw soup down her neck rather than acid. In doing this, we are healing ourselves. When her face is bruised from taking home the wrong trick, who steals our VCR and other electronics after he is satisfied he has beaten her enough, fucked her enough, we bathe and change her as gently as if she were a baby; the intruder's scent static in the air – sweat and spunk – clinging to our walls and furniture for weeks afterwards. We clean the mess, saving our admonishments for a time when she can hear our words over a feedback of shock, which threatens to deafen her – how her face has stiffened from it, defensively locked and unable to meld. Again, we are healing ourselves.

'... but I was wearing chandelier earrings.'

'In the wrong bar. Those places aren't meant for us.'

'You didn't see the ends of them. Sharp as a blade.'

'Death by your own hand, Sherry. Listen to your mothers.'

'Who used to pick up milk at the store in nothing but Chanel No.5 and a smile? I heard those stories.'

'AIDS era. We needed to be unafraid.'

'And not now? I should heed you bitches?'

'You broke a couple of toenails on that run, huh? Learn.'

They disappear, the children. Feeding from our table but living by their own advice. They were safe at the vogue balls. Outside of that, we had no dominion, legal or pastoral.

We called ourselves Mothers for we ran the vogue houses.

You joined our house – to dance or walk in drags – and you were our child. You took direction, and followed our rules; dressed for competition, in the category we groomed you for: femme, banjee, high fashion, executive, street walker. Category variations the way France has cheeses. But outside of that, how to mentor those out of sight; who will take dinner when it is offered, and a bed when it is needed but disappear the rest of the time? How to read those who yearn for family yet still run from it?

We are not cut out for parenthood, too deeply marked by all that has shaped us, but here we are, coddling and giving shelter because we're here, and because there are no others to ask. We will not turn those away in the manner we were abandoned; our clothes thrown into the street; how inaction is a cruelty in itself.

For all the trouble children can bring, fractiousness that follows them to our homes, it gives us life to see the house filled with spirit. Sherry could growl and still light up the room. We think of her often, recognising that there was much we could not decipher during her time with us; how the things that she asked for we found it hard to give.

'This bed is one thing. The shelter is another. But I don't feel anyone's arms around me. Never felt for one moment I could relax because someone had my back. It's arched too high for anyone to reach, from being forced into a defensive position from such an early age. Almost turned into a hunch-back from how I was raised. Sugar Loaf Mountain in wigs and heels. You were weaned similar. I see it from how you are with me. Neglect recognises neglect, and all the ugly shit that comes with it. The easy part is telling me I'm beautiful. You mean that, and I hear it from you. Listen, this bitch is stunning. A heartbreaker. I know that, but still I need to hear it from your cracked lips. Makes me believe it more, somehow.'

Soft times like these, nothing like she was at the dinner table, brittle and argumentative one moment, slyly teasing the next. Nor how she was at the balls, walking as if her life depended on it; her very future resting on the attention spent on her outfit, the intensity of each step and pose. She threw poses as if she carried a pocket full of grenades, taking out the competition one category at a time. We trained the children as soldiers; how werk was work; the ballroom our battlefield. If you could find something of yourself there, that was all well and good, but the ultimate purpose was to slay those competing in rival houses. Glory was all.

Sherry was a natural competitor.

'When you grow up tussling for even the smallest piece of bread, it makes you a fighting bitch. Steal me a pair of Chanel earrings and watch as I clear the floor. You want trophies? Give me two hours to get this hair piled Empire State high on top of my head. Crown me with those earrings. A flash of Chanel and a smile. Giving face, and thigh, and ALL the glamour. Teddy, pocket me them jewels. Face like a choirboy from the tropics. Walking in, in your Brooks Brothers shirt, those damn owl glasses. They won't look twice at you.'

Teddy, always shy when called out from the glare of the dinner table, his face moving further towards his plate, retreating into himself.

'When I win the lotto, you can have all the jewels you want. I'll buy you anything. Until then . . . '

His smile was clear nevertheless; embarrassed for the attention, his neck red with it, but pleased to be needed, a spotlight on all the traits he tried to bury among the children's noise. They looked for characteristics other than reliable; loathing all that was nondescript and attentive, not understanding that it was these qualities they would gravitate towards once Sherry and the others disappeared. They would appreciate loyalty above all else; need level-headedness, and someone with an organised mind. They would welcome good sense and empathy; that wisdom could stem from somewhere beyond anger; studious coldness to their heat.

What made Teddy boring at the dinner table, some-one to taunt mercilessly – even with affection – was what they would hunger for later. Even when they hated Teddy, whether jealous or indifferent to his path, they would always have need of him.

'Teddy's sweet on Sherry! Look at his eyes on her!'

'Gurl cast a spell on the innocent. Draining that goodness.'

'Tranny chaser up in here!'

'As long as that's all she doing. Old enough to know better.'

'They ain't dissimilar in age. Some folks had a harder life, is all.'

'Not when we're eating food! It's disgusting. Get them a room!'

'Leave the boy his crush. Lord knows we all need some innocence around here. Hush now and eat. Let his eyes roam where they want.'

And his eye did roam, roving faster than his blood rate and his teenage growth; eyes travelling across the city and back, from the river's end point to its origins, as if determining whether what he pined for came from nature; before they relaxed and finally settled on the troublemaker opposite. Relishing the mayhem, Sherry cackled in response and kept badgering whoever would listen for her right to Chanel.

10.

'Why can't yous speak? Is it illness?'

'They've chosen to stay silent as a mark of their protest,' says Teddy.

'How the fuck can you protest if you can't tell people what you're protesting about? Are we missing something here?'

'I'm their voice. If you have any questions, come to me.'

'With respect, son, we needed answers in the middle of the night, when one of them wouldn't stop crying. Where were you then?'

'I speak for them, but I'm not them. You understand the distinction, I trust?'

'We see a group that refuses to move. You're in there

somewhere. There's no room for individuality within a mob. If that's what you're looking for, son, you should go home and express yourself elsewhere.'

'They're my responsibility. That's to say, I feel responsible for their well-being. Nobody else here . . . there are few others who will make sure that they eat, are warm enough.'

'Yous their social worker?'

'I work for the City, officers, but I'm cut from their cloth. Pulled-off the streets and given a home. A bed to sleep in and a warm room to study in.'

'Breaking the law to repay a debt is misguided. Go back to your desk and let this silence play itself out.'

'Not when they feel this so strongly. Driven in a way I've never seen, or maybe wanted to see. We hide much of the truth of our parents from ourselves, don't we? It hurts less that way.'

'Wigs with baseball caps attached. Is that their thing now? What they all wore yesterday.'

'They're messing with you. Aware that you notice these things.'

'Lined up like soccer moms on too many steroids. It can frighten the shit out of you if you're not used to it.'

'Recognise that they sometimes feel insecure. It's not easy sitting up there. It makes them comfortable in a place where there's none.'

'Battle ready?'

'Stop seeing everything in fighting terms. They're just trying to be brave, is all.'

'Yeah, well. I guess it takes bravery to pull off a curly red wig with a green cap on top. Real guts.'

'Now you're just being mean. Do you want me to douse you with wig water?'

'Now who's messing with us? Ignorance is something we shy away from on the force. You can't serve and protect through ignorance.'

'I thought that's what you were doing.'

'You getting clever now? I thought we were reaching an understanding.'

'Force of habit. Force of mindset, I should say. Hard to shake these things. You mean well. I understand this.'

'We ain't bastards. It's the uniform that makes us appear so. The baton. And hood. We'll keep an eye out for your old men when we see an absence. At night, especially.'

'I'm grateful. I realise that I'm needed here, whether I believe in the enterprise or not. The reality, however . . . '

'We're not tucking anybody in. Don't get ideas. If they breaks the law, they've had it. But I think of my pa getting his shut-eye on the sidewalk. How I'd feel. The vulnerability of the group of them sleeping out there tears me up. But, their choice. Their choice.'

11.

We left Teddy to his own devices those times when he was not responsible for our care, hourly intervals of respite where he could concentrate on his job, or extended to selfish luxuries such as the food he wanted to eat or a new boy that he wanted to give his focus to. We never anticipated the mental energy or the sheer timescale it could require on his part to attend to our basic ministrations: the half-hour he spent in our apartments delivering and storing away groceries, the pans and glasses scrubbed and rinsed, the trash emptied, our light bulbs changed. We did not factor in the distance from his apartment to ours, or the time lapsed in the supermarket queue.

All that was tangible to us was our precious thirty minutes where we could either show our love or air grievances; mostly a little of both, anxious as we were for time with our prodigal, hungry for his attention, all the while aware of the rescinded space that would once again grow before his return. For as much as we cherished silence, the blank spaces in our apartments frightened us; an abyss that only his sheer presence could fill, reassured by his muscular physicality and the confidence in his voice.

To rely on someone so openly requires a confidence of its own; the belief that family springs from a place beyond your genes and loins. Our need for Teddy went beyond the practicalities, more that his presence – a constant mind from the ephemera that marked our history – gave us the freedom to live well. His strength and ability nourished ours.

We think of elders we see in the neighbourhood, parents and grandparents still tap dancing in the park, or working the same job, running companies, even; how simply knowing that your children are near allows you to flourish. How the energy of these elders still burns brightly for the familial backbone is assured; growing, altering to the dictatorial march of age, but strengthening in spirit. For the times Teddy was around, we too shone.

For everything we knew about Teddy – the knotty hair we washed clean; the crescent-shaped scar on the outside of his left hand, marked from climbing out of a broken window to escape his angry mother; his refusal to let a childhood of violence shape him into anything other than a campaigning moderate; the almost imperceptible intake of breath before involving himself in an argument, his tone always even but incisive, raising his voice with authority when needed, but never anger; how a plate of meatloaf topped with cornflakes and ketchup could make him the happiest man alive, a taste unchanged from the kid of six-teen who appeared at our table the day after a ball, already marked by his origins, but burning even then with a deter-mination that this would not define him. All this we know, yet he remained an enigma.

Away from us we were confident of his demeanour and aptitude; how the City would not have hired him for any-thing less. He would discuss work at our table, that which was safe to disclose: unscrupulous employers flouting labour laws; how he played his role in closing down filthy and dan-gerous working conditions, and put fear into those who paid

pennies off the books. We were sure of his beliefs, proud of
the contribution we'd made, but we did not know his mind;
all that he absorbed when he did not speak. How his eyes
would sometimes fall upon us in the midst of our vanity and
eccentricities. The conclusions he would draw.

One time, walking us across the block to the late-night
pharmacy, we were accosted by a group of college boys, out
of their depth in our neighbourhood, but drunk and still
vocal in their derision.

'Ask those queers if they have any drugs to sell.'

'Who wears those kinds of theatre clothes at this time
of night?'

'Unless their assholes are for sale, too.'

'A kimono? For real?'

Teddy's body had changed little since we'd first known
him; though the chubbiness came, went, and reappeared
again, his frame remained broad and muscular, and tall
enough to silence bullshit as it reached his ears.

'I'm sorry, guys, would you mind repeating that? Didn't
quite catch what you were saying about my Mothers here.'

His moves were nothing more aggressive than a steady
pace or two towards them, his face open but authoritative.
Though in his early thirties he was still of their generation –
wearing near identical sneakers; on their level yet still above
them, occupying a space they were yet to understand.

'Who they fuck d'you think you're talking to . . .'

One of them starting with cleverness, but all running

within moments because even in their inebriated state, they did not trust the look in his eyes as he stepped forward.

'They could wear nothing but a pair of bedsocks and a smile, and you still wouldn't have the right to say a word. Watch your mouths the next time we see you down here.'

We saw satisfaction flash across him in their retreat, but also longing too for one of the youths that caught his eye, something we discussed afterwards between ourselves but never brought up again. Reminding us of the gift he opened that first Christmas with us, a coveted digital watch with calculator buttons; the same look: brief moments when he was happy and unselfconscious.

Other times we saw a more measured contentment from him; understanding that feeling secure and safe was the yardstick from where his satisfaction grew. In adulthood the same: open, unguarded, yet still a degree that was unquantifiable. The other children were open wounds: they gave without reservation, unafraid of the ugliness that came with living. By this example, he was ruled by fears of imperfection, less to do with success, more the drive to control his demeanour; that capability and trust depended on holding something down within his core; an absence that could never be explained.

Teddy was not a participant in our conversion, his only role was to escort us to church when we asked. He did not comment or ask about our experience, but something stuck. Soon afterwards he was spotted by the children, kneeling at the foot of church benches in the city during his lunch hour, or early evening before his journey home.

'Most of the time he was sitting. Just sitting. The way you see an old man at the bus station taking a breather. Nothing on his mind. Nothing on his face. Having his moment in the quiet.'

The children left no patch of the city unturned in their daily hustle. That they spotted him in various churches from the garment district to far uptown came as no surprise. We had drilled them in the fluidity of how to turn a buck; how to create opportunities when 'Situations Vacant' was closed to us. 'Situations Vacant' could be aspired to; adhered to with devotion; starched shirts and crisp résumés; clear eyes and a firm handshake – everything Teddy managed to reflect and achieve.

But what was meant to happen in the meantime for those less able? Those whose eyes were muddied from the balls, who would never complete their GED; those too immature to rise at the appointed hour; who could C.E.O. and C.O.O. multinational companies had their working hours been from midnight to six. How to fill time and make money when money needed to be made?

So Teddy was spotted at church but never approached for we had raised them better. They were puzzled by and enjoyed the secrecy of it, never having found a place for themselves outside the balls. Something childlike asserted itself in their need to preserve his sanctuary, possibly discussed and agreed between themselves out of our ear-shot. Consequently, reports on Teddy slowed and then fell away completely, when we felt in our bones that he was still practising and seen.

Though we read the untrustworthy children, they had nothing but our love; having been charmed by liars all our lives. We swallow lies even as the fabric of their sentences disintegrates before they are even completed; their breath becoming like hydrogen, igniting as each word expels into the air. How can we do otherwise?

When we talk of the unknown we think of Teddy holding our hand on the subway as he escorted us to a meeting at the housing office or medical centre; how we could read the lines on his palm without sight; draw them on sidewalks from memory, but were still afraid to ask what was on his mind as he sat in church; what drew him to the bench; why he would never sit with us, preferring to wait in the atrium until the service was over. Was it from a sense that his faith could not match ours, a sense of unworthiness, or that his faith surpassed ours? (We noticed that the apples on his kitchen table differed to ours – red and organic; how the milk in his refrigerator was more expensive.)

Was it about faith at all, or another feeling not yet understood? In lesser moments we would identify this as weakness, proof that he did not have our strength, for he would take the vow of silence, if so.

Vanity debilitates as much as piousness; our voices shrill

with both as we belittled all that Teddy had done, and of the time and care he continued to take over our well-being. He was merely punctual when he should've been early, controlling our diet, and passive over our indulgences to the point of contemptuousness.

He was a hindrance rather than an aid; a spy for the children losing interest in our shelter, their responses growing leaden as they became distant to our sphere of influence. Countless children had left us over the years, born from their frustration that we did not know them significantly; struggling with issues of trust and obedience; reaching too for something akin to our conversion: the blind worship that precedes enlightenment. In adulthood, Teddy was a special boy and could not be treated like the others. We loved and needed him. Still, we complained.

TEDDY'S CITY [i]

Boy

1.

When did Teddy start lying to the Mothers? That afternoon he returned from school, bloodied in the face, blaming it on boisterousness on the basketball court? When he started work after college, intercepting their letters before they hit the stoop, opening final demands and setting up payment plans to cover historic arrears, telling them their debts had been written off? Or later, when he lied about what happened to Sherry? A black lake of untruths, slowly becoming a cesspool, where he repeatedly dives.

He thinks about where the propensity to lie originates from; whether it was born of necessity, or more tightly woven into his fibre; whether lying is part of his DNA, a splinter from a greater shard, for which he has either his mother or his father to thank. How did it start? He is not anxious to be liked, untroubled by his ability to please. When he returns from school with a flatter nose and blood smearing his shirt, the falsity of his story comes from panic; hearing the rise in the Mothers' voices as they take him in, the speed at which they leave the table and rush towards him.

It's their swiftness that makes his heart pound inside his chest, these oldsters who shuffle and rise for nothing outside of the balls, now moving like sprinters to check him over. He's overcome by their force, the sheer physical strength shrouded by muumuus and food-stained housecoats; the solid heat that seeps through their clothes as he is held, the smells that mark their undeniable adulthood over his unwelcome adolescence.

What repels him is the loss of equilibrium in the room; how the atmosphere changes because he was stupid enough to get beaten up for standing up to a senior. A guy calls you out for being a faggot, must somehow recognise that he's a faggot too. I tried to be smart in that moment, he thinks, now understanding that the immediacy of his backchat in the hall corridor reaches beyond the confines of the school; how the Mothers are affected by the blood, the mood despairing and funereal until he pulls the basketball story out of his ass.

It was a lesson in consequences: by protecting the Mothers from truth, he was also shielding himself from a darker fear he was still unable to articulate. All that emanated was the primal impulse to banish it to where it could not be found.

He wished to avoid disturbance; ripples to fracture all that made him secure. It had taken a minute to find a refuge as safe as that which the Mothers provided – passed from one

unsuitable relative to another, before running away entirely
from the side of the city which had negligibly reared him.
The peace he found here he was not prepared to risk. Easier
then, to create harmony, even if there is none outside; where
new schoolmates would still torment him for being different;
the poverty of his clothes outshining theirs; mocking his
earnestness, and his lack of participation at the bullying of
others. If he can talk his way out of trauma – his, theirs –
then all the better for it.

He equated this to being an adult; proof that he was
capable, and trusted to do no harm. In explaining how victory on the b-ball hoop was worth getting the full force of
rubber bounced off his nose jumping to make an intercept,
he forced himself to be there on the court, nauseous from
the thick musk of the competing boys, his ears ringing from
the clink of his watch strap as it slammed against the hoop.
His body was damp with sweat, how it matted the hair in
his pits and groin. He was there, and as his story finished,
so were the Mothers.

He understood the importance of a sense of place in telling his stories; that if he did not feel it, how impossible it
would be to convince others. He did not look actively to lie,
more to spare the Mothers from hurt; not beyond finding
them foolish, but still in worship and awe, thankful for all
they'd given. They did not search him, those times when
he fell back upon this comfort of saying what they wanted
to hear; more that he learned to become adaptable – more

learning – realising that at least one of the children needed
to be so equipped.

He always thought on his feet, so he figured it may as well
be him; how he became adept at hiding truths; how withholding became itself a comfort, one that could easily stray
into piousness – a religion of his own – if he were not constantly mindful. The reality he spared them: eviction notices
frantically remedied from the privacy of his desk; children's
various illnesses from too much fucking; the escalation,
decrease and escalation again of neighbourhood robberies
allowed them to stay in the realities they had constructed
for themselves. It was impossible to keep the greatest grief
from them, the children who flashed in and out of their lives,
some leaving by choice, others not.

He was unable to carry the weight of their uncertainty
and grief; fathomless in its capacity to swallow them whole.
(It's what brought him in adult life to tell the lie about
Sherry – as much from selfishness as for the need for the
relief.) At times he felt they were permanently stranded in
black lakes, brought to insanity from tiredness and cramps,
ready to drown. How they lived in near trances for weeks,
the glassy eyes and near shutdown of their bodies, the only
way they could communicate their pain. Other times they
were roused, calling him at all hours with their plans –
instructions – for legal and other procedural challenges to
the precincts and community bodies for their negligence in
handling these cases. Their anger was a storm, a hurricane

whose eye was a calm and omnipotent grief; a living grief that needed to be fed, and understood.

'Are you taking this down? It must be transcribed to the very letter. Don't be tempted to make it pretty. We've tried doing it in your language and they ignored us. Forced us into their drag, only to be patronised and belittled in their space. No more. Time to give them a taste of ours. Real talk.'

For every letter he transcribed, there was another he wrote to conventional standards. For every crank phone call at the apex of their frustration – do your fucking job, goddamn cocksuckers – was his patient fielding from one precinct to the next; shaking hands with whoever needed to be met, lobbying various departments for access and/ or manpower, chasing those departments and decision-makers, following through, and finally threatening when City handshakes were dishonoured, something he took as a personal insult.

At times he felt as though he was attempting to shift a monolith with his bare hands, from the alleys behind their apartment blocks to the steps of City Hall. His palms were calloused from effort, his muscles torn and strained. But who else would do this for them? The children, those who were around, had interests of their own. Their sense of history did not carry the same weight; living through similar wars but bound by the optimism of ignorance and tender skin. Their love for the Mothers was avowed, yet they were still prone to vanishing when they were truly needed; finding something distasteful and unwanted in a grief so raw. Who else to tend, mop and sweep away?

'You they gatekeeper, Teddy. Like a bouncer in that suit.'

'You the voice behind their throne.'

'Their favourite. The one who had a desk and chair bought for them at the Goodwill.'

'I'm no such thing.'

'We see no other desk and chair here.'

'A furniture set, your Royal Baby Highness.'

'They put their money into you, boy. Investing in your studies.'

'And look how you turned out.'

'They invested something in everyone, whether it was their time or their dollars. How am I the one singled out?'

'Whispering in their ears, Teddy. Getting us kicked out of the apartment.'

'How can you say that when you know that their door is never closed?'

'You're a gossiping muthafucka.'

'They need help sometimes. Their decisions, from their mouths. Nothing to do with me.'

'Watch, Teddy. Keep up your chat and watch the children leave one by one. Apartments emptying one bunk at a time, until you are the only one they focus their ire on. See what you enjoy about that.'

Not so much prophecy as inevitability: Mothers getting older and children younger; less comfortable in sharing their homes; sometimes lacking the motivation to parent, preferring the solace of ghosts. The children for their part, unwilling to take accommodation from queens so old; willing their own space into being where they could live and misbehave.

What he learns is the quick-measure of relief that comes with a lying mouth; how everyone can breathe once he provides false reassurance. The Mothers would tell him that reading was fundamental; the ability to cut a bitch with vocabulary and wit, but in reading, lying was essential to his survival. To read was to reveal truths, and this he spared them.

Three days later, they stand taller on hearing of another uncoordinated b-ball move striking him – heavily bruising his arm and possibly dislocating his shoulder – believing that he can handle himself in his quiet way; how he will not give them cause for worry like some of the other children, like Sherry. What he hides is honestly intended, wishing not to upset them in the moment, but not realising how presumption will creep upon him over time; a slow, decaying creep; how he is no better than the children in playing the Mothers when he trots out his lies.

'I found Sherry, on out-of-state tax records. She's filing nails on the west coast.'

To his mind, the children are brazen and impulsive, knowing the hurt they can cause. He differs, knowing that there is no hope for Sherry; instead, wanting to save them, the way he was saved. He has the information but who does it benefit? A bloody matador jacket found in the sewage pipe that runs to the ocean; TyTy stabbed in a motel on the interstate; Diamonds' ID buried in the concrete foundations of an office building. Records pieced together in the dank of City Hall's basement; imagination filling in gaps where other documentation was destroyed. Perpetrators unknown; jacket's owner unidentified; whereabouts of body unknown. Sherry, possibly alive, or her body ground to dust. His certainty that she would never have taken off the jacket; that whatever was going on in her mind in those last moments, matador realness remained her world.

The Mothers already pray to a god that doesn't exist. What good does it do to take away their totem; all that gives them comfort and strength? He is not playing God, only sparing them a crippling truth. Let them deal with what they can see with their own eyes; what is happening now: children brutalised in the street or in their home. How they are targeted by those who hate their kind: strangers, lawmakers, blood parents, lovers. What happens now they can act upon. The historic: that which has been recorded and purposefully buried, he will shoulder; has long shouldered. His frame is built to take the weight.

2.

Sleeping on his cot in the living room he was happy and secure; the weight of his anxiety in finding shelter dissipating after the first week, understanding what the Mothers provided was to be respected, their rules adhered to. Carefree now, as he walked through the neighbourhood; jovial in the barber's chair, feeling part of the community in every goof and cuss; out and out free as he sat with the gurls getting their nails painted at the Korean salon, staffed by quick-witted women with good humour, who paid them no mind; still frightened on walking through a crowded school corridor, but that would never change; gripped by near paralysis at the edge of the voguing runway, aware that his drag had been clocked by his competitors but not seen, that victory lay in pushing aside paralysis and stepping out, owning the damn thing, the promise of euphoria acting as the carrot on a stick that got him moving, the memory that he loved to dance, no matter what trash he was persuaded to wear.

He saw adulthood clearly now that he was no longer self-sufficient, scrabbling around for food and a place to wash. The Mothers had rules and these were welcome. He did not wish to push against boundaries, as other children often tried, instead grateful for knowing what was expected of him; how there was a consistency in care and attention if he was polite, made up his bed each morning and stuck to the chores assigned to him. Parenthood was best respected when it was uncomplicated. How he had longed for uncomplicated guardians; those who would not rouse him out of bed in the small hours to rail about misdemeanours he had neither committed nor understood; who would not withhold food or heat as punishment; who kept their fists to themselves.

He would still sleep with his back against the open room, for lifelong defensives would never truly leave, but he recognised that his posture became less hunched over time, allowing his frame to elongate and stretch the full length of the cot; how softening was a luxury he could now afford under this roof. The street and its attendant darkness became adventurous terrain rather than a series of trapdoors to be navigated. He was never far from the older children, the banjee boys in particular, whose raucous protectiveness he looked up to. Affiliation to those boys conferred an autonomy that allowed him to travel across their part of town unscathed; from late-night bodegas to buy snacks to keep him going while studying, to short cuts from the subway where crackheads roamed for naive tourists.

Do streets bring fortune? They can if you have confidence, he thinks; every step filled with wonder and possibility. More than once he is chased home from school, frightened but exhilarated knowing that he has a place to go, and people to share his worries with, if he chooses. Stunted, in this respect. Ever reaching, but hindered. How much more he's able to accomplish with his studies just from having a bed and knowing that he has regular meals. For these reasons he takes a seat at a church on the back strip, blocks away from the eyes of Mothers and children.

He goes not to pray but to acknowledge his good fortune, knowing it is the sanctity of space he wishes to commune with, rather than a higher being. Where else can he give thanks but here? Where else will he find the space; this peace? The noise from the Mothers' apartments fill him, even when they are at their most argumentative, he is happy there, flooded with life and sound, but the peace he finds there is in snatches: the total quiet that comes at four in the morning when there are not vogue balls, ten in the morning when there are.

The attraction of church is that its silence is a constant. He doesn't care about God, but understands how it's possible for people to make their weekly appointments here. Sixty minutes of respite and solitude from a week of noise. He shows gratitude when he's dancing, but that is something different, a partnership between his mind and body and the music. What he gets from a hard church seat is pared down even further, down to his elements.

He does not come to church to pray, more searching for ways to escape. He remembers looking at his grandmother with bewilderment as she walked so piously to and from services, following tremulously in her wake; seeing how she was simultaneously lifted yet still weighted with the burden of what awaited her at home; the foolishness of believing in this nonsense; how even the most whip-smart could lean so heavily on this dishonest crutch. He could not understand it, but would support it, for anything that gave her comfort was welcome; she, the only one who had comforted him. If she found a space to carve within this hypocrisy, then by following her example, he can find a similar strength.

3.

He skipped school on two afternoons looking for the Chanel store, knowing that he could steal nothing, yet still compelled to stand outside and watch those who could afford to buy pour over glass counters and racks. He studied those women intently, their clothes and mannerisms, hoping for knowledge he could share. It was as if standing under the Chanel awning made him closer to Sherry, even though he was certain that she'd been never close to the shop floor either; how in making the pilgrimage to Fifth Avenue he was earning her respect, making a concession to what she found important.

What would actually happen if he returned home with a pair of Chanel earrings? Grudging respect, a deeper path to his further servitude, or something unknown? It was the latter that rocked his stomach as he stood and watched, understanding that his future could be decided in what he did next.

He walked the block three times before deciding to go inside, smoothing his hair and straightening his tie in a shoe store window on the neighbouring street. Still, he was cautious, waiting until there was a woman to follow who looked as close to him as possible in skin tone and features; the one he chose was leagues away in body and years, but there was a meandering beat to her walk that he identified with, a rusty note in the scent that trailed in her wake, suggesting to his mind that she was capable of marrying down. (The stories he needed to create in order to enter spaces closed to him. It was still happening in his adult life. Would always happen, uncertainty diffused through his blood.)

Her countenance also was indifferent, bearing neither worship nor hatred as she entered, making it seem that to her Chanel was as important as the dime store – convenient, standard, boring but reliable – and something in that deduction, however mistaken, made her an ally. Never was he so grateful for his uniform and the origins it could hide; how the two balls he'd attended to date had already taught him lifelong rules of posture, so that he was able to walk tall and hold the doorman's gaze as he followed her, five or so steps behind.

'I'm with my mother', the mumbling as authentic as it was fearful; embarrassed to be there at all, let alone with her. Still, he was inside.

Teddy was not green. He had shopped in department stores, spent afternoons criss-crossing the great totems on Madison and Fifth, taking advantage of either the heat or the air conditioning in those places, depending on the season.

He was not intimidated by the beauty of Chanel; indeed, he responded to the beauty, magnetised by all that he saw; handbags and accessories only on this floor – all that glittered seemingly made for his body, or Sherry's; the hallowed clothing traced to the staircase below but immediately decided against, feeling a step out of bounds.

The difference in Macy's or Bloomingdale's, even Bergdorf, was his ability to pay for something, whether it was a candy bar or a pair of socks. There was no opportunity here, acutely aware of the barrenness of his pocketbook; how it was possible to be both ashamed and brazen simultaneously, again questioning his reasons for being here, whether gazing at chains and sparkles could justify the lessons missed – classes he enjoyed – all for the sake of having a story to entertain Sherry.

'He's smitten!' the boys would chide.

'He's woke!'

But what was he woke to? He wanted to impress those boys too, only in a less complex way. They could be pacified with a joke or a hoop from the twenty-yard line. His studiousness was mocked at the table, yet there was a stoic respect when they passed him at the bus stop in his school uniform. He'd been living with the Mothers for two months and in that time this group of boys, banjee, rowdy boys, had his back.

Sherry appreciated a joke but they rained off her back; she was drowning in jokes and cheap lines from every man who passed her on the street. It took a lot for her to belly laugh at the table, and he was aware that he often lacked the wit to try. I'm a workhorse, he thinks. Everything I come up with is laboured and predictable. But there remained this driving need for her to acknowledge him, eating into his school day and life outside the apartment. He was here for this reason, an adventure to pique her interest, something that would mark him out from the others.

'Good stuff, right?'

'What?'

'They make nice stuff.'

The woman he'd followed inside, now following his tentative steps around the floor; her eyes trailing his as they ran over a wall of quilted handbags, leather, nubuck and suede dyed in every which colour. If you had one of everything from this palate you could never want, he thinks, channelling Sherry. You could never walk a ball feeling something was missing or compromised in some way, if you had a bag for every colour. Would a closet crammed with twenty-five identical bags be enough to stem her wandering? If he built shelves to accommodate a bag display such as this, would she be satisfied enough to stay?

'I, er . . .'

'Spoilt for choice, right?'

'So many. Are there people who buy the complete set?'

'They're Chanel bags, kid. Not baseball cards. You buy the one colour you or your loved one likes most. That's the idea.'

'But if you wanted one in every colour? Like guys have with sneakers. They'd sell them to you, right?'

'That would make you incredibly rich. It would also make you an idiot.'

She's amused at his line of thinking rather than mocking; nose wrinkling as she considers this possibility; her eyes brilliant and direct as they roll over his uniform and his bag still mud-stained from an evening in the park.

'You're a long way from the neighbourhood, cowboy. Must be here for something special.'

'A present. For a friend.'

'She must be a special friend if you're considering one of these babies.'

'Oh no, I . . . She likes the earrings. That's what she always talks about, anyway.'

'She probably talks about more, but all you hear are the earrings. Relax, I'm kidding! I'm here to get a bracelet mended, all that stuff's towards the back of the store. Unless you know where you're going?'

'No. First time out.'

'Come on, then. I'll take you round. Don't be shy, I don't bite. You wouldn't be scared of your mother now, would you?'

'You heard that?'

A rush of blood heating his face, wanting to run but paralysed in this woman's orbit.

'How would that look, a boy walking ten petrified steps

behind his mother. I mean, I've seen women like that. I know kids like that, but I don't think that's the kind of mother I'd want to be when the time comes. Ah, don't look so mortified, son of mine! I'm playing with you. Kids don't have a sense of humour nowadays?'

They walk in sync now, moving past cabinets and shelves of endless bags – sixty-four varieties – not realising that her arm has looped through his, until he feels her gloved hand resting on his sleeve. He clears his throat self-consciously on seeing it, elongating his posture to give her the support she demands. He thinks of the men he sees on Sunday morning taking their mother or grandmother to church; how a strong back and direct gaze would be appreciated, giving her less to tease him about.

'Does she have a particular style, or can I help you choose something?'

'I'm not taking up your time?'

'I'm good. And what mother is going to abandon her son at this rite of passage? I'm guessing this is your first time here, the way that you're looking at everything. Oh yes, you said that, didn't you? I need to listen more to my children, don't I?'

'I get told off for mumbling.'

'Ah, same as my husband. Tell me to mind my own business if you like, but I'm happy to help if you need it.'

'I do. Scared to get it wrong.'

'You'll never get it wrong in here, kid. A gift box from this joint can make anyone happy.'

'I'm not sure I believe that.'

'Ah, a philosopher! Well, let's not get ahead of ourselves. A pair of earrings isn't going to solve world hunger, but it will make a girl you care about feel good about herself.'

Ingrained criticism burned across his face and chest, as he continued to play out this fantasy, unsure as to where he was headed or how far to go. How to turn and leave the store before he made a greater fool of himself; searching desperately for an emergency he could manufacture that would take him out of there.

He would never see that woman again, certainly, so why was it important that he extricate himself without disappointing her? She was easy company, comfortable with the awkwardness of his age, reading more into his situation than he at first realised. When she held on to his arm, it was as much for his reassurance as hers. Also, she was close in age to the Mothers, making him wonder why she had no children of her own, that when she'd spoken of having children, it was in an unreachable future tense; the familiarity of this from his own childhood now striking a chord later than it should've.

How quick he was to judge her when she had spared him the same unkindness. The kid's not a pushover, he thinks. I'm tougher than I realise. Everything I've been through will never stop my wits from working overtime. I will always be suspicious before I learn to trust, because that's how I was raised. For all the softness in her hold, he still extends his legs until almost rocking on the balls of his feet, ready to run should she turn.

'Want to see what I like? It might give you some ideas.'

'Sure. You keep it fairly simple from what you're wearing now.'

'Good eye, kid. This is how you impress girls. Observation.'

'I did?'

'You got it right without being a smart-ass. I like that. You're not going to have any problems. Heartbreaker in basketball sneakers.'

'I'm not the only one who notices things.'

'Because I saw you're wearing Pumas? Chanel's not quite the street, but we're no backwater. Pumas and Nikes get seen around these parts.'

'Sherry's not interested in Nikes.'

'Ah, that's her name! Your intended.'

'Not intending anything. We're just friends.'

'Of course you are. Though, listen, kid, even if that's not the case, there's no reason to go overboard and spend a chunk of money that you might regret later. A boy I barely knew from my college class once turned up at my door with plane tickets to San Francisco. Thought we could tune in and drop out together. I had no idea why he thought that might be a possibility. In three years of class I'd never spoken to him.'

'I'm not so blind.'

'She'd want it? Not throw it back in your face or dump it in the trash?'

'Sherry's not like that. Anyway, isn't the pleasure in giving a gift to someone as important, no matter the response?'

'The basketball philosopher strikes again! That is always true, so long as it's not a way to pressure anybody. Never learn to take pleasure in that.'

'Sherry can't be persuaded into anything.'

'Sounds like my kinda gal. Look at these. Do you think they'd suit her?'

'Don't think so. They're too . . . '

'Decorative?'

'They seem old fashioned.'

'Too much for a teenager?'

'They'd look at me funny if I handed over a box like that. The other guys.'

'You must never let what other guys think detract you from following your choices. So long as they're the right ones.'

'Now who's the philosopher?'

'Sorry if I'm getting all big sister. Over-stepping, right? Just your face lights up every time you mention this girl. Makes me want to help.'

'You're helping plenty. I wouldn't have made it this far without you.'

'I've walked you twenty metres, not reinvented the wheel. Now, over here. I think you might be interested in these. They're fun, right?'

What she points to is a tray of plastic earrings, fluorescent hoops studded with the Chanel logo through their centre, bulbous and immovable like the centre of stoned fruit. Only now does he notice that the sales girl who has trailed them along the counter all this time has yet to acknowledge him.

Usually, he would break into a sweat from this kind of stonewalling but here he lets it pass such is the tangible relief he feels in saying her name without mockery or judgement. The arithmetic that would be going on if he spoke this way around the Mothers or at the dinner table, making 5 from 2 + 2, muddled in their excitement and nosiness. Have you never bought a gift for a friend? he wanted to tell them. Is your life so reduced that simple unreciprocated generosity has withered to the same pathetic state as the unattended plants on your stoop?

But he stops himself from descending into shade, never far from remembering that their apartments were nothing BUT an act of generosity; how the evenness he feels, the joy of a routine as mundane as school and home, peppered with the excitement of the balls, was down to them alone. The brattishness of the teenage mind was still a luxury he couldn't allow himself, so thankful was he for his good fortune in finding them. Still, there were moments, kept solely in his mind.

'I think I saw pictures of these in a magazine she showed me. It's meant to be junk jewellery, right?'

'But with a touch of class. Look at me roll my eyes while I said that. You could probably pick up some banana clip-on earrings for less than three bucks on Lexington, but here at this rodeo ... Don't think about that, just gravitate towards the ones that you like. She got long hair? Short hair?'

'Long. She wears it up most of the time.'

'In which case, something like these might be what she needs.'

He's intoxicated by the Chanel fantasy, believing in his right to stand at the counter and choose whatever he desires. Before finding the Mothers he lived on cans of tuna and cheese slices, sleeping on whichever sofa he could find that was furthest from home. This new guardian he stands with, clipping and plucking fruit and vegetable shapes from her earlobes at speed, appears similarly dizzy with endeavour.

Why are the Mothers not as carefree? It should be them causing a riot at the counter, not a stranger, he thinks. What other rites of passage have been lost because the way is barred to them; enjoying himself yet still aware that he has lucked upon his seat at the Chanel table; that he could still quite easily be standing outside. Better to think of this than acknowledge the vacuum in his pocket; how a ten-dollar bill and some loose change is tantamount to a wing and a prayer. How much further can he go?

Sooner or later he will have to make a choice – or his excuses – and what then? He realises that he is no longer worried about embarrassing himself, more that he wishes to prolong this high. Though he talks of Sherry, he is frightened of how another woman can leave him rapt in such a short space of time. Is it confidence I'm responding to, or something else? he wonders, knowing from the outset that the attraction is not physical, rather an essence, her apparent mastery of the adult world he wishes to claim. Sherry's knowledge is equally powerful, offering something more than the cerebral, but that too is in danger of diminishing, at once aware of the natural end of things; all from a few earrings that will be forgotten in a month's time.

His mood begins to subside, feeling both helpless and foolish. The jewellery itself becomes tatty in his eyes, an easy trap for fools to part with their money. He resents the false serenity of the store, wishing nothing more than to burn it down. He pines for the sanctuary of a library desk, a space he can claim for his own, free from chaos. What's in my nature to run from one impulsive act to another? he thinks. When I should be thinking solely about my work, I'm straining my eyes reading under streetlights as I follow Sherry around, prepared to haggle for tasteless jewellery with money I don't have. Where does that come from? My mother – or somewhere deeper down the family line; characteristics that were never known or explained in the momentary trysts that brought about life. How much can you prepare for your actions if their precise origins are unreadable? Somewhere there is self-preservation, which has kept him safe thus far.

Now he is only filled with regret as the woman continues to fidget at the counter; the sadness of a schoolboy on the boardwalk who knows that his holiday is coming to an end.

'I thought you needed to get your bracelet seen to?'

He speaks weakly, not wishing to rile her, merely to hurry her along. The sooner she is distracted, the quicker he can escape; something in the mirrored surfaces and the powdered scent distressing him beyond their ostentation. He gags on the false promise of it all, understanding that a ribboned white box under Sherry's bed would not wipe the unease marked on her face. Sure, she would be enamoured, vocal at the scale of his generosity and effort, but the house would soon be distracted by something else, a crisis taking precedence over his boyish attempt to buy favour.

She would wear other trinkets, would be similarly careless with their upkeep. Jewellery can only be treasured if you know when and where you last saw it, and Sherry was care-less like that; managing to be both territorial and wilfully neglectful over her stuff. But what swells his chest is the idea that generosity is not closed to him; hunter-gatherer on Fifth. It outweighs the nervousness he feels, and the knowledge that he is moments away from a decision being expected of him and transactions made.

The woman continues to wave samples before his face, moving from earrings to necklaces – pineapples hanging from chains, charm bracelets laden with miniature quilted bags; references it is assumed he knows or has an interest in – but her voice now passes over him, as he fidgets from side to side, in his head strutting like a peacock, imperious and divine. The strength of his walk as he will return to the apartment; from the firmness of his steps up five flights to the reassuring click as he shuts the door, non-threatening but decidedly masculine. Daddy's home. Giggling to himself that he could be a provider. Baby wants Chanel, Baby got Chanel, no problem.

'Come back to earth, kiddo. You're miles away. Am I hypnotising you?'

'Trying to figure out what she'd like best.'

'Now you're talking. We need to make some decisions. Get moving.'

Later, he will replay what she says and analyse the meter of her words, and her body language. The apparent carelessness with which she discards one piece for another, the sales girl left to collect the tagged detritus; how she still speaks to him so easily and without agenda, lulling him into a nascent passivity with her friendliness, making him briefly wonder whether they could ever be friends on the outside; if a life raft in Chanel could translate into a coffee somewhere every now and then; the need for new figures in his life, and the thirst to learn all that he doesn't know. For now, her eagerness to shake him off has more to do with returning to her original business before she was obliged to his guardianship. Fair enough, he thinks. She's shown me enough kindness and given her time. But afterwards, there're possibilities.

'I feel terrible for taking up so much of your time. Your bracelet . . .'

'It's a boring gift from my mother-in-law. I'm only

dragging out the alterations so that I don't have to wear it. Just by standing here you're saving me from mediocrity.'

He wonders whether there'll be a time when he speaks with a similar authority and confidence; for to be generous, you must at first be at ease with yourself, and he still feels so uncertain as his adolescent frame continues to stretch and break, wanting to be heard but uncomfortable in his skin.

'I shouldn't keep you any longer. I need to get to the library to study before dinner.'

'But your gift for Kerry!'

Her tone indignant and disappointed; face starting to flatten, as if tiring of her indulgence for the first time – or perhaps just the first time that he notices.

'Sherry.'

'Yes, of course. She'll be expecting something now, won't she? If you've been talking about it.'

'Sherry doesn't know that I'm here. I came on the off-chance. Even now, I'm not sure why.'

'So you're not going to get anything?'

'I don't want to make a mistake.'

His chest beating now, because every word that tumbles from his mouth is leading him into one. Just turn and walk, he thinks. Give your thanks and find the door.

'You understand I was looking for a happy ending, right? I don't find it much elsewhere.'

'Not sure.'

'You're still a kid, but you'll grow into a man who can't make a decision soon enough.'

She's stopped looking at him now, fingering the edge of the glass case in irritation. He's reminded of various teachers whose good intentions are pushed to their limit by challenging classrooms; whose snarl when it arrives comes less from his actions, more his physical presence, representing an unnamed demon not disclosed to him.

Would it make a difference if he showed a renewed interest in the jewellery again or has the moment passed? He struggles for options that offer the least chance of humiliation at her hands, knowing that only courtesy prevents her from commenting on his filthy shoes or the crumple of his blazer; how his school books, those that don't fit inside his bag, are held in a grocery carrier ripped on one side.

He remembers now that the doorman too passed no comment, neither the sales girls who hover at each counter, as if somehow it had been agreed that he was the woman's responsibility, meaning collective affirmation or criticism would only come from her mouth.

'Thanks for your time. I've lots of options to think about.'

Speaking as brightly as he can in order to detract from the mood; his spirit as sterile as his surroundings. He feels dull, an object of disappointment, where he should have delivered adolescent optimism. He worries about the impression he will leave rather than surveying the ruins of a deflated fantasy. There's enough of a story to regale Sherry with later, he thinks. Street espionage in Chanel; passing for one of these folks. That must count for something.

If he feels hurt in losing the woman's interest, it must be his fault for both provoking her enthusiasm and the need for validation which she so quickly filled. Am I so trusting that it only takes ten minutes with a woman in a store for me to feel that I am living a good life? he thinks. What was so different to life in the half-hour before that made me less satisfied? He hates himself for being seduced by trinkets, hungover now from sparkle and the unreal. He wants to leave the store but at the same time, never to leave; how first time at a ball he felt the same: these bubbles which envelop and shield you from real life.

As he gets older, he reads this as weakness, looking for satisfaction only in the tangible; how fantasies are for those with feeble minds, fractured by the pressure of their upbringing; those who cannot find a way to transcend their origins.

'Let me buy you the earrings. You liked the bananas, right? Saw your eyes light up when I had them on.'

'I can't. We don't know each other.'

'What does that have to do with anything? We're at the same store at the same time, that's enough.'

'You didn't come here to buy me an expensive pair of earrings.'

'I'm buying your girlfriend an expensive pair of earrings. Big difference. Will be to my husband, at least.'

'I-I-I . . .'

'Kid! I'm getting you the earrings and that's the end of it. Remember what I said about happy endings?'

'Does that include charity?'

Finding his voice now, understanding what must be accepted if he takes them. Sherry wouldn't care how those bananas fell into her lap.

'The goods is the goods, boy. People see what you have, not the backstory behind it.'

He would, though. Does. When the store owner from the bodega lets him take a soda if he's five cents short, he's burdened for the rest of his walk home; hole burning in his pocket from the debt, cheeks flushed from the greed that made him grab the tallest can from the store fridge in the first place. The debt he already owes the Mothers can never be repaid. He cannot take on another.

'What's going on? You don't have to back away, you know. It's junk jewellery, not grenades.'

'Might as well be. They're too expensive for me to accept . . .'

'From a stranger? That's what you're about to say?'

'Yeah.'

'Don't be so old fashioned, kid! You're standing in the middle of the greatest city in the world where anything can happen. People meet the love of their life waiting to cross the street. Hot-dog sellers become millionaires.'

'Those are just stories. No one ever knows those people.'

'The man who became my husband once gave me a package at the opera. Changed my life.'

'What was in the package?'

'That's for me to know ... What I'm saying is, you should always stay open to the prospect of opportunity. Allow yourself to be surprised.'

He remembers street hustlers trying to sell their bags of rock outside his last school using the same patter: hawking suspension of disbelief and expecting him to swallow it; to exercise wonderment over long-held notions of right and wrong; asking people who had no faith left to trust in storied futures. What this woman offers is no different. He thinks of whether he would do the same if Sherry or one of the banjee boys needed him to shop a rock, and he knows that he would run a mile. Chanel ain't no better, honey; just another pusher in a city of many, working for their dime.

'You've been helpful, really, but I'll come back another time.'

'You won't be here again. Let's not waste each other's time.'

Surly now, not to have her way. Something of Sherry's obstinacy he recognises in her body language: how her body turns away from him to roll her eyes at the sales girl, and the thinning of her closed lips; a challenge he's ready to take on when Sherry acts that way, only here he's chilled by the woman's response, his legs heavy and rooted to their spot, when he needs speed and lightness to get the hell out. Is it fear that makes him stay or curiosity, deliberately slowing his movements, the way a car eases along a traffic queue for its passengers to gawp at a collision? In much younger days, barely a sapling, when he knew that a beating was coming from his mother he never ran, even if there was opportunity; fascination lingering behind his nausea, intrigued as to by what means a conclusion would be reached.

'Let me put it another way. Do you want to make your girl happy?'

'Yes.'

'Then give her the damn earrings. I'm taking the other three for my nieces, so one more pair won't add anything. Come on, now. I insist.'

'Only if you let me pay you back in some way. I can trim a hedge or wash cars.'

'We have people to take care of those things, but if you think of anything else. Can you speak French?'

'Er, no.'

'I want to speak better French. I sound like a schoolgirl whenever I try to ask for anything. Decent French lessons with someone who won't look down their nose at a bored American woman is what I'm after. Can't think of anything else I need.'

'I don't even know your name.'

'What d'you want, kid? A handshake? A written contract? This is my attempt at romance here – the anonymous benefactor. You've heard of *Great Expectations*?'

'The book? I know of it.'

'That's good. Knowing that books even exist is half the battle. The city'll go to ruin if we stop acknowledging books.'

'I guess.'

'You're trying to act cool, but I see you're carrying half the library with you. Makes me hopeful for the future. So, are you going to indulge me?'

His life is bound by unwritten contracts: with the children who protect him on the street, with the Mothers who house him; an unspoken intimacy with Sherry, this undefined space where it's possible to open up, even when he's saying nothing. What is one more contract to add to this debt? Everything that he's been given must be repaid, knowledge that does not stop him from sleeping easy, but still he's aware of it in the mist that fogs his eyes on waking: how his freedom has come from the hands of others.

By rights it should make him cautious, but he feels happy and reckless. The giving of kindness – or charity – is down to the will of the beholder. He can refuse it, but is powerless to stop the offer. It's a pair of fucking earrings, he thinks, not an oil well. She's buying into a dream as much I am when I hand them to Sherry over the dinner table, or wherever. Will talk about it for weeks.

'OK, let's do it. Thank you, ma'am. It's not something I was expecting.'

Relief floods his face, surprised at the lightness he feels now that the decision is made. In moving in with the Mothers, there was only sickness which did not fade until after the first week. Has he lightened up over these past weeks, their shelter healing him in some way, or is he actively courting disaster? Who cares? The shit is pretty. He will not feel guilty for liking pretty things, and in his right to own or gift them.

Just standing in Chanel brings about a quiet revolution, an understanding that he and those he loves are good enough for these things, and how he'll work hard to obtain them.

'Don't call me ma'am unless you want me to change my mind. It makes me feel decrepit. Now, is it definitely the bananas, or would you rather a pineapple?'

'The bananas, for sure.'

'You're right. They're the best of the lot. So, we'll take two bananas and two cherries, but if you can package the young man's fruit separately.'

Hands reaching for boxes; for tissue; the sales girl disappearing into a back room so that her packaging work cannot be seen. All that is mundane banished from view, leaving his eyes to rest only upon beauty, more things to covet and dream of, and then moving towards her puzzled face.

'Something wrong?'

'Only that I've left the receipt for my bracelet repair in the car? Would you mind waiting for me? I'll be two minutes.'

'Sure.'

Taking a seat on the adjacent sofa to wait for a woman who will not return. How he will wait for close to an hour before the truth becomes clear. Only when grown would he understand this, looking back at the Chanel boxes piled on the counter awaiting a buyer who had either changed her mind or was merely being cruel because she did not like how he looked.

Learning to wait, and to moderate disappointment, became a religion of its own standing. He'd started the day thinking of a gift for Sherry, but what he left with was something lasting for himself. Here began his lesson. Easy to lie about being hurt by a stranger's cruelty in Chanel. He still cannot walk through that side of town without thinking of his pastoral education: where he learned to shut down. Just being on that street sets his teeth on edge; how green and trusting he was; only that way because he felt safe, how being with the Mothers and Sherry made him happy. Easier to stomach City Hall bullshit when it can't touch you; that in making these mistakes before he was fully grown he'd rinsed all its meaning and humiliation, satisfied he'd felt all there was to feel.

4.

He loved parties, from the first balls where he spoke to no one to those under the Mothers' care, walking for them in drags, where he still largely kept to himself. The effort it took – the bravery – to walk a cleared dancefloor in an outfit conceived by another's hand weighed more than socialising with the group.

He'd stand with the children from his House, but was too

nervous about what would follow to engage, nodding and smiling instead at everything they said, so that they would not think him rude. Self-conscious, too, of the clothes, which were pulled and tucked to accentuate his frame. The Mothers' eyes were on point: always a deep V slashed to show off his chest, jeans or trousers cut high to best display the musculature in his thighs; maybe an earring clipped at one or both lobes, hair pulled back into the shortest of pony tails, giving him a headache after several minutes, but he was too wary of complaining.

He wanted to be there, no question. Relished how alive he felt in the heat and noise of the room. Though was it possible to have stage fright when there was no stage? He was simply required to walk and dance, but the weight of those requirements in the moments before he took his place – the expectation, also – was immeasurable, feeling as if he would cave under it.

'Book boy, you need to deliver. Walk as if your life depends on it. Take no shit from the vogue caller, the crowds, no one.'

'We want to walk home with those trophies.'

'Snatch dem trophies, boy.'

'Teddy boy, dance to the tune you like. Show them shapes. Show them face. You've the shoulders of a football player, but you can still be graceful.'

'We've seen you practising in the apartment when you think no one's home. You're no Nureyev, but you got some chops.'

'You wouldn't be competing for us otherwise.'

'Lighten up, Teddy boy. It's fun you're meant to be having.'

He thinks of soldiers laughing with each other before they head into battle, for this is similar, surely; the feeling that he must pull himself out of the trench and make himself known.

'What if I freeze? That must have happened before? What? Stop laughing.'

'No one freezes on that dancefloor, boy! Got too many attention whores in here. Don't make us think that you different.'

When his moment comes, he is deaf from noise: screaming, insult and proposition. Walks like a blind man, informed only by spatial sense. Somehow he makes it.

This was the fear: their discovery that he was different enough to be kicked out of the apartment. Not everyone who passed through their homes walked in the balls. The children were not hustled to participate, but somehow the like-minded gravitated in their direction. Those without dance skills or the ability to wear clothes the way they should be worn were made to distribute flyers at bars and stores, or work the coat check; their voices and influence lesser than the more able children. He did not wish to be relegated, wanting so desperately to preserve what he had. When they asked him to dance, he danced, jerking to their tune.

The Mothers were the gods of the room, worshipped as such. He could not always equate their divinity with the mess they wore at home: housecoats most often, and loose pyjamas of any fabric they could find. They could wear the same housecoat for days, crusted with food stains and heavy with musk, burrowing deep inside their apartments in the weeks outside the balls, as if hibernation was essential to protect and restore the energy they brought to the dancefloor.

They could be playful, but they were not there to play. Play was for children, and they were grown. He was awe-struck by the concentration on their faces – more than their actual dance moves, in some cases. The moves slayed, but their intensity was the greatest revelation: how their vogu-ing ascetic married with the music; how instinctual each pose looked as they moved from one to another, but how well thought out against the draping of fabric across their shoulders or around necks; how the tossing of a pony tail or wig was a move in itself, a riff of voguing poses centred around a plait and a house beat; all of it graceful, all of it inspired, feeding off the crowd's energy and noise and yet somehow moving independently from it, feet planted in an alternate universe.

Again, wondering where the vision came from when there was no sign of it in their domestic lives. Can this be what made painters great, he thinks, the separation of the two worlds? If this is the case, does that make the Mothers artists too? He was anything but: a boy in a fur coat and braces, or a borrowed suit and tie, who moved as he saw fit, but with lumpen gestures, lacking a more practised finesse. There was validation when the crowd cheered at a look or move, or if the vogue caller spared his walk a mauling, encouraging him over the mic rather than berating:

'. . . and work, and serve, and turn, and work. Baby drags at the 7/11 realness. Cashier shade realness. She bags more than just your groceries. Work, baby boy, work. Now prance! Prance! Prance the runway, bitch. Straddle that runway like it's the checkout desk. Twirl for the children. Twirl for the children. Twirl for the children. Faster, bitch. Faster! Walk that conveyor belt like the manager's in the office and your pay check ain't due till next week. Work. Work, I said! Serving it up, bless him. Turning it out.'

Even in kindness, he leaves the dancefloor bruised and terrified; elated from the noise, heartbeat battering his eardrums, yet deeply slashed by each comment. What separates him from the Mothers is that he's unable to rise above the vogue caller's barbs; his inability to harness the praise and snipe, and work it to his advantage as he moves. The other children treat it as a battle and act the part; the definition of fierce, ready to take no shit. Somehow he is paralysed to follow their lead; words leaving their mark too easily on his face. He is neither regal nor ethereal, his eyebrows raising at every insult that reaches his ears. Out here, he cannot hide.

'Quit crying and watch me walk out. I'm ready to murder these bitches.'

If Sherry had any fear she didn't show it; her face a palate of gold-brushed cheeks, kohl eyes and deeply red lips, mir-roring the fashion magazine spread she'd spent days pouring over. Standing tall from both pride and the exertions of her costume upon her; a riff on matador realness, embroidered high-waisted pants which the Mothers had stitched her into, and a bolero jacket fastened tightly across her chest, bare underneath. She never showed skin in the way they expected, mostly covered up whenever she took to the floor.

'Always a preview. Never a full show. You keep these bitches thirsty. That's why they don't turn their backs on me when I come out. Always wanting more.'

He, like the children, wanted more, an illumination or explanation of parts yet to be revealed. He could draw on a mannequin the areas he had seen so far. Knew it by heart: left shoulder with a mole at the base of her neck, right shoul-der with a dry patch of skin moisturised into tomorrow, the contour of her back and hips when an open dress gave her room to breathe, the sheen across the outside of her thighs when a gown was slashed just so. Composite parts, flashed weeks apart, fitting a jigsaw he had in his mind, every piece puzzled over and cherished.

He heard that she walked naked in other apartments, opening the door to the pizza delivery guy in an open house-coat after encouragement by her roommates. There was none of that now, and especially around him, he was aware of how she was often buttoned up; always a coat or jacket, a sweater or scarf to absorb his gaze.

At the balls she walked rather than danced, despite the Mothers' cajoling and threats.

'You walk like a dancer, so why can't you move your ass like one?'

'I sell enough already. That's not what I'm here for.'

'You're lazy, Sherry. Don't think we don't notice. There could be so much more potential if you listened to our suggestions.'

'I'm giving them fashion, old women, not a gymnastics show. You're kidding if you think I'll drop to my knees in this dress, and demonstrate how I feel the spirit. Let them feast, and use their imaginations.'

Always walking her best immediately following an argument, the hint of a smile on her face as she moves into the light, relishing the tease, and the catcalls from the crowd that encircles her. No one could compete fairly in her categories because they were unable to replicate her lightness: their smiles too tight to look natural, walking with poise but not grace. In every ball Teddy had seen, Sherry's breeze across the floor, so transparent as to be a sprite, was a moment. It did not detract from the Mothers' power, but it was a perfect bubble to foolishly grasp and remember. She was life.

'Boy! Get yourself together. Dry your eyes and watch me.'

'Can't. I still feel sick.'

'Have some liquor and follow me out.'

'Like that's going to make me feel any better. Get that bottle away from me.'

'All right, moody man. You've made your point. Come join the grown-ups when you've stopped being a baby.'

She knows that he will follow because his curiosity is greater than the weight of his outburst; knows that he will run after her as she sets a pace towards the dancefloor. I'm no different than a crying toddler distracted by a shining light or toy, he thinks. Tears easily dried because they meant nothing in the first place. Unsure whether he resents Sherry for knowing how to turn him, or worships her more for the easiness of her insight. He feels dumb for knowing so little about people's natures; how everything must be spelled out before it is clear.

'Category is: femme realness. Crème de la femme. None of y'all butch bitches get near this floor or you will get read to filth. If you wear lipstick but have a hairy toe, then this walk is not for you. If you have a Marilyn Monroe wig but prance like a lumberjack, wait your turn. Only the femme ladies here. No cock-dragging, beer-bottle-holding hoes to get in my sight. I ain't playing. Be prepared.'

Sherry walks after two others from rival Houses have their looks cussed to the moon and back: one for wig slippage, another for wearing a man's watch. The Mothers and children join in the uproar, enjoying that it is not one of their own who is penalised. The Mothers especially, congratulating themselves on their eye for detail, aware that they would never let these smallest details slide. A cocktail dress with a man's silver Timex strapped to the girl's wrist! What low-density mind sanctions that shit?

Teddy is agog, believing their words; that the misfortune of those of who bomb on the floor lies in their own hands.

'Knowledge, Teddy boy! They gotta have some knowledge of what they doing.'

'There's freedom of expression, and there's a hot mess thrown together because they have no clue.'

'You can be beautiful here and still end up a failure because you did not think your look through correctly.'

'When we say head-to-toe consistency, we mean it. How many times over the dinner table have you heard us say it?'

'These sloppy bitches ... I feel for them; only, learn your lessons, fool.'

'Look, a queen can try her best and not get bussed up over it. But if the next competitor does it better ...'

'We fight, Teddy boy, but there is always love here. The balls started because we needed to find love. Ways to love ourselves and be proud.'

'But competition is competition.'

'That's right. We'll cut a bitch if they drag us down with their sloppiness. Damn straight.'

'Hug them afterwards, but in the moment of combat, rip them to shreds. Tear through flesh to get to the bone.'

Sherry didn't wish to simply pass. She wanted to be. Teddy saw that as she walked the floor, in every gesture and sway of her hips. She could've padded to accentuate further but that was not her way.

'I'm not a drag queen, Teddy. I'm not a club kid trying a few crazy looks. What this is is all I have.'

'Fucking with people?'

'Ha ha! Cute. I'm being myself, is all. Working this snatch. Walking the floor the way I would if I was catching a bus or pushing a trolley down the supermarket aisle.'

True, this. If she wanted to fuck with people she would do the grocery shopping in drags; teased hair and full make-up, in an outfit least suited to the time of day: ass on show and pushed-up tits at the deli counter, or her ass bouncing out of hot pants as she berated the butcher to keep the cuts lean. Her interpretation of the essentials: corn chips, cans of tuna, and,

'. . . really good bread, because I read somewhere that it's this that separates us from the animals. I can't afford shit, but those bitches at the checkout line should know that I understand what good bread is. Having knowledge is what makes people respect you. Same with you and your books.'

Teddy accompanying her, thrilled at the ruckus, enjoying how she performed for both his amusement as well as hers. I must figure in there somewhere, he thinks, otherwise she wouldn't go to all this trouble. It's not something she would do with the Mothers or any of the other children. His uneasiness only came once he registered the hostility of some of the shoppers they passed, realising that it was his job to protect them both should an incident occur; how he was as much her armour as her audience.

Walking the floor now, she has no need for armoury. She knows the space intimately. Rules it without title: visiting royalty at best, so as not to take anything away from the Mothers. Same as the street, she clears a path just by putting one foot in front of another, here as the matador, at home as the simple neighbourhood girl who tried to be extra from time to time. How to hold three hundred people in the palm of your hand simply by walking back and forth across the dancefloor; only, her definition of walking was designed to make the crowd reconsider themselves and how their bodies moved. To walk in her shadow was to admit a deficiency, either that you lacked her easy physicality or that you were simply less alive.

'Work. Work. Girl is looking for her bull and will stalk the floor to get it. I will warn you now, if you have crossed this bitch, protect your chest and private parts. Put a hand across your jugular, and pray to any gods you've been raised to fear. This matador queen is hunting for prey and she is not afraid to get her hands dirty. Work and turn. Let us all be amazed.'

Even the vogue caller, putting his nasty mouth on hold for a beautiful moment couldn't be sullied with blandishments. Within the chaos of the balls, the noise and heat, tensions between rival houses spilling on to the floor over the correct cut of a man's coat to the width of a belt – magnitudes, he discovered – there were rare moments of stillness that nulli-fied the storm and unified all comers. How a girl struggling to breathe in trousers a size too tight brought the crowd to their knees, seeing the luminescence that he saw, ethereal and without a place on this earth, bar this space, this home. He never wished to leave.

Afterwards, in the hurricane that is victory, Mothers and children celebrating from every fibre of their being, the pair of them slip away; she, flushed with dollars but wanting to make more another way. He, filled with happiness, ready to follow her anywhere.

'Teddy boy, you did good! Now. Get! Take this twenty, and don't come back until you got either my pizza or an apartment. And if it's a slice, make it light on the cheese. None of that greasy shit they throw over everything.'

She has already turned from him as she speaks, the park waiting for no man; opportunity and self-improvement in using her mouth and her behind. She's free, he thinks. Free in a basic way that I am not; how she follows her instincts and plays by rules that only she knows.

Your capacity to disappoint others can only happen if they are made party to those rules, and she will never allow anyone that close. Not even him. For all the intimacy the bushes afford, he is satisfied that no one else sees what he sees, what she's revealed. Queens the city over can flash their tits and people won't bat an eye. What she shares, her fears, the future that lies beyond being pushed hard against a wall or tree trunk. Means to an end. Victory through war. He's growing up good, he thinks; if he can handle these realities and not be destroyed by them.

But why then does he shiver as she fades from sight, as if it's left to his body to indicate the frailty of his thinking? If receiving bruises and STDs from strangers paying for sex is ultimately part of fighting the good fight, why is he filled with the urge to run after her, protect her from those both attracted to and repelled by her physiognomy; those who will harm after fulfilling what pleases them? What is he normalising by letting her walk away?

'Sherry! Hey! Sherry!'

Calling after her finally, his voice taking leave of all that he's rationalised; that she walks, not to turn out in a shift at the bar or grocery, but somewhere worse; how he's normalised where she goes and what happens to her.

'I'll be there soon!' he tries again. 'Usual spot!'

But her ears are filled with traffic noise and catcalls from passing drivers who only see her legs and the glitter of city lights against the jewels pasted to her bolero jacket. If he knew then that this would be the last time he saw her, he would have shouted louder, chased her up the road so he could see the brightness in her face, dragged her to the pizza joint so she could complain about his choice of toppings. Would he have kissed her? He has years to obsess over the permutations: whether a difference could've been made from something so simple, all from the courage it takes for a boy to kiss his girl on the street. The city is united in its opinion of her as hot stuff; the magic she casts as she walks the route to the park.

VOGUE CALLER [i]

1.

Category is: fierce. Category is: FierceNest. Category is: shy bitches get to the back of the line realness. Category is: we ain't here to play, realness. Category is: IBM are relocating 'cos we mean serious business realness. Category is: rolled-up sleeves and sweat realness. Category is: she pulled herself out of the gutter realness. Category is: attention seeker realness. Category is: she come out of herself realness. Category is: free from the grind realness. Category is: she came to grind realness. Category is: backstreet dancer realness. Category is: what she do in her time is her business realness. Category is: factory floor by day, dance hall by night realness. Category is: women's panties under my overalls realness. Category is: Len or Le'Netta realness. Category is: confused by the size of my hands realness. Category is: I change lorry tyres with these hands but I use tongs to put sugar cubes in my tea realness. Category is: does she fuck in drags realness. Category is: fuck this shit, I came to dance realness. Category is: fuck this shit, I came to work realness. Category is: I was looking for love but I found dance realness. Category is: voguing gave me life realness. Category is: voguing is my truth realness. Category is: house music all night long realness. Category is: you can't fuck to Detroit techno realness. Category is: gimme a beat and I'll ride it realness. Category is: the beat is life realness. Category is: gagging on the beat realness. Category is: dance with soul realness. Category is: jungle fever realness. Category is: dance like the devil's watching realness. Category is: dance like your mamma's watching realness. Category is: dance like your pastor's watching realness. Category is: dance on that church organ in heels realness. Category is: coil your hair and dance realness. Category is: fix your bun and dance realness. Category is: crimp your bangs and dance realness. Category is: clip your bangs and dance realness. Category is: Marcel wave the fuck out of your bangs and dance realness. Category is: just dance, fool! realness. Category is: seriously, just dance, fool, and stop looking round everywhere realness. Category is: voguing is like communing with the spirits realness. Category is: speaking in tongues realness. Category is: more sense than a Buddhist retreat realness. Category is: holy brothers realness. Category is: monks in drags realness. Category is: the nuns is haterz 'cos we got all the false eyelashes realness. Category is: nuns be hatin' 'cos they're heavier realness. Category is: Mary Magdalene is my homegirl realness. Category is: Martha and Mary drags realness. Category is: if there was a spotlight and a beatbox at Gethsemane, we'd work around those crosses realness. Category is: pick up your sticks and walk realness. Category is: heal all lepers realness. Category is: remember our lepers realness. Category is: we will honour them realness. Category is: fight until our last breath realness. Category is: see you in the afterlife realness. Category is: dance on my grave realness. Category is: haunting your dreams realness. Category is: haunting your mamma realness. Category is: Beach Barbie realness. Category is: tropical realness. Category is: cocoa butter bitch realness. Category is: back to Africa realness. Category is: civil rights realness. Category is: Black Panther realness. Category is: Malcom X is my homeboy realness. Category is: prison wife realness. Category is: conjugal visit realness. Category is: country realness. Category is: barefoot and pregnant realness. Category is: *Gone With the Wind* realness. Category is: Rotary Club realness. Category is: bridge club realness. Category is country club realness. Category is: tennis club realness. Category is: bridge club at the country club realness. Category is: polo club realness. Category is: polo club ball realness. Category is: charity chair realness. Category is: ladies who lunch realness. Category is: PTA president realness. Category is: slutty PTA mom realness. Category is: suburban women realness. Category is: virgin bride realness. Category is: unfaithful wife realness. Category is: the other woman realness. Category is: Millie Jackson realness. Category is: the wronged wife realness. Category is: TV villainess realness. Category is: I'm the baddest bitch realness. Category is: Susie Homemaker in her finery realness. Category is: working woman realness. Category is: PR executive realness. Category is: beauty editor realness. Category is: fashion director realness. Category is: fashion editor realness. Category is: Diana Vreeland realness. Category is: Irving Penn realness. Category is: Janice Dickinson realness. Category is: Milan go-sees realness. Category is: Paris go-sees realness. Category is: working model realness. Category is: broke-down model realness. Category is: rookie model realness. Category is: Diane von Furstenberg realness. Category is: working designer realness. Category is: international designer realness. Category is: a tribute to international glamour realness. Category is: international collections realness. Category is: fur coat and a smile realness. Category is: swimwear realness. Category is: party girl realness. Category is: two-bit hooker realness. Category is: street corner realness. Category is: mama running her whorehouse realness. Category is: street walker from out of town realness. Category is: high-class escort realness. Category is: mile high club realness. Category is: international airlines realness. Category is: hostess realness. Category is: daughter of the rodeo realness. Category is: South China Sea oil leases realness. Category is: Denver Carrington realness. Category is: Colby Co. realness. Category is: oil heiress realness. Category is: agricultural heiress realness. Category is: Park Avenue realness. Category is: Lexington Avenue realness. Category is: poor little Edie realness. Category is: Russian Tea Rooms realness. Category is: hat check girl with a dream realness. Category is: bar girl paying the rent any which way realness. Category is: conservatoire realness. Category is: barre realness. Category is: *Swan Lake* like your mama realness. Category is: understudy with a grudge realness. Category is: *All About Eve* realness. Category is: *Cleopatra Jones* realness. Category is: the Hope diamond realness. Category is: Cartier realness. Category is: cat burglar realness. Category is: confirmation realness. Category is: bride of Christ realness. Category is: devotional realness. Category is: epiphany realness. Category is: ascension realness. Category is: full evening dress realness. Category is: dinner and dancing realness. Category is: cocktail dress realness. Category is: at the opera realness. Category is: Met gala realness. Category is: Black and White ball realness. Category is: Fire Island realness. Category is: in the Pines realness. Category is: Tom of Finland in drags realness. Category is: Provincetown bear trap realness. Category is: summer at Martha's Vineyard realness. Category is: sorority realness. Category is: kappa alpha beta realness. Category is: hunting tweeds realness. Category is: winter sports realness. Category is: Aspen realness. Category is: opera gloves realness. Category is: bra and panties realness. Category is: T-shirt and pannies realness. Category is: foot job realness. Category is: bar-room stripper realness. Category is: Gypsy Rose Lee realness. Category is: burlesque realness. Category is: Celia Cruz realness.

Category is: merengue realness. Category is: Mambo Queen realness. Category is: samba realness. Category is: calypso realness. Category is: carnival realness. Category is: favela queen realness. Category is: queen of the projects realness. Category is: closet queen realness. Category is: only at weekends realness. Category is: your mamma doesn't know realness. Category is: your bachelor uncle realness. Category is: confirmed bachelor realness. Category is: go-go money realness. Category is: millionaire from go-go tips realness. Category is: go-go dancer down on her luck realness. Category is: out calls only realness. Category is: he buys me gifts realness. Category is: kept woman realness. Category is: I'm spending his children's inheritance but I don't care realness. Category is: dance on his wife's grave realness. Category is: too rich and too thin realness. Category is: veiled realness. Category is: veil and train realness. Category is: plastic surgery convalescence realness. Category is: glamour on a dime realness. Category is: Upper West Side bankruptcy realness. Category is: Long Island foreclosure realness. Category is: Hong Kong layover realness. Category is: one night in London realness. Category is: tea with the Queen realness. Category is: auction room realness. Category is: blitzed the auction room realness. Category is: art bitch realness. Category is: art opening realness. Category is: downtown studio realness. Category is: Studio 54 realness. Category is: Halston realness. Category is: Liza realness. Category is: Bob Fosse realness. Category is: Fosse in Detroit realness. Category is:

Warhol Factory realness. Category is: Viva realness. Category is: Candy Darling realness. Category is: space age realness. Category is: east–west space race realness. Category is: first queen on the moon realness. Category is: first heels in space realness. Category is: all Martians are drag queens realness. Category is: dark side of the moon realness. Category is: the aliens are among us realness. Category is: intergalactic federation realness. Category is: drag wiped out the dinosaurs realness. Category is: asteroid hair realness. Category is: lace front realness. Category is: private hairdresser realness. Category is: hair hopper realness. Category is: beehive sistren realness. Category is: funeral of the President realness. Category is: funeral for the disappeared realness. Category is: femme realness. Category is: butch femme realness. Category is: full-time femme realness. Category is: weekend femme realness. Category is: first time in drags realness. Category is: second time in drags realness. Category is: butch realness. Category is: banjee realness. Category is: college grad realness. Category is: college grad with debts realness. Category is: boy at the store realness. Category is: homeboy realness. Category is: boy from the block realness. Category is: he's just my nephew realness. Category is: cop realness. Category is: rogue cop realness. Category is: attorney at law realness. Category is: pro bono realness. Category is: Supreme Court realness. Category is: prison drags realness. Category is: chain-gang banjee realness. Category is: gang banger realness. Category is: bandana realness. Category is:

motorcycle boy realness. Category is: leather queen realness. Category is: leather daddy realness. Category is: hoist glamour realness. Category is: dominatrix realness. Category is: broken-down John realness. Category is: prairie couture realness. Category is: Great Plains realness. Category is: Mount Rushmore realness. Category is: founding fathers realness. Category is: wagons roll realness. Category is: frontier saloon glamour realness. Category is: forty acres and a mule realness. Category is: Saturday night at the plantation realness. Category is: river fugitive realness. Category is: Freetown realness. Category is: Yankee Doodle realness. Category is: mammy's got the run of the house realness. Category is: Josephine Baker in Paris realness. Category is: Josephine Baker airport press call realness. Category is: *Gilda* realness. Category is: mulatto realness. Category is: down Mexico way realness. Category is: Frida Kahlo opening realness. Category is: Louisiana swamp realness. Category is: Florida Glades gold-digger realness. Category is: Miami gigolo realness. Category is: Ocean Drive John in a hurry realness. Category is: Miami Jewish matron realness. Category is: retirement home slut realness. Category is: self-obsessed geriatric nurse realness. Category is: Daddy Warbucks realness. Category is: Annie gone bad realness. Category is: juvie realness. Category is: teenage mom realness. Category is: biker girl realness. Category is: biker girl with regrets realness. Category is: the Shirelles realness. Category is: Brill Building realness. Category is: Times

Square realness. Category is: garment district realness. Category is: rag trade realness. Category is: international furrier realness. Category is: diner counter realness. Category is: twenty years in a Denny's uniform realness. Category is: Russian princess at Denny's realness. Category is: homeless princess realness. Category is: mad woman with shopping trolley realness. Category is: mad woman on subway with amazing shoes realness. Category is: restrained by medics realness. Category is: Bellevue couture realness. Category is: drunk tank realness. Category is: cold turkey realness. Category is: ten-step evangelist realness. Category: wife of a TV evangelist realness. Category is: dime-store preacher realness. Category is: TV evangelicals on the run realness. Category is: head-hunter glamour bitch realness. Category is: private dick in drags realness. Category is: butch fraud investigator goes undercover in evening wear realness. Category is: fall winter realness. Category is: spring summer realness. Category is: *Harper's Bazaar* realness. Category is: *CosmoGirl* realness. Category is: Gucci Pucci realness. Category is: Chanel realness. Category is: Yves Saint Laurent lost in Brooklyn realness. Category is: nickels for dimes realness. Category is: catwalk after 8-ball realness. Category is: Playmate from the wrong side of the tracks realness. Category is: full pussy centrefold realness. Category is: Dolce Vita realness. Category is: *Never on Sunday* realness. Category is: *West Side Story* realness. Category is: land of Oz realness. Category is: *Attack of the 50 Foot Woman* realness.

Category is: female raging bull realness. Category is: hulk realness. Category is: Godzilla drag babe realness. Category is: Penelope Pitstop realness. Category is: suffragette city realness. Category is: femme emancipation realness. Category is: marching for your rights realness. Category is: pride in your love realness. Category is: bravery in drags realness. Category is: uncompromising bitch realness. Category is: independent business woman realness. Category is: femme d'esprit realness. Category is: pardon my fucking French realness. Category is: secrets known only to a woman realness. Category is: best friend glamazon realness. Category is: women hold up the sky realness. Category is: law-maker realness. Category is: truth tea realness. Category is: cheerleader realness. Category is: track and field realness. Category is: soccer mom realness. Category is hockey mom realness. Category is: hula gurl realness. Category is: hula, gurl! realness. Category is: shake it to the beat realness. Category is: Toro! Toro! Toro! realness. Category is: matador realness. Category is: perilous drag but beautiful with it realness. Category is: graveside glamour realness. Category is: fierce and FierceNest. Dressed for battle and ready to slay.

2.

Floor fantasy, right now. She walks. She works. She vogues. Triple threat, bitches. This is a four-minute warning. Watch your backs, 'cos she will eat you alive. Work it. Work it out.

Work it out, gurl! Work. Show us why you a legend. Makes these children GAG on the eleganza. Turn those moves like you in Carnegie Hall. Precise, like you engineering the Golden Gate Bridge from matchsticks. Huh! Work. We see the fan, gurl. We know a matador has no business being in the bullring without a fan to create a little breeze. Is it me or is it hot in here? Wave that fan, gurl. Create your breeze. If your personal breeze is on point, then your life is on point. Tens across the board for walking through that breeze. Turn those steps now, gurl. Twist dem heels. Oooooweeee, this matador is steppin'! That bull better be fast to keep up with her! Yessssssss, work. Work, bitch. Show that bull who's the boss. Make that bull your bitch. I want to see that animal on suicide watch 'cos he can't keep up with you. This is some hot shit we have on the floor. Gurl is working my last nerve with the cape. Swing that cape, gurl. Swing it like you 'bout to lasso yourself some freedom. Attack that bull with your cape, bitch. Let him be afraid of you. Same as I'm afraid a you. Running into this gurl down some dark alley. It'd be death by cape, I'm tellin' you. She'd take an army down in that cape. And pose. And pose. And pose. And pose. Give some face to the children, gurl. Give them cape face realness. Give them night train to Madrid realness. Give them tapas and fino sherry bitch realness. What? I wouldn't know sherry if I saw it? I got my education, muthafuckas, so y'all better hush your mouths. Work. Work, gurl. Yesssss! Drops the splits like she doesn't care. Like she's shopping for groceries.

Splits down the aisle realness. Yessss! Show them, gurl. Keep
giving them face, even if they don't deserve it. Gurl doesn't
drop a beat. Slick with dem moves. She perfect like she
battery operated. Did this one come out of a box? Someone
needs to check. Work. And work. Vogue. And pose. Spanish
Vogue realness tonight. Barcelona street scene fashion editorial realness. Drinking with Hemingway as the bombs fall
realness. Simple matador fleeing Europe in just the clothes
she stands in realness. Gagging on the bullfight fantasy. If
you children are not gagging you are deaf, dumb, and blind.
Gag on it! This is not your average bitch. Recognise. Yessss!
Keep making that noise. Louder than the bull. Louder than
these beats. Clap like you're queens of flamenco with wet
panties for her brave, butch matador. In time, for crissake.
She's run ragged from the bullfight, but she hasn't lost her
memory. Recognises claps out of step with the beat when
she hears it. It's OK, honey. You're not hallucinating. They're
really that stupid. Work it out, girl. Finish your gig. Keep
clapping, muthafuckas. Clap her out.

Now. Here come these legendary bitches. Turn the music
up! Drown in the entrance here. Walking in their line like
they supermodels at Versace. These bitches will cut each
other for the glory of their house, and now they walking
the floor like they bed buddies? This blows my mind. This
is Berlin Wall realness right now. This is drag glasnost. Who
got they cameras? Snap this shit and snap it good. Snap the
line, kid. The line, before they reach the end of the runway.

Don't you children appreciate a moment? Recognise when the Mothers of legendary houses come together. If you can't learn to love your enemy, you don't deserve Holy teachings. In the age where we have seen everything, five queens can walk a runway hand in hand and blow your mind. You blown? Then show it! Make some fucking noise. Y'all too quiet in here. Either you've had too much to drink, or not enough. If you have your pills, then take your pills. Legends deserve our respect and you show them nothing by holding your tongues. That's right. That's what I'm talking about. I want to hear ringing in my ears. Make these bitches deaf before they take another step! Deafen them. Respect your legends. Without them you have nothing. There was only wasteland before they came along. Recognise. Without these bitches, you'd be voguing in the kitchen when your family's at church. Wearing lipstick in the bathroom. These Mothers unshackled you, so give it up. They create the space to be your queer selves. Keep it up. Turn it up. Rock star moment realness. Where yo' lighters? If you don't have lighters, throw money. Tina Turner with more make-up realness. Hair so turned, it's turnt. Turnt. Pull it off they heads, and the hair will walk off the stage unaided. Yesssss. They bringing it. Work. Work. Petal formation like they synchronised swimmers. Janet Jackson tour, only Janet wore less jewellery. Shy with how they showing face, or are they fucking with us? Give them face, bitches. We're parched and need your wig water. If you start your walk like that, then you have to deliver. Don't keep us hangin'. Don't lose your nerve or your concentration. You seniors now, so I guess that happens. Huhhuh! States of death. Extermination by wig water. Just playing, bitches. Filling these airwaves while you vogue to glory. They doin' it. Doin' it right. Work. And work. And serve. And spin. And cut these bitches with your moves. Cut these bitches. Slay the children. Their arms folding over one another's head, like they a Hindu statue or a praying mantis in hoop earrings. Work those earrings, Ma-Ma. Work that finery. I'd say borrowed finery, but I'm not as low down or as jealous as these bitches walking after you. Bitches'll need to step their game up! I'm telling you. Work. And work. Can we turn the lights up please? Let these queens see their subjects. Know who you're voguing for. What you're straining muscles and purse strings for. Your Mothers are your lifesavers. Whichever House you belong to, prepare to kneel at any of their feet should they pass. Mothers bring life into the world, and here into your muthafuckin world. Without them you'd be banjee queers, robbing cars and looking for back-room hook-ups. Or sissy queers who could buy lipstick but have no place to wear it. And work. These are our idols. We hate them as much as we love them. We want to fuck them as much as we want to drop their carcasses down the bottom of a well. Y'all are quiet bitches with the noise you're making. Open your muthafuckin mouths if you agree. That's more like it. You can turn the lights down. A queen should always see her subjects as they truly are. Goes the other way.

And work. See how they sweatin'? The work they puttin' they bodies through? Work. And work. And work. And turn. They will pull a muscle if it means getting the right move. They'll bust a ham string if it means keeping the beat. When did you last see them breathe? Who can breathe when their corset is on so tight? You want commitment, bitches? This is commitment, here. Serve. And serve. And walk. And turn. They're giving you legs. They're giving you waist. They giving you silhouette. Slicked-back, hourglass realness. They walking in flats and they cannot breathe. They twisting on the floor. Turning and spinning for they life. Not breathing properly for over an hour, and still dem hoop earrings in place. Tens across the board for these legends. Nothing less than tens. Nines not accepted tonight. Nines for the upcoming legends or the children who luck out on a good ensemble and a good walk. Not this, which ... elevates us. Don't you bitches feel lifted? Me in my Bass Weejuns, starting the night at gutter level, but now feel raised to the gawds. Amen up in here? And work. And turn. Make some noise if you're with me. And tens. Yesssssss. Tens for these bitches. These founding sisters. Clear the path, now. Clear the path! Let these legends through. Let them get to the back so they cut themselves out of those damn corsets. Give them space to breathe, and throw up, and reapply the paint that's sweated from their faces. Let them recompose.

TEDDY'S CITY [ii]

Between

1.

He searches: after school; after dark; same streets where he left her; spots around the park; all the places she liked to go, around the pier if the company was good, Penn Station if not. She stood in the midst of the commuter rush and liked to take it in, she told him; that particular station because it was closer than the airport, and even if the trains were only destined for the wastelands of the suburbs, they were at least travelling somewhere; rolling stock standing for escape, an adventure outside of her own experience.

In following her traces there he could only increase his anxiety, falsely recognising her frame in dozens of finely boned women, well turned out and confident in their bearing. Was she studying them as much as the departure boards overhead? What fantasies could be revealed in a fake Chanel jacket and an office-regulation court shoe? He understood that everyone hid their unhappiness most of the time – the goodwill of the Mothers' apartments allowing them all to heal and get by. But what travelled alongside that sadness, what dreams or regrets could also not be shared?

He waited outside apartment blocks on the Upper West Side, calculating that if you found a way to leave your life behind, the fabled Sugar Daddy comet, this is where you'd be found. Scooped off the street in a limo to live like a queen for however long the hotel room was rented, or the family were away. She'd described one such incident in the months before the Mothers welcomed her, and felt sure it could happen again. If Sherry believed it, she who was smart and averse to bullshit, why not he?

It was his responsibility to keep these beliefs alive; in the early days especially, it felt like a disservice not to. He still thinks that way when he walks past certain apartment buildings now, even knowing what he knows. Habits are engrained through process, and what he chooses to believe. Years of thinking that Sherry's disappearance was of her own volition, making it possible for her to reappear.

'Where was she going when you saw her last?'

'What was she carrying? 'Cos there's money missing from this house, which has to point to something.'

'Was she pissed that we were holding on to her money from winning her ball category? Because we wanted to make sure that she would spend it on something good, and not fuck it all away on Lexington Avenue crap.'

'Is she making a point because we decided on her behalf?

You kids ain't got no savings. Don't crucify us for trying to put small sums by.'

'This wasn't our money. It was her money, and she knew that. So when it disappeared . . . '

'We ain't detectives yet, but the clue trail leads to her door. Don't have to dust fingerprints to know.'

'You get angry because you don't yet have a grown mind. She was simple in her reasoning, sometimes. That's not a read; we're just saying how it is.'

'Sherry gets mad, so Sherry goes into hiding. She's textbook. We'll let time pass before we panic.'

Days passed before there was panic. Just Sherry being Sherry. There'd been stories of her taking off for three weeks after a row in her house before last but this could not be corroborated. Folklore woven across the laminate table. Every child had a legend of some kind; the Mothers attracted to vulnerability as well as notoriety.

She had a temper, this they did know. It made many things possible, theories and suppositions they presented to each other long after the visible pain subsided; gurl becoming a hero in the story of her disappearance, neighbourhood wrongs righted; a Good Samaritan in wigs and heels. In chaining himself to his desk, and the pile of textbooks that warranted his attention, he gave his strongest refusal to participate; hearing how they laughed as they threw conspiracies back and forth across the kitchen table: she either started a fight or stopped a fight; she robbed money from someone who deserved robbing – a stack of bills large enough for her to kiss everything off, including this apartment and the family who put food in her belly.

Sherry is not the first child to disappear, but the first that he knows of, whose flesh-and-blood presence still lingers in the apartment; strands of hair pooling into dust balls along the skirting, her voice almost tangible in the air, as if you could grab one of her insults with your bare hands to cradle and keep safe. He feels her in every empty space around the apartment; the space behind his desk she would sometimes hover around; the seat at the dinner table, a red-legged stool, left empty for several weeks before it was filled. Life moves, like water, always pushing, flowing towards the elemental, the ground or the air.

The pain felt by all was acute, a period where he stopped sleeping, ripping pages from his school books in frustration, one of the few ways he could think of punishing himself. Also, a string of nights in the park where he stood in her spot in an attempt to take her place; in his street clothes rather than drags, but needing the taste of gravel and soil to cut his young lips; to be pushed down and pounded into the dirt; the hole in his backside reflecting a greater abyss; never complete, never filled.

For the remainder of his growing years he tortured himself with his failings as her keeper; how he was not watchful as he should have been; his vigilance dulled by simple happiness and unfulfilled desire; that she'd been endangered by both his shyness and his horniness around her. Pathetic how he'd failed.

'No one looks after me by myself. You put your trust in someone and all of a sudden they ain't there. Don't need to feel that panic, boy, or that disappointment.'

'The buck falls with me. I keep my own counsel. Run safer that way. Means I don't have to look behind me, save those who need saving.'

He wanted to tell her that she would never need to turn with him; that she could run in the confidence that he would remain her shadow; that it would never need to be questioned or acknowledged, just accepted for what it was: protection and freedom to be; an immodest angel sitting atop her shoulder.

How is it possible to know someone so briefly and their life to leave such a mark? He feels not so much haunted as branded, stains that permeate deep into the epidermis and pollute his blood, a mixture of guilt and unrequited love. He knows that if Sherry had stayed around she would have moved on of her own volition, her attention mercurial, his dissatisfaction, ancestral and chronic. He would always be unable to mend what needed to be mended; neither youthful optimism nor a mind filled with college learning could soothe so wired a state.

It will take years for him to understand the truth of this: that nothing he could have done would have changed her actions. When she leaves him to get pizza she walks with freedom of choice – whether she went to the park or sat at the bus stop makes little difference. She walked and kept walking. In the same way being an obedient child never stopped him from getting beat, his mother sticking to her map of rages, her way and logic, so too with Sherry.

'People gots their own minds. In some cases, that's all they have. In wearing this wig I choose to separate myself from the rest of the animals. If I pull on these hot pants where my butt cheeks bounce out, the same. This is life, Teddy, and I am liv-ing.'

Where the Mothers fail in their immediate response, they make up for in their action once three weeks becomes four and it is clear that she is not staying away because of a tantrum. As a child, what Teddy wished for most were parents who acted decisively, confident of their decisions and the actions they could take. At home, adult decision-making and anger were locked tight; with the Mothers too, frustration marred their judgement at times, reeling from perceived slights against their Houses, and falling into the ghetto of vendetta and gossip. (It wasn't until college that he saw first-hand what he had long wished for, able parents tending able-handed kids, but the warmth he saw there was sterile and hard to fathom, whereas the Mothers' love, if clouded in judgement, was visceral; once given, it strengthened bruised, faltering hearts.)

They live at the police station and the youth services at City Hall, pounding steel desks with their fists until the soft skin there cracks and bleeds. They fill out every form there is to fill, telephone day and night, chasing, chasing; any fragment they remember which could be a clue – places she liked to go, bars she mentioned, restaurants or holiday destinations she dreamed of.

They hold interrogations of their own, pushing the children into chairs and mining them for all the information they have, where she went and who her tricks were; turning the space in her bedroom upside down, hunting for clothing receipts, cash and unfamiliar keys. (It would be a further three months until the police would decide to do the same thing.) Teddy was yelled at, prodded for his stories; threatening to burn his desk, throw him out if he was unable to comply.

'No one is interested in having good kids in this house. The good-kid act is bullshit. Brooding at the desk all day when you should be outside. Disappearing at night, Lord knows where.'

'We got eyes, boy. You think we're in the back room fooling around with wigs, smoking our weed, but we hear you stepping out. Saw how you looked at her.'

'Were you jealous, Teddy boy? Was that what you wanted to be? So thin, and fine?'

'Did you want to walk like she walked, is that it? She blew you away at the balls, right?'

'Blew your mind.'

'Should we be jealous that it was her walk which had that

effect on you over ours? What are we, pigs in heels? See how they treat us in the street? We are fucking worshipped. Why not you?'

They are acting out, this he knows. Still, he feels their insults tearing his flesh, their contempt cutting him to the bone. He remains safe in the apartment but understands that he is despised, for not making his fears clear earlier.

'You should've been jumping on this table and shouting out, not gently pulling our hems. How are we meant to hear you in the midst of all this noise? We use our voices in this house, Teddy boy. We can't see brains. They count for shit.'

Also, he was the last person to see her, and this weighs heaviest of all. In later years, they will apply salve to his wounds, reaffirming that it was his good sense that had held body and mind together; of how proud they were. But he would not forget that time.

In walking the streets he saw her at every corner: waiting to cross the street in midtown, behind the counter of the dry-cleaner's, at a window seat of a passing bus, submerged deep within the crowd at the balls.

He knew to put faith in mirages was on the path of madness, but each apparition was so deeply felt; the thickness of her eyelashes magnified through the bus glass; her scent, musky and sweet inside the dry-cleaner's. For a period he walked with the sole intention of summoning her ghost, thinking that if he sat long enough at the pizza bar she would somehow appear, triggered by sense memory of pepperoni and cheese; sprinting the stretch of road outside the apartment, her route home, as if speed would bring a faster resolution – her return through kinetic energy, and sweat. He could neither cry her back nor rub a lamp. How can you long for something that was never real in the first place; almost translucent as she waves him off, the city running by and through her; carrying on.

'Boy is like a hunting dog set loose on the fields.'

'You got the scent, Teddy boy? Are you on the trail?'

'There's only one scent he was after, and that puss has long gone.'

'Huh! No different to every other man in the city. You manly now, Teddy? You grown?'

The children alternated with solidarity and bullying, themselves hiding all that they feared. Sherry was simply the next in line to disappear, a signal that their position at the head of the queue was getting ever closer. They handled this in the way they knew how, through acid mouths and smoke. They lived, because living well was the only response they had; as vigilant in this as he was in his daily, twice-daily, skip-school-daily, hunt. Only they did not hunt, but chose to protect themselves.

Easier to spend less time with him, finding reasons to leave the room when he returned to the apartment, qualifying this as letting him study without disturbance; how it was only his best interests they had at heart.

'You the bright spark, boy. We proud.'

'Don't let it fade, brah. Get your work done. Polish that peanut head.'

They did not want to hear about where he went and the strangers he questioned, from showing pictures to random passers-by to revisiting the same people again and again: the hairdresser, the manicurist, the man at the bodega, the lady at the pharmacy. Someone must remember something, however insignificant the fact. No interest in his theories of where he should try next, which agency the Mothers should badger, which other cities were viable search areas. They read this in his face, could feel them reading him as he hunched over his desk, with textbooks that no longer made sense, that were now as indecipherable as hieroglyph-ics. Leaving him to his silence as they played music in their room, getting ready for parties that he could not attend.

It was as if in looking for Sherry he was unpicking a wound they wished to heal. Normality – security – could not resume while he combed the streets. If he was unable to stop this, torturing himself for something out of his control, their only choice was to ignore it. Turn the music up. Party on.

There was freedom in being more like them, for sure. He could drink and fuck it away. Where they were right was in that working helped him; algebra and history something to cling on to; somewhere to dive. An hour lost in equations or essay-writing centred him, grateful for the discipline it required; the order it gave to his mind. If he could raise himself from his desk he would have willingly joined in with their ramshackle wake; less to do with celebrating her, more getting their stories straight; rewriting the history that would be remembered later: petty squabbles over the dinner table becoming full-blown fights in their nostalgia, resentments into treachery, brief moments of consideration into selflessness, sainthood.

They had guilt of their own, too busy to hang with Sherry, and stealing her clothes, but it was a shame easily smothered by liquor and the misadventure that came with that. What he carried was far greater and they all knew it: he was the last person to see her; how a word one way or another may have changed – or delayed – things.

'The two of you, thick as thieves. How come you don't know nothing?'

'You've been here two minutes, Teddy boy, but you were tight. Stuff she musta told you.'

'Peanut Head knows where the bodies are buried. All the darkness in her head. Dem secrets. You know she was calling herself She'dith before she decided on Sherry, right? Ran a few balls like that before realising that it didn't suit her. How old was she then?'

'Fifteen.'

'Yeah, she was fifteen. Baby drags. Gurl's grown now, though.'

'Let's get one thing straight right now. Sherry doesn't do drag. You're misunderstanding her.'

'Look at the fight in this one! Ready to throw me off my

chair! Relax your bones, boy. We know who Sherry is. We respect that. All I'm saying is, putting on baby drags helped to work herself out. Ain't no diss.'

'Some of us in this room remember her with boy hair, so you can drop that face. You have your history with Sherry, as we do ours. One ain't superior to the other.'

'Unless you were the last one to see her.'

'Oh! He went there!'

'Huhhuhhuh. Butch queen with a bitchy mouth.'

'Don't be cunty with the boy, now. There's shade, and there's pain. We all making amends.'

Several nights of spontaneous wakes, when the Mothers were already deep in their oblivion, leaving him at the mercy of the children's loose tongues. He welcomed the company as much as the punishment, thinking that if he kept putting himself through it, he would wake to lightness one day, his footsteps less heavy; allowing him to stand at the corner of his block and look up, nose to the sky with the wind lashing his face. Just to feel something. Freedom of sun and wind; the study of how everything buried must rise: hair, ashes, dust.

But that moment would not come, not in the first year, or the second. Lightness in his fingers as his pen raced across an exercise book each night, but that was all. His brain, heavy with facts; congestion in his chest with memories of Sherry; a constant weight on his sternum making it hard to breathe. If he lived on an island without people, it would be easier; her face turning away from him on a crowded subway platform; her wig in every blonde woman he passes. But where? Drained by recollection, wishing for its clarity to blur and fade. He feels like a man with ailing health, forcing himself to run around the park each morning; a further lap to make him well; for blood to start moving around his body, the warmth stinging his skin as it thaws all that is frozen. Pushes himself hard. Pressure of another kind.

2.

It takes eighteen days after they report the disappearance for the police to visit the apartment. Teddy's initial hope on seeing two uniforms at the door lessens as the officers, dopey with sugar and desk duties, commandeer the sofa without it being offered; all promise expiring as they start growling, making it clear that neither wants to be there: their enquiries a sidebar on a lengthy call sheet, needing to be ticked off by day's end.

The officers' bodies betray their lack of interest to procedure; their posture slack, with arms extended over the sofa's back rests, as if they're relaxing in a bar; how they will only pay lip service to their obligations, and for the Mothers and children to be visibly grateful for it – their appearance and time. And while the intermittent brightness in their eyes shows how high they are to be in the company of the Mothers, betraying private fantasies, the pucker of their lips indicates a more public disgust, investigating the lives of people who do not deserve their care. From his position in the doorway, Teddy sees it all.

'Yous can't say shit. Four weeks this man's gone before yous think something's wrong and call it in, and now yous want to be mad about the City dragging its heels?'

'We need you to answer our questions as fully as we'll attempt to answer yours.'

'Can't see that happening, Fred. We got an apartment of comedians here. Too caught up in themselves to tell one day from the next. Do any of yous have jobs?'

'Let's try, then. All of us, including my colleague here.'

'How many of yous live here? Who pays the rent? Can that person step forward?'

'This a rent-controlled apartment? Do you have the relevant documentation?'

'Are there any minors present? If so, we'll need to know yours relationships.'

'Again, documentation. We need to see proof of these things to move the investigation forward. You've told us that a man calling himself Sherry had disappeared, but your details in the original filed report are hazy.'

'Tells us nothing. Someone who was living with yous but yous don't know their full name? What kind of toytown set-up is this?'

'He means their real name. Legal name.'

'Or their gender. Have yous remembered anything more on that?'

'Was this person paying rent? Or contributing? Did he have a bank account?'

'Were yous provided with any documentation to support he was who he said he was? Driver's licence or social security card.'

'Did he have a passport?'

'Ever travel abroad or talk about it? A chance he's dancing the hula around a volcano somewhere? Those floral skirts look pretty, this time of year.'

'If he likes holidays then we have nothing to worry about, right, guys? We can wait it out.'

'Was there any mention of a motherland or ancestral home? It's where a lot of the kids are going now, what with all the rappers talking about it.'

'Was he into rap?'

'Was he into drugs? Did listening to music get him into drugs, or was he always into drugs?'

'Will we find drugs in this apartment if we produce a search warrant?'

'I'm wondering why it would be that a man of his young age would be sharing an apartment with much older persons if it wasn't about drugs. Yous not family, are yous? No Thanksgiving pictures on yours sideboard. No school photos.'

'By family, he means blood kin. If any of you are the man's biological father, you should make it known. Pull out a birth certificate if you have one.'

'Documentation.'

'All co-ops in the city have a rule of conduct book for their tenants. You're provided with this when you begin your tenancy. It has strict rules regarding drugs and other behaviours. You're aware of this, I take it? There's nothing happening under this roof that would be in violation of the co-op's guidelines or that would hamper our investigation?'

'Have any of yous here been summoned to your co-op boards in the last five years?'

'Let me put it another way, has any of the legal tenants of this apartment been brought to the co-op board?'

'Can someone bring the rent book? We should take a look at that.'

'We're not the housing board, just gathering information to help us help you.'

'Yous want us to find this young man, right? Terry who calls himself Sherry?'

'Cooperate as much as you can and watch things speed up.'

'This is how we run things. Simple cooperation to get results. Yous didn't think you could leave us to do all the work, did you? The City can barely pay for itself, let alone its police services. We're wearing five-year-old uniforms and driving ten-year-old cars. Yous think the City has time and resources for this, with the full information?'

'We got parents, real parents, on our doorstep screaming when their children take off. Mothers and fathers in pieces over the loss of their flesh and blood. People who bear children show true pain, like you wouldn't wish on your worst enemy.'

'No sign of that pain here. I see people troubled but not destroyed.'

'We see them at their most frantic. Hammering down our door.'

'Dry-ass skin and their hair falling out from one sleepless night. At their wit's end with fear. They don't wait four weeks before they decide something's up.'

'They're quick on their feet. No fooling around.'

'What were yous doing in those four weeks is more the question. How have yous guys been spending your time?'

'Splashing the cash lately? Any sudden windfalls?'

'Anyone here been buying expensive gear in the last four weeks? Stereos? Computer games? I'm guessing no cars, because no one drives in this city, and yous don't look like you'd have those skills.'

'Who got new kicks recently? Sneakers are your thing, right?'

'And ghetto jewellery. Show us yours rocks. All that gold yous like to wear in yours teeth.'

'Enough of that.'

'Which boy bought himself a fancy new dress?'

'That, too.'

'Terry called Sherry had money put aside, did he? Would someone be after that money? Or did he decide to kiss yous off and take his money elsewhere?'

'What made you think after all this time that him taking off wasn't a possibility? It seems like the straightest theory to us.'

'Bored of yours company? Found himself another boyfriend? Which one of yous was the boyfriend to start with?'

'Again, we need confirmation of his date of birth. If he's found to be underage, then this will be another investigation entirely.'

'We will come after yous if the boy is underage. Believe that. He won't be the only one who might need to think about a holiday, or a walk down the street to meet a friend for pizza. Start getting creative.'

'Don't look so worried. These are simple enquiries. We're not going to start following you around.'

'That comes later. When yous keep giving us nothing, and we get tired of waiting around.'

'Ignore my man here. He's trying to scare you into giving us more information. Truth is, we don't have the resources. A homicide and everyone's out. Cases like this, less so.'

'He's the one yous need to ignore. The mouth on it.'

'I don't think this is the right time . . .'

'Brothers because of our badge, Mike? You're dead to me. Extra stripe on your shirt and you think you know it all. There's a talk we need to have in the car later.'

'There surely is.'

'Fellas, look. Nothing you're telling us is adding any further credibility to the original report. We can write up a charge sheet for wasting police time and no one would question it.'

'If we have facts we can get to work. Without those we're shooting in the dark.'

'Sending us on a wild-goose chase. I got hobbies of my own, right? Better ways to spend our working hours.'

'Not enough information leaves us open to coming up with theories of our own.'

'Like yous making the whole thing up.'

'Among other possible scenarios.'

'Yous wanted the attention. Was that it?'

'You've heard of similar cases? The City's sent men to jail who thought they could play foolishness and pervert the course of justice.'

'There's easier ways to get two strapping members of law enforcement up in yours apartment. We could just give you a ride home one night. Pick yous up from your street corner. The piers, right? Or behind the rail yard? Yous know all those places. Conduct your work there. We get a call to this particular neighbourhood, we see an apartment filled with men and boys, conclusions are made. If you have any complaint about that, please speak to your representative.'

'Statistically speaking. No one is making any accusations.'

'We're teaching you history. Queers in the neighbourhood who've previously wasted our time. Know their rights but not their manners. Happy to play with us as street justice for slights against their community that we know nothing about. No idea.'

'Help us out.'

Teddy's ideas of history bounce across the walls; of the community he came from, and the one he belongs to now; of the bullying of both; how easy it is to dominate when you come from a world outside of those struggles; the power a man can wield when accountability is erased. He sees the tension in the Mothers' bodies as they stand and take this; how they had claimed the right to live and walk on these streets by marching against these ignorant goons. Laws were on their side now, but the cowards who sat there, farting into the couch, would deny that, choosing instead to hide behind other laws, those that favoured their picket-fence morality.

He wants to pull them up by their too-tight collars and throw them down the stairs; to drag them by their scrappy tufts of hair, anything to banish their cynicism and hatred from the room. He knows not to get picked up by the cops when he's out; to have eyes in the back of his head, ears alert for unwelcome movement ahead or behind him, primed for the pitch and crackle of police radios, the blanket deafening of their sirens.

Teddy knows right from wrong, is cautious rather than rebellious, inclined to follow the rules, will look up to those teachers who have wisdom and show them respect, yet still he understands that this means nothing on the street. Ninety-two per cent on a math test counts for nothing; that he held open the grocery door for an old lady, or carried a child's stroller down the subway steps for a laden mother. He once found a wallet in the library crammed with theatre stubs and sixty in small bills, and handed it in; no other thought than the desire for its owner to successfully retrace their steps. He cannot carry that history in his face, his origins telling another story, a louder story, one that fits the suppositions of these fools on the couch.

The rawness of feeling in that moment; how everything he has achieved and will achieve will always be reduced; negated by strangers because of his skin tone and how he speaks. Even in absence – death – he'd be denied a voice and an acknowledgement of his history just for being who he was. He is not so much angered as decimated; the truth of their place in the world, and their safety, clear to him now and painfully undeniable. Shocked by the acuteness of the pain.

'You're talking about her like she's a piece of crap, but Sherry's a good person. You should know that.'

'Teddy . . .'

'You should know that. Shading her with drugs and everything else. How is that helping to find her?'

'Teddy. Come and sit down. We can handle this.'

'Calm your boy. Walking towards us like that. He can see that we're armed.'

'He's upset by what's happening. We all are, even if you think otherwise.'

'We have to ask these questions. They'd only be asked later on. Why delay it?'

'But this isn't just about Sherry. You're enjoying yourselves, aren't you? Making us uncomfortable in our home.'

Uncomfortable, too, on the street. The iciness he feels as a squad car pulls up alongside. The focus it takes to fix his face and control the shaking in his legs; finding ways to hold Sherry's tongue if she was with him, or that of the other boys. For all the street smarts they possessed, there was something defeatist in their shutting down whenever the police were on the scene; from the basic differences in their voices and posture, but also what was unspoken in their eyes: how crossing the line was all well and good, but not in that moment if you wanted to stay alive.

'Sorry we got yous riled, kid. But upset or not upset, that's a stinky tone you're taking with us. So think hard about what yous want to do next.'

'He'll be fine, officers.'

'If yous know what's good for yous, leave the talking to the grown-ups. Unless you got something valuable to say.'

'Everything I say is valuable. Our statements have value. Is that not why you're here?'

'Oh, a smart guy? Angry and better spoken. Odd combination in this neighbourhood.'

'Sit, Teddy boy, and let us speak. Mess you're making, now.'

'I would take that advice, kid. If you won't take it from me, hear them. Oh, and now you're curling your fists? See, we have methods to deal with that. Clock all the toys hanging from my belt. Take your pick.'

'You think this is funny? Sherry is not some joke!'

He has never raised his voice in the apartment, and the tininess of his voice is what he's first aware of; that he lacks the richness and life he hears so readily from the others, in his face and through walls. To shout is to expose your strength or weakness, he realises, feeling the puniness that burns behind his anger. He's aware that Mothers, children and law turn to face him; how he's shaking properly now, unable to add weight to the feather of his legs; that he will ascend if he does not control himself and take root. To fly, as if as transient as his status within their home.

If I left now, who would search for me? he thinks. Who would crowd around the sofa when the police come, and where would it be? What questions would they ask? He is respected by certain teachers for his attentiveness to study but otherwise keeps his distance; there is rarely company to acknowledge him during his respite visits to church; his mother, in hell for all he cares. It leaves these people here, this family: who he stands before is all that he has.

'You think this case is garbage so we're not worthy of your time.'

'With respect, son, we're here.'

'And we should take comfort from that? Speaking to us in our home like we're dirt? Because you've used all the polite language up on the nice families on the other side of the park? Someone's daughter goes missing and you're combing the streets. Our sister has vanished and you do nothing?'

'Are yous taking in anything we said, kid? We've been sent here to investigate our asses off. We'll be so thorough in your business that you'll wish you never let us enter this apartment.'

'The threats don't stop, do they? Just get out of here and do your job.'

A scuffle of movement in both sides: chubby cops rising from their stupor, and the insistent pushing against his frame as the children drag him to the bedroom.

'She is our sister. She she she! Learn to say it! Start memorising it when you're sent on door-to-door calls. S.H.E.R.R.Y.!'

'Teddy! Enough. Time to cool it.'

'There are people on this earth too fierce for a surname. Understand that!'

He's high on his anger now, and righteousness; understands how the other children glow with exhilaration when they act out their feuds within these walls. He wants them to choke on the apartment's odours, the perfume from burning oils, and sweat. If I look in the mirror now, I'll see the eyes of a heavyweight, he thinks. I have the strength to take this chump duo out, and the balls to ride the squad car afterwards. Sirens blaring as I ride across the expressway. Rushing to the city line.

'Do your fucking job! Get out on the streets and start

looking! You ain't going to find her under the sofa, or hiding behind the closet.'

'BOY! HUSH!'

'We're out of the closet in this house, officers. You're in Oz now.'

Channelling Sherry in her mockery, but finding the strength in his voice to keep challenging the ugliness of the visit.

'We don't come and shit in your houses. Why do you shit in ours?'

From the bedroom he hears their footsteps coming closer along the hallway, his heart rate quickening to an impossible speed, before making a left and then down the stairs; the crack of those flat feet snaking through the children's noise as they try to calm him, and that of the Mothers, who apologise and strike whatever deal there is to be made. This was the first failure: his fault at exacerbating their distaste; angry when he should have been cooperative, wise enough to handle their ignorance if it meant instigating a wider search for Sherry. As such, he'd blown it, and the entire apartment was aware and would hold him to it; Mothers, especially.

'You think we had no tongue in our head? That we woke mute? There's times to talk back, boy, and that weren't it. Six months you lived in this apartment now, and you ain't picked up how we operate with these folks? Have your ears been closed all this time? We pay for your books because we've been thinking we might cultivate a genius, the way some folks grow orchids. Today we find ourselves with the stupidest of the lot. There's things we could say to you, that we know you're hurting about Sherry, and that you spoke the way you did because of that pain. How pain motivates everything, to the point where you're capable of all kinds of foolishness, but this ain't the time, understand? The police were in our house and you wanted a lullaby? Wake up! Open your eyes to how this city treats us when we don't take care. We wish a nasty death on those muthafuckas, but for now they are all we have. We work with those pigs or we don't find Sherry, it's that simple. In making a fool of yourself, you disrespected us. Were you raised not to speak until you'd heard from your elders? The chaos you bring into this house. Confusing our noise at the table with a lack of manners. The chaos you sometimes find at the balls. Recognise, and learn from it. We won't tolerate backchat and attitude.'

'Sherry spoke to you any way she liked. I can't?'

'She had reasons for talking how she did. You don't. And lower your voice. They've gone, so there's no reason for you to still be shouting. Your tone, too. We don't appreciate it. You could've given us a chance, Teddy. We know how to act in order to change minds. What to say and how to appear. They wanted us low and grateful, and we'd fake it that way if we needed to, if that was the humiliation needed to get them to work a little faster on Sherry. You saw them. Never done a proper day's work in their lives. Hiding behind a uniform and a gun. But we need those muthafuckas. We needed them.'

'I'm sorry.'

'We're angry enough to beat you, now. If someone fetched us a belt from that closet there, new leather with a strong buckle, we'd turn your skin black and blue. Fifty lashes until our arms gave out. But we're not torturing bitches. Figure you're doing a good enough job of torturing yourself.'

'You got their details, at least?'

'Hey, we were serious when we talked about that tone. But yes, we got everything, if that makes you feel better. They leave business cards now.'

Years from now, hurling over exams stretching miles, and the sacrifices associated with that; learning to button down with each step, how to give less away, Teddy has those two officers fired during a secondment to their precinct. For weeks afterwards, he took solace in dreams; scenarios where he had the power to strip complacency from the over-fed faces.

When it finally happens in adult life, it is purely by chance; six months of sitting in the main operations room, observing the culture-wide negligence there; fungus, growing from rot. He had neither the status nor the access to effect any significant change, but rooting out certain disruptive elements hostile to new ways of practice was the best he could do. He did not look for the men, but seeing them on his third day there jolted him alert, shocked that they were still in their jobs and needing to act upon it.

Feeling like a puny child as they walked past his desk,

his stomach hollow with memory; not recognising him, but instantly familiar with the laboured bottom notes of their breathing as they laughed between each other, and the heaviness of their steps. They were thrown out not for this conduct, but for mishandling loose cash taken from suspects during street arrests. If they'd ever beaten him in the Mothers' apartment that day, nothing would have ever come of it. Thieving was different; the one code which the City could not endorse.

If he could know this then, a justice of sorts, as he kicks and grapples the wardrobe door in frustration until it sways loose from its hinges, he could temper that fire and look for more constructive ways to explain his loss. Instead, the first roar of adolescent insolence, the children's encouragement ringing in his ears, with the hollow chastisement of the Mothers not far behind.

'Batter that door if it makes you feel better, Peanut Head. Use that energy. Don't hold on to it, else it'll go somewhere dark, and you don't need that darkness. Listen to your brothers and sisters when we're giving good advice. Hammer that door. Tear it to pieces. Cut your fingers and splinter your palms. This furniture is shitty and no one will miss it. Laminate wood isn't the same as flesh and blood. It can take your frustration. Better the wardrobe than someone on the street. Maybe if more people punched their wardrobe some kids might stay safe. Maybe Sherry ... No, scrub that. We didn't mean anything by that. Brainstorming in the wrong

places. Keep going. Drain that anger. You'll feel better afterwards. Not happier. Lighter. Able to get on with other things.'

'Open this door, Teddy boy! Stop your destruction. What
angered you has left the apartment. Breathe deeply and let
your temperature drop. Count backwards from ten. It'll slow
your heartbeat and mind. Don't be breaking things without
knowing how you'll replace them. You break it, you pay for
it! This is no hotel we're running here! Cut this nonsense
and open the door! We credit you with more intelligence.
You can't get angry when we still have no facts. Sherry could
walk in at any moment to see you making a fool of yourself.
This is how babies behave, and you are grown. Let us in
before you tear this apartment to pieces.'

When they are finally allowed in, he is sitting on the bed,
panting and exhausted. They will not look him in the eye,
their faces turned to the destruction of the room, the wardrobe door that now lies flat, the clothes within strewn over
it; ball clothes, valuable to them, and the place that made
Sherry most happy. It is her presence they feel most strongly
in the eventual quiet of the room; how they trample over
her grave and memory with their frustrations and misunderstandings; how their incredulity at what has happened must
turn into credence – a party line they can agree and act upon.

He knows it does them no good to be fighting with each
other, but still feels residual power in the warmth of his
hands, ready to slap the Mothers awake, and any other child
who refuses to act. He will tear their hair out in the same

way as he attacked the door, for he is woke too now, and will not sleep again.

3.

He can pass exams, but there are twenty-four hours in a day; ample time to be used. He compiles lists of advocacy groups from library records and passes these to the Mothers. He finds the names of their elected representatives and calls their offices from a pay phone outside the school during lunch breaks, arranging meetings for the Mothers to attend and speak on their behalf. He creates a poster which they pin to every tree and newspaper bin on their block. He distributes leaflets outside the subway, and enlists the children to do the same at other points in the city, uptown spots she talked about and may have taken a chance upon. He changes the design of the poster for a second round, and then a third. They letter-box the neighbourhood, partnering with a boy who drops pizza leaflets into every home. He takes an hour a day to run in a different part of the city, the exercise clearing his head from study, his eyes taking in every detail of bars and back streets, opportunities she might have taken had she been there from free choice.

He presses the Mothers to call the advocacy groups again; to go in person; to turn up alone; to turn up in groups; to attend in full drags; to bring a beatbox and vogue the fuck out of their offices; to invite them to the balls; to give trophies to the elected representatives; anything to frighten or cajole them into action.

The Mothers were confident again as they took to the streets in their garms, purposeful in their step, strong in voice as they gripped hands and made their agenda known. They flushed away various pills or did not renew certain prescriptions when they expired. There was less weed in the apartments, but whether that was theirs or the children's doing, he did not know. Clear-headedness ruled their home; they were not always active, but they did not bury themselves in sloth, writing letters from bed, or spending the day in their housecoats glued to the telephone.

He did not direct, merely encourage; once they saw that their letters received replies and phone messages returned. The words themselves were meagre and disappointing, lip service to keep prospective voters sweet, but they understood that results bore greater fruit so long as they remained present, running a campaign to their tune, of its own logic and meter, but undeniably driving forward. From their bedrooms and the sofa, they waged, pushing, and then pushing further, heady now with the power of their voice.

Evenings, their recollections of Sherry dominated talk at the dinner table, the children's indulgences neglected or ignored; the Mothers rewriting their history for those who would be around to tell it; that through their imperfections they had fashioned a diamond from concrete, a girl too precious for these streets.

'Gurl had the best of everything. Whatever we could afford was hers. Time we went without eating if it meant filling hers.'

'What you talking 'bout? She ate like a bird. Only touched food if she felt faint.'

'This is what we remember. Are you saying our memories should be insulted? Many of you children weren't here when Sherry came to us. Stop hatin' and talk of what you know.'

'We know bullshit, so we talk of that. Sherry weren't no fan of sitting around the table . . .'

'That's a lie!'

' . . . only if she got something out of it. A jacket she saw in the store window she hungered for the balls. Cash to ride the bus some place, or to fix her hair.'

'We fixed her hair good. She never had to ask.'

'You did. But gurl was no angel. Remember that. She fought like a beast. Liked it best when peeps were feuding, not 'cos she was nasty, but 'cos the energy excited her. She liked the cursing and the noise. Kept her brain working. Kept her here.'

'These are your memories, not ours, based on your own mental states and prejudices. Children be high at the dinner table sometimes. Don't want to hear no different.'

'We were never fried. Even after weed we notice things. Burnt potatoes at the bottom of the stew. Blue and green spots across the bread crusts. Your cooking stank!'

'You got fed! Where else would that happen? Emptying

every last cent from our pockets for the smallest piece of meat. Racking our brains how to fill a pot each night with the meagre provisions we had. Ever notice how much we ate?'

'No!'

''Cos y'all were too busy gobblin'! Ha! Occupied with stuffing your faces to register that we went without. Settling for coffee and those bread crusts you're so bitter about. Hunger clawing at our bellies but knew that you kids needed it more. You want to know what it means to be an adult? To know when to put selfishness aside.'

'If you say so.'

'Working my last nerve here. What d'you say, Teddy boy, sitting there so quiet? Settle this argument before I find a stick from somewhere to make these children see sense.'

'Come on! You're not seriously expecting me to get between the pair of you? I value my life too much.'

'Your eyes never rest, boy. You woulda seen what the others can't.'

'I don't know about that.'

'You saw the bread, at least. Please tell us you saw the bread.'

'Yeah, Peanut Head. Tell us how you saw them chewing that mouldy-ass bread. Moistening that dry crumb with their selfless tears.'

But he would not be drawn, never allowing himself to take one side over the other, even when the Mothers were at their most ferocious, and the children, their most petulant. What harmony existed in their homes was dependent on someone with peace-making qualities. In periods of sustained fighting, it was always the peacemaker who outlived them all. He was only of use if he stayed alive; studying towards a future he couldn't yet picture, helping out at the balls, still looking for Sherry. It was this which determined his fence-sitting most of all, not realising how this would help him so greatly in adult life, in City Hall chambers, where the ones who survived civic backstabbing or regime changes triggered by the ballot box were unreadable. He would make a name for himself just by giving nothing away.

If I keep out of this squabbling no matter how much I want to wring their necks, he thinks, the way they throw her name around like she's just been sent to the store on an errand and will appear at any minute with the smallest loaf of bread and no change from a twenty. If I breathe and hold that rage down, stamp it under the table, kill it, then I'll have more energy to look for Sherry.

There was two hours before dark, ample time to head uptown and run a few laps around the brownstone squares and the lower end of the projects. How could he do that if still fuming from an argument he had no business in joining but still speaking out because he liked the sound of his own voice? Why should he use that energy to act smart, when he needed to conserve everything he had, stamina and clarity of mind, for being on the street?

'Peanut Head. Hey! You dreaming. You gon' fix this?'

'I can't fix something that ain't broken. You're perfect.'

'See! That's our boy, right there. Man's correct. He speaks correctly. His judgement is correct. That settle it for you?'

'Teddy boy! Don't tell us that you're siding with these hooligans, whose brains have turned to bubble gum from all their mischief. You no longer recognise common sense when it's spoken, or is that now too simple for your expanding mind?'

'Nope. You're perfect, too.'

'Flattery will always work with us, we can't lie. But don't take us for stupid. You weren't raised by mules that see no further than the carrot being fed to them. We made sacrifices for all you kids, not because we had to, but because we wanted to. When you reach our age and see what awaits those coming up under you, how easy it is to be lost without guidance, you may think differently.'

'The hand is ashy dry and needs moisturising, brah.'

'Hush, fool. I'm speaking to Teddy. You understand what we're saying, boy?'

Teddy smiles with as much light as he can spare, as if this will settle things on both sides. Times when words cannot summon the depth of judgement they require. How can he draw a line under something when the ground keeps shifting? His search widening, frustration growing, anger at the nostalgia that dominates table talk; of Sherry now spoken of in the past tense, and how that is unchallenged, even by him, because he has no answers to give. But for all this, he still notices a Mother's head turning to the door at every sound, for he still does the same. They speak in the past tense, but the draught pushing against the door frame, the click of a Yale key before it turns in the lock is ever present and cannot be consigned.

He understands the cosiness of their reminiscences, designed to put the children at their ease. There are no fools at the table, but the young are spared the tenseness that greets their phone enquiries, the meetings with City or community officials where they are stonewalled by crossed arms and hastily made promises that are never honoured; middle-aged men who sweat over the amount of cosmetics they're faced with, and who will say anything to get these clowns out the door. If the children are given constructive tasks they have something to take pride in, positive contributions in what is a hopeless cause.

Sherry cannot be found because Sherry – as they know her – does not exist, and there is no appetite or resources to look beyond a mirage. Teddy knows this but he does not waver. A person can be found outside of City records and police muscle. He will look where they cannot, rely on intuition as his guide. He still feels like a child to be so easily irritated by the dinner-table sing-song, another reminder of how much growing he has to do. If he can keep himself in check, stop the blood from rising to his face every time he is riled, then he has a chance; the need to stay focused is paramount in his mind. Cold, like the best investigators.

Cold, like her body. Without this, he's a boy detective, nothing more.

'Teddy boy. We're waiting on you. Stuck on dreaming. You understand what we're saying? Put down your pork chop and look at us.'

'Like gospel. You can't learn any important lesson if you're not grateful for it. My math paper. This pork chop. Sherry. I appreciate everything.'

4.

The lightness he feels when other children start to disappear; how guilt can now be shared. No longer under scrutiny for his last movements with Sherry, because the comings and goings of the new kids take precedence – who last saw who at the club, who sold the poisoned weed, who fucked around on gentler hearts who could not take the disappointment – but he does not torture those who have lost the way he was tortured. He's growing some. They have need of his mindfulness and organisation. Sherry's image has form; something to hold on to as he searches in the dark. When the other children vanish, their ghosts are fleeting and insubstantial. He should be offended that Mothers appear to feel the loss more: that greater tears are shed for Diamonds and TyTy; how they are set to riot after kids younger than that fade on their way to work or after the club. With every disappearance he feels a door closing; how her scent becomes dryer, her image milky and rippled. He dreams of her being hunted, Sherry. The others don't haunt him in the same way.

She cries of being hunted. Sherry. The weight of unseasoned eyes upon her as she leaves the bar; a cigarette packet crunched under rolling tyres as they follow her up the road. The shoes were the prettiest she had: white mesh pumps punctuated by silk-woven birds of paradise at her toes; floral and feminine in size tens. Still she was made to run. The choice – to slow down and unstrap the sandals, or to keep moving; a shuffle warming into a run; muscle memory overtaking what the heels were telling her; that her ankles would not take the strain, how she would at best trip, at worst, shatter bones in her failure to stay upright. But memory is the thing. It sees past common sense. Safety over common sense. Fuck everything else. We've all felt hunted, he wants to tell her. Nights when we were all perilous with our safety; the satisfaction in how we looked overcoming practical considerations. At one time or another we let down our guard and because of it, we were made to run. Drag is nothing but family. Drag is everything but family. Remember this.

VOGUE CALLER [ii]

1.

Walk. Walk. Walk. Walk. Walk. Walk. Walk. Walk. Walk.
Walk. Walk. Walk. Walk. Walk. Walk. Walk. Walk. Walk.
Walk. Walk. Walk. Walk. Walk. Walk. Walk. Walk. Walk.
Walk. Walk. Walk. Walk. Walk. Walk. Walk. Walk. Walk.
Walk. Walk. Walk. Walk. Walk. Walk. Walk. Walk. Walk.
Walk. Walk. Walk. Walk. Walk. Walk. Walk. Walk. Walk.
Walk. Walk. Walk. Walk. Walk. Walk. Walk. Walk. Walk.
Walk. Walk. Walk. Walk. Walk. Walk. Walk. Walk. Walk.
Walk. Walk. Walk. Walk. Walk. Walk. Walk. Walk. Walk.
Walk. Walk. Walk. Walk. Walk. Walk. Walk. Walk. Walk.
Walk. Walk. Walk. Walk. Get your money, gurl. Walk.
Walk. Walk. Walk. Walk. Walk. Walk. Walk. Walk. Walk.
Walk. Walk. Walk. Walk. Walk. Walk. Walk. Walk. Walk.
Walk. Walk. Walk. Walk. Walk. Walk. Walk. Walk. Walk.
Walk. Walk. Walk. Walk. Walk. Walk. Walk. Walk. Walk.
Walk. Walk. Walk. Walk. Walk. Walk. Walk. Walk. Walk.
Walk. Walk. Walk. Walk. Walk. Walk. Walk. Walk. Walk.

Walk. Walk. Walk. Walk. Walk. Walk. Walk. Walk. Walk.
Walk. Walk. Walk. Walk. Walk. Walk. Walk. Walk. Walk.
Walk. Walk. Walk. Walk. Walk. Walk. Walk. Walk. Walk.
Walk. Walk. Walk. Walk. Walk. Walk. Walk. Walk. Walk.
Walk. Walk. Walk. Walk. Walk. Walk. Walk. Walk. Walk.
Walk. Walk. Walk. Walk. Walk. Walk. Walk. Walk. Walk.
Walk. Walk. Walk. Walk. Walk. Walk. Walk. Walk. Walk.
Walk. Walk. Walk. Walk. Walk. Walk. Walk. Walk. Walk.
Walk. Walk. Walk. Walk. Walk. Walk. Walk. Walk. Walk.
Walk. Walk. Walk. Walk. Walk. Walk. Walk. Walk. Walk.
Walk. Walk. Walk. Walk. Walk. Walk. Walk. Walk. Walk.
Walk. Walk. Walk. Walk. Walk. Walk. Walk. Walk. Walk.
Walk. Walk. Walk. Walk. Walk. Walk. Walk. Walk. Walk.
Walk. Walk. Walk. Walk. Walk. Walk. Walk. Walk. Walk.
Walk. Pray your maker sees you. Walk. Walk. Walk. Walk.
Walk. Walk. Walk. Walk. Walk. Walk. Walk. Walk. Walk.
Walk. Walk. Walk. Walk. Walk. Walk. Walk. Walk. Walk.
Walk. Walk. Walk. Walk. Walk. Walk. Walk. Walk. Walk.
Walk. Walk. Walk. Walk. Walk. Walk. Walk. Walk. Walk.
Walk. Walk. Walk. Walk. Walk. Walk. Walk. Walk. Walk.
Walk. Walk. Walk. Walk. Walk. Walk. Walk. Walk. Walk.
Walk. Walk. Walk. Walk. Walk. Walk. Walk. Walk. Walk.
Walk. Walk. Walk. Walk. Walk. Walk. Walk. Walk. Walk.
Walk. Walk. Walk. Walk. Walk. Walk. Walk. Walk. Walk.
Walk. Walk. Walk. Walk. Walk. Walk. Walk. Walk. Walk.

Walk. Walk. Walk. Walk. Walk. Walk. Walk. Walk. Walk.
Walk. Walk. Walk. Walk. Walk. Walk. Walk. Walk. Walk.
Walk. Walk. Walk. Walk. Walk. Walk. Walk. Walk. Walk.
Walk. Walk. Walk. Walk. Walk. Walk. Walk. Walk. Walk.
Walk. Walk. Walk. Walk. Walk. Walk. Walk. Walk. Walk.
Walk. Walk. Walk. Walk. Walk. Walk. Walk. Walk. Walk.
Walk. Walk. Walk. Walk. Walk. Walk. Walk. Walk. Walk.
Walk. Walk. Walk. Walk. Walk. Walk. Walk. Walk. Walk.
Walk. Walk. Walk. Walk. Walk. Walk. Walk. Walk. Walk.
Walk. Walk. Walk. Walk. Walk. Walk. Walk. Walk. Walk.
Walk. Walk. Walk. Walk. Walk. Walk. Walk. Walk. Walk.
Walk. Walk. Walk. Walk. Walk. Walk. Walk. Walk. Walk.
Walk. Walk. Walk. Walk. Walk. Walk. Walk. Walk. Walk.
Walk. Get your money, gurl. Walk. Walk. Walk. Walk.
Walk. Walk. Walk. Walk. Walk. Walk. Walk. Walk. Walk.
Walk. Walk. Walk. Walk. Walk. Walk. Walk. Walk. Walk.
Walk. Walk. Walk. Walk. Walk. Walk. Walk. Walk. Walk.
Walk. Walk. Walk. Walk. Walk. Walk. Walk. Walk. Walk.
Walk. Walk. Walk. Walk. Walk. Walk. Walk. Walk. Walk.
Walk. Walk. Walk. Walk. Walk. Walk. Walk. Walk. Walk.
Walk. Walk. Walk. Walk. Walk. Walk. Walk. Walk. Walk.
Walk. Walk. Walk. Walk. Walk. Walk. Walk. Walk. Walk.
Walk. Walk. Walk. Walk. Walk. Walk. Walk. Walk. Walk.
Walk. Walk. Walk. Walk. Walk. Walk. Walk. Walk. Walk.
Walk. Walk. Walk. Walk. Walk. Walk. Walk. Walk. Walk.
Walk. Walk. Walk. Walk. Walk. Walk. Walk. Walk. Walk.

Walk. Walk. Walk. Walk. Walk. Walk. Walk. Walk. Walk.
Walk. Walk. Walk. Walk. Walk. Walk. Walk. Walk. Walk.
Walk. Walk. Walk. Walk. Walk. Walk. Walk. Walk. Walk.
Walk. Walk. Walk. Walk. Walk. Walk. Walk. Walk. Walk.
Walk. Walk. Walk. Walk. Walk. Walk. Walk. Walk. Walk.
Walk. Walk. Walk. Walk. Walk. Walk. Walk. Walk. Walk.
Walk. Walk. Walk. Walk. Walk. Walk. Walk. Walk. Walk.
Walk. Walk. Walk. Walk. Walk. Walk. Walk. Walk. Walk.
Walk. Walk. Walk. Walk. Walk. Walk. Walk. Walk. Walk.
Walk. Walk. Walk. Walk. Walk. Walk. Walk. Walk. Walk.
Walk. Walk. Walk. Walk. Walk. Walk. Walk. Walk. Walk.
Walk. Walk. Walk. Walk. Walk. Walk. Walk. Walk. Walk.
Walk. Walk. Walk. Walk. Walk. Walk. Walk. Walk. Walk.
Walk. Walk. Walk. Walk. Walk. Walk. Walk. Walk. Walk.
Walk. Walk. Walk. Walk. Walk. Walk. Walk. Walk. Walk.
Walk. Walk. Walk. Walk. Walk. Walk. Walk. Walk. Walk.
Walk. Walk. Walk. Walk. Walk. Walk. Walk. Walk. Walk.
Walk. Walk. Walk. Walk. Walk. Walk. Walk. Walk. Walk.
Walk. Walk. Walk. Walk. Walk. Walk. Walk. Walk. Walk.
Walk. Walk. Walk. Walk. Walk. Walk. Walk. Walk. Walk.
Walk. Walk. Walk. Walk. Walk. Walk. Walk. Walk. Walk.
Walk. Walk. Walk. Walk. Walk. Walk. Walk. Walk. Walk.
Walk. Walk. Walk. Walk. Walk. Walk. Walk. Walk. Walk.
Walk. Walk. Walk. Walk. Walk. Walk. Walk. Walk. Walk.
Walk. Walk. Walk. Walk. Walk. Walk. Walk. Walk. Walk.
Walk. Walk. Walk. Walk. Walk. Walk. Walk. Walk. Walk.
Walk. Walk. Walk. Walk. Walk. Walk. Walk. Walk. Walk.
Walk. Walk. Walk. Walk. Pray your maker sees you. Walk.

Walk. Walk. Walk. Walk. Walk. Walk. Walk. Walk. Walk.
Walk. Walk. Walk. Walk. Walk. Walk. Walk. Walk. Walk.
Walk. Walk. Walk. Walk. Walk. Walk. Walk. Walk. Walk.
Walk. Walk. Walk. Walk. Walk. Walk. Walk. Walk. Walk.
Walk. Walk. Walk. Walk. Walk. Walk. Walk. Walk. Walk.
Walk. Walk. Walk. Walk. Walk. Walk. Walk. Walk. Walk.
Walk. Walk. Walk. Walk. Walk. Walk. Walk. Walk. Walk.
Walk. Walk. Walk. Walk. Walk. Walk. Walk. Walk. Walk.
Walk. Walk. Walk. Walk. Walk. Walk. Walk. Walk. Walk.
Walk. Walk. Walk. Walk. Walk. Walk. Walk. Walk. Walk.
Walk. Walk. Walk. Walk. Walk. Walk. Walk. Walk. Walk.
Walk. Walk. Walk. Walk. Walk. Walk. Walk. Walk. Walk.
Walk. Walk. Walk. Walk. Walk. Walk. Walk. Walk. Walk.
Walk. Walk. Walk. Walk. Walk. Walk. Walk. Walk. Walk.
Walk. Walk. Walk. Walk. Walk. Walk. Walk. Walk. Walk.
Walk. Walk. Walk. Walk. Walk. Walk. Walk. Walk. Walk.
Walk. Walk. Walk. Walk. Walk. Walk. Walk. Walk. Walk.
Walk. Walk. Walk. Walk. Walk. Walk. Walk. Walk. Walk.
Walk. Walk. Walk. Walk. Walk. Walk. Walk. Walk. Walk.
Walk. Walk. Walk. Walk. Walk. Walk. Walk. Walk. Walk.
Walk. Walk. Walk. Walk. Walk. Walk. Walk. Walk. Walk.
Walk. Walk. Walk. Walk. Walk. Walk. Walk. Walk. Walk.
Walk. Walk. Walk. Walk. Walk. Walk. Walk. Walk. Walk.
Walk. Walk. Walk. Walk. Walk. Walk. Walk. Walk. Walk.
Walk. Walk. Walk. Walk. Walk. Walk. Walk. Walk. Walk.
Walk. Walk. Walk. Walk. Walk. Walk. Walk. Walk. Walk.
Walk. Walk. Walk. Walk. Walk. Walk. Walk. Walk. Walk.
Walk. Walk. Walk. Walk. Walk. Walk. Walk. Walk. Walk.

Walk. Walk. Walk. Walk. Walk. Walk. Walk. Walk. Walk.
Walk. Walk. Walk. Walk. Walk. Walk. Walk. Walk. Walk.
Walk. Walk. Walk. Walk. Walk. Walk. Walk. Walk. Walk.
Walk. Walk. Walk. Walk. Walk. Walk. Walk. Walk. Walk.
Walk. Walk. Walk. Walk. Walk. Walk. Walk. Walk. Walk.
Walk. Walk. Walk. Walk. Walk. Walk. Walk. Walk. Walk.
Walk. Walk. Walk. Walk. Walk. Walk. Walk. Walk. Walk.
Walk. Walk. Walk. Walk. Walk. Walk. Walk. Walk. Walk.
Walk. Walk. Walk. Walk. Walk. Walk. Walk. Walk. Walk.
Walk. Walk. Walk. Walk. Walk. Walk. Walk. Walk. Walk.
Walk. Walk. Walk. Walk. Walk. Walk. Walk. Walk. Walk.
Walk. Walk. Walk. Walk. Walk. Walk. Walk. Walk. Walk.
Walk. Walk. Walk. Walk. Walk. Walk. Walk. Walk. Walk.
Walk. Walk. Walk. Walk. Walk. Walk. Walk. Walk. Walk.
Walk. Walk. Walk. Walk. Walk. Walk. Walk. Walk. Walk.
Walk. Walk. Walk. Walk. Walk. Walk. Walk. Walk. Walk.
Walk. Walk. Walk. Walk. Walk. Walk. Get your money,
gurl. Walk. Walk. Walk. Walk. Walk. Walk. Walk. Walk.
Walk. Walk. Walk. Walk. Walk. Walk. Walk. Walk. Walk.
Walk. Walk. Walk. Walk. Walk. Walk. Walk. Walk. Walk.
Walk. Walk. Walk. Walk. Walk. Walk. Walk. Walk. Walk.
Walk. Walk. Walk. Walk. Walk. Walk. Walk. Walk. Walk.
Walk. Walk. Walk. Walk. Walk. Walk. Walk. Walk. Walk.
Walk. Walk. Walk. Walk. Walk. Walk. Walk. Walk. Walk.
Walk. Walk. Walk. Walk. Walk. Walk. Walk. Walk. Walk.
Walk. Walk. Walk. Walk. Walk. Walk. Walk. Walk. Walk.

Walk. Walk. Walk. Walk. Walk. Walk. Walk. Walk. Walk.
Walk. Walk. Walk. Walk. Walk. Walk. Walk. Walk. Walk.
Walk. Walk. Walk. Walk. Walk. Walk. Walk. Walk. Walk.
Walk. Walk. Walk. Walk. Walk. Walk. Walk. Walk. Walk.
Walk. Walk. Walk. Walk. Walk. Walk. Walk. Walk. Walk.
Walk. Walk. Walk. Walk. Walk. Walk. Walk. Walk. Walk.
Walk. Walk. Walk. Walk. Walk. Walk. Walk. Walk. Walk.
Walk. Walk. Walk. Walk. Walk. Walk. Walk. Walk. Walk.
Walk. Walk. Walk. Walk. Walk. Walk. Walk. Walk. Walk.
Walk. Walk. Walk. Walk. Walk. Walk. Walk. Walk. Walk.
Walk. Walk. Walk. Walk. Walk. Walk. Walk. Walk. Walk.
Walk. Walk. Walk. Walk. Walk. Walk. Walk. Walk. Walk.
Walk. Walk. Walk. Walk. Walk. Walk. Walk. Walk. Walk.
Walk. Walk. Walk. Walk. Walk. Walk. Walk. Walk. Walk.
Walk. Walk. Walk. Walk. Walk. Walk. Walk. Walk. Walk.
Walk. Walk. Walk. Walk. Walk. Walk. Walk. Walk. Walk.
Walk. Walk. Walk. Walk. Walk. Walk. Walk. Walk. Walk.
Walk. Walk. Walk. Walk. Walk. Walk. Walk. Walk. Walk.
Walk. Walk. Walk. Walk. Walk. Walk. Walk. Walk. Walk.
Walk. Walk. Walk. Walk. Walk. Walk. Walk. Walk. Walk.
Walk. Walk. Walk. Walk. Walk. Walk. Walk. Walk. Walk.
Walk. Walk. Walk. Walk. Walk. Walk. Walk. Walk. Walk.
Walk. Walk. Walk. Walk. Walk. Walk. Walk. Walk. Walk.
Walk. Walk. Walk. Walk. Walk. Walk. Walk. Walk. Walk.
Walk. Walk. Walk. Walk. Walk. Walk. Walk. Walk. Walk.
Walk. Walk. Walk. Walk. Walk. Walk. Walk. Walk. Walk.

Walk. Walk. Walk. Walk. Walk. Walk. Walk. Walk. Walk.
Walk. Walk. Walk. Walk. Walk. Walk. Walk. Walk. Walk.
Walk. Walk. Walk. Walk. Walk. Walk. Walk. Walk. Walk.
Walk. Walk. Walk. Walk. Walk. Walk. Walk. Walk. Walk.
Walk. Walk. Walk. Walk. Walk. Walk. Walk. Walk. Walk.
Walk. Walk. Walk. Walk. Walk. Walk. Walk. Walk. Walk.
Walk. Walk. Walk. Walk. Walk. Walk. Walk. Walk. Walk.
Walk. Walk. Walk. Walk. Walk. Walk. Walk. Walk. Walk.
Walk. Walk. Walk. Walk. Walk. Walk. Walk. Walk. Walk.
Walk. Walk. Walk. Walk. Walk. Walk. Walk. Walk. Walk.
Walk. Walk. Walk. Walk. Walk. Walk. Walk. Walk. Walk.
Walk. Walk. Walk. Walk. Walk. Walk. Walk. Walk. Walk.
Walk. Walk. Walk. Walk. Walk. Walk. Walk. Walk. Walk.
Walk. Walk. Walk. Walk. Walk. Walk. Walk. Walk. Walk.
Walk. Walk. Walk. Walk. Walk. Walk. Walk. Walk. Walk.
Walk. Walk. Walk. Walk. Walk. Walk. Walk. Walk. Walk.
Walk. Walk. Walk. Walk. Walk. Walk. Walk. Walk. Walk.
Walk. Walk. Walk. Walk. Walk. Walk. Walk. Walk. Walk.
Walk. Walk. Walk. Walk. Walk. Walk. Walk. Walk. Walk.
Walk. Walk. Walk. Walk. Walk. Walk. Walk. Walk. Walk.
Walk. Walk. Walk. Walk. Walk. Walk. Walk. Walk. Walk.
Walk. Walk. Walk. Walk. Walk. Walk. Walk. Walk. Walk.
Walk. Walk. Walk. Walk. Walk. Walk. Walk. Walk. Walk.
Walk. Walk. Walk. Walk. Walk. Walk. Walk. Walk. Walk.
Walk. Walk. Walk. Walk. Walk. Walk. Walk. Walk. Walk.
Walk. Walk. Pray your maker sees you. Walk.

TEDDY'S CITY [iii]

Grown

1.

'What was this about working for the City?'

'The City pays my wages, officers. Same as yours. That same brown envelope on the last day of the month. Same blue slip. Same deductions.'

'Well, you're not a cop.'

'Clearly not.'

'If I had ten dollars for every jerk who claimed to be undercover as we booked 'em, I'd be living with the family in St Barts. If I had fifty dollars for every time I heard that line, I'd ditch the family for a washed-up supermodel.'

'Making more undercover cops than hoods.'

'Exactly that. They see the badge and take us for clowns. Think we can be talked out of anything.'

'Even with the gun?'

'Even with the gun. Fear of the barrel sharpens your wits. Makes them think fast. If you're coming up with excuses, better make it the best excuse you've ever had. Let the words distract from the stink that's coming from everywhere else. Their eyes are yellow with it. Choking on the smell of their own bullshit but talking like there's no tomorrow. Looking for any loophole they can find.'

'My fragrant Mothers will never yellow. I trust you've already determined this?'

'Hard as nails, your mothers. Susceptible to the weather, but otherwise they can take anything we throw at them. We're including you in their number, also. You're talking up a storm, but you're unafraid. Is this what the City hires you to do? Talk?'

'Industrial and civic policy. You've been brought in from outside the precinct, which is why I'm a stranger to you.'

'We can find out for ourselves but it will be easier on you if you tell us. We'll be busted for filing an incomplete report without these details. Your name doesn't sound right for a start.'

'On that brown envelope handed to me on the last day of the month, it says Teddy on the front. Ultimately it doesn't matter what I do. I work for the City same as the garbage men work for the City. No more or less important than that. What your report includes or doesn't include regarding my name and occupation should have no bearing on the tone or content of what you write up. It will be backed with independent evidence to that effect.'

'You're submitting a report?'

'It's what's expected of me. You see how there are over

one hundred people joining us today? Tomorrow it will be closer to two hundred. By the end of the week, more. Movements grow. It's the natural order of things.'

'Mobs grow, too. This is also the order of things unless nipped in the bud.'

'The City isn't getting a mob. It's accommodating peaceful protest. One where no one says a word. How is that a mob? You see them as a group of old men, but to me they are my Mothers. This is a family, sitting peacefully with their friends. The City has no problem with that. None whatsoever.'

'See the flowers that flank the building on the left sidewalk? A month ago they were white, now their petals have turned blue. The City can change its mind, son. Today you're a hundred red roses, I'll give you that. But tomorrow your precious two hundred will switch to blue, and you'll struggle to explain why.'

2.

Back at his apartment, Teddy smoked on the balcony he shared with his neighbour, a woman in her seventies who never left the house aside from Christmas and saints' days. He would make notes on his report later, but for now he only had a mind for the slow-burning rush of his cigarette and to watch the sun disappear over his building before sinking into Queens. He was at the apartment so rarely at that time of day he had forgotten that the golden hour he so cherished in the early years of his tenancy could still hit this backwater between Hells and uptown.

The light that bathed the Mothers as he left them was similarly flaxen; combined with their poses on the steps, they briefly became statues of piousness and sacrifice. A century ago and more, they would have been either celebrated as saints or burned at the stake. Both, most likely. He was loath to return inside because his notebook was waiting, and once within the proximity of his desk he could no longer deny his obligations. He'd been asked to observe the movement and to participate as his origins dictated, in so long as it curtailed the protest morphing into something unpalatable.

All the work has been for this: an avalanche of lies and shit that come with a City pay check. The sacrifices, so that he can improve life for certain parts of the community and irreparably damage others, through compromise or lack of will. For all the boxes he can open, the one that explains what happened to the children – most of them – remains out of reach, if it exists at all. Children run away. They get bored and move on. They tire of the scene. They look at the balls with maturing eyes and feel sickness lodge in their stomachs; bile ducts flooding their denial of who they are, washing it away. He cannot write policy for their disgust. This is something they must deal with themselves. What he can do is strengthen the rights of communities within existing licensing laws, enabling clubs to operate with bullshit raids that are conducted for fear and spite. He can install more prominent cab ranks in the hubs of uptown neighbourhoods, so that kids can get home safely; no more Sherrys being chased home after midnight. This is how he starts at City Hall, with trifles that mean nothing to those at neighbouring desks, and upwards from there.

The City asked much of Teddy, firefighting so that they could keep their hands clean. Many times he was burned, but never did he shirk his responsibility. He understood that he was lucky; the opportunity afforded him had fallen to few others. He was here because he was observant and could be trusted, and because he had worked hard. His desk at City Hall was not due to the lack that marked his background, but in spite of it. There were those in the team who did not see it that way, preferring to acknowledge his assignments with barbed references to affirmative action; seniors who were considered no longer valuable to the field, shitting their pants at that thought muddying their hands. Mentors who had previously dispensed advice freely, assuming they were passing tips that would never be used, ignored his calls and made themselves unavailable.

This distancing is a trick of another kind; if you were not in the room you could claim no responsibility when things went wrong; miraculously reappearing for the clean-up and insincere wringing of hands. Inside City Hall, among friends, his guard was constantly up for fear of making a mistake; blank faces and statutory jargon chipping away at his confidence.

Only out on the street did he truly feel himself and have faith in his capabilities; able to quell the mood at a union meeting or picket line. That he was known and respected; that he could be confided in; how he was able to make himself invisible when the situation required, all imbibed him with a sense of strength. You find a kid in trouble and you lift them up, somehow; the way he too was lifted. It was in his grasp to change the city to his vision so long as he knuckled down and took action when it needed to be taken. Direct change gives him the most gratification but his head fizzes with the opportunities creating policy can provide. Wonk at the vogue ball, wonk at the policy desk. Every environment he cares about is touched by his wonkiness: the balls, finally made profitable in their last years; the city, a living, breathing organism, to be pored over and understood; for weak spots to be identified, assessed, and then attacked. He was learning about their weaknesses; wormholes through which he would burrow and hide.

He was asked to find a way to stop the protest before it grew out of hand.

'These are your people, kid. Best you're the one to clean it up.'

'Postpone your operation following around undocumented builders and look out for some of your folks.'

'Would you rather they were treated fairly or unfairly? Is family dealing with family never the gentler option?'

'If I had kin on those steps, I would want to be the one

to turn them away. My hand on their shoulder rather than law enforcement.'

'Think of the experience. Something to take on to the next job.'

'It'll read better from your touch. Photograph better.'

'No one's asking you to put on disguises. Just to keep a handle on their trouble.'

'If they're unable to properly identify those alleged young people who've gone missing, how are we?'

'What makes them think that now is the time to wait at our door? Is it compensation they seek?'

'Have their TV shows been cancelled and they're looking to pass the time?'

'Is this new to you? Have you heard this problem discussed before?'

'We take a dim view of inside jobs, son. You've heard stories about your predecessors, I take it? Of course every bastard wants a tip-off. Doesn't mean they get it.'

'Let them know they can't make their noise here. Make it clear the steps are neither their lounge nor their pulpit. We can host them for this short time, if only to show that the City is listening, but we will not engage further.'

'We don't engage or indulge. Remember your teachings.'

'Kid, make it go away. Get your experience and move them on before everyone looks like an ass, the City included.'

The Mothers would hate him in time – before they understood, so he was making the most of the hours spent with them in their ignorance; studying each as they sat there, from the shadows under their eyes to the way each cleared their throat; the way they expressed their care and annoyance through silence; how everything was communicated through the hands and eyes. (Their bad humour being as precious as their joy.) He absorbed it all, something to treasure when they would no longer speak to him. He was not yet close, still warming up, but understood how relentless the operation would be; how all was governed by this need to fuel. He was doing it for them, in the end.

3.

The restroom was their cheat space; the stink-hole a floor below the burger fryers at the joint across the street. Two visits at three and nine o'clock, policed by Teddy but with a degree of self-enforcement once they realised the relief it provided: to piss, cry, wail and cuss in the privacy that basement afforded. Teddy examined the bruises on their knees and butts, massaged the circulation back into their extremities, and watched as they paced the corridor until pins and needles ceased. Their tears came from anger and tiredness; their cussing from the same place also, but with greater relish, he noticed, on the days when their bodies felt less punished and they were able to acknowledge the mischief being served.

'Muthafucka on security barring the door to City Hall like he's the last Injun. Thinking he's back on the frontier.'

'He has the same tight, sunburnt face as the rest of the wagon rollers. Put a bonnet on him and he'd be panning gold and fighting whoever got in his way. Little bastard.'

'He's just pissed that they won't let him carry no gun. You can see in his eyes how quickly he would've seen us away.'

'Manners is manners. He should know his station.'

'He does: to keep us out. He'll kill us with his bare hands if he has to.'

'It's fucked-up that we're relying on the police to protect us. They'd bring me down if I even looked at them the wrong way on the street.'

'But out here, look how they cluster around us. Like we're a pack of endangered zebras.'

'Girl, we are endangered. Last of our kind.'

'Who the fuck are you calling a zebra? We're peacocks, aren't we? Look at our legs.'

'We're old buzzards with half our feathers falling out. Broilers ready for the pot.'

Teddy presides as they confer over their position and say their prayers; generals in their war room, moisturising ashy arms and elbows. They will kick the trash can in frustration or perform another act of minor vandalism to burn off the latent energy that continues to fizz. In those fifteen minutes they exercise their mouths like they're on the sprint-track:

fast burn, talking whatever pain may come later to the muscles in their throat and jaw.

On and on; all that is ugly and blinds them to their purpose. Something sincere, even in their petty hatreds: feeling unable to complain that donuts delivered by the police that morning were stale; how the biggest threat to breaking silence is often the nausea brought on by the foul gases emitted by one or other of the Mothers. They jump and holler their frustrations like frat boys waiting for girls to arrive at a party; they pluck and preen as if backstage at the balls. Serving beauty to moments that were never beautiful, he realises. The best they managed with all that they had. They return, determined and silent once more, any unresolved argument saved for the next six hours of silence.

By nature they are not disciplined people, Teddy writes later in his report. What they have achieved is largely down to a combination of tenacity and mistakes. Putting the balls together, running their households, was born from pride and stubbornness. An innate narcissism also placed them at the head of their tables; similarly behind why they were always the last to walk at balls.

Once they saw what had been created, how it was valued in the community, they were motivated by duty and love; but throughout their greater years, their well-intentioned infrastructure was marred by chaos and laziness. They were capable of organising, but the slackers among them would unravel their work in an instant: costumes not being made because of domestic troubles with unsuitable partners; children going into hiding, who decided that the street was a greater draw than their table; ball judges from the fashion world who tried to steal the best walkers for no money; their dead-of-night belief that they were still worthless and not capable of anything.

Others would lay different charges at their door, a litany of grievances, but still all the while proclaiming that their achievements should be recognised; that without the balls and Houses, many children would have been lost, Teddy among them, and their culture undeveloped and unrecognised. Maybe that is what he is doing, he thinks. That by writing reports he is forcing recognition on to those who have no clue. If he breaks the movement but gives their achievements the credence it deserves, will that not be worth it?

The Mothers' untended grief over the lost children, undimmed by their conversion, is informed by their ongoing silence. Of this he takes note. They do not understand this as a discipline but as something elemental, as necessary as breathing or sight. They are prepared to lose both if a further difference can be made. They are guided by what they have been taught in Sunday mass: that the differentiation between a well-meaning individual and a saint lies in such decisions; lessons too from their brothers on the street; on amassing street corner power quietly and without fuss. Any means.

Teddy understands all this, but knows too that an explanation without words is open to interpretation. His eyes are not theirs. Whether college has changed his perception of where he comes from, or if the logic that governs their action remains an implicit belief that cannot waver, he is unsure. What he fears is their disappointment if he explains in too-simple language – in writing or otherwise – the strength of their action; though ultimately, it is his decision, for this is what their parenthood has prepared him for.

4.

Teddy fulfilled his obligations on both sides; his keeping watch on the steps served him well. The officers he'd been speaking to, bored out of their minds; the children having no provocation, subdued. He wonders whether the essence of protest – and wars – lies in these lulls. How conflict is essentially inertia interspersed with fighting. And of what ratio – 70:30, 90:10? His mind wanders as the others' seem to do. What powers a man to fight other than adrenalin if stupor and hunger marks the remainder of his day? Where does the energy come from – fear or the pleasure of distraction?

He has difficulty envisioning the children getting to their feet, sleepy and underwhelmed. Even those he counts as family: troublemakers who raised hell at the dinner table are now pacified by silence. Those fast to quarrel or seek attention in more dramatic ways, sweeping plates from the table when they felt misunderstood or ignored, rifling through pockets whilst others slept, bringing home tricks who were decades past the parameters of young manhood, all nullified by the movement, whether in delayed response to the abrupt disappearances of their brothers and sisters, or in bemusement that the action itself existed; executed and brought to their door by the crazy house mothers they were trying to escape. Their faces were marked by surprise: awed that the old men had the wherewithal to pull it off, and how they found themselves genuinely drawn to it, recognising the pull the mothers still exerted on their lives. The pull existed for him also, but unlike the others he chose not to deny it. Though loathed at times, it was needed.

The reinvigoration of the movement came from an unexpected place: a cab showboating back and forth past City Hall in an attempt to get a better view of proceedings, and hitting a bus pulling out of its stop as it did so. The sound was of metal scraping metal, the crunch of the actual impact rose up the steps to reach his ears in successive waves; the children getting to their feet at once and moving towards the kerb.

'Where were you going, you dumb fuck?'

'Where were you going, you blind fuck? Did you not see me pulling out?'

The bus driver dazed, the cab driver unhurt, entering into a protracted argument that prefaced the eventual use of fists. A Russian and a Pakistani, not yet separated by the police, hurling insults across vehicles and continents; notes of entitlement and grievance that were familiar to Teddy, a freeform score that sound-tracked his movements around the city.

Somehow the soundtrack had been forgotten, eclipsed by the pallor silence brought to their skin and minds. With the crash, their memories returned. The two men broke off of their own accord moments before the police reached the bottom of the steps; one pointing to the other that theirs were the only sounds on the street. Traffic aside, the eighty children had lined the sidewalk to watch them silently. The sheer weight of eyes upon them, seeming to shine brighter as they absorbed the energy before them; every insult and car horn from backed-up traffic recharging all that had been depleted.

Teddy could see how they were slowly unfolding back into themselves with the kinetic movements in their arms and legs, aware of their obligations, but remembering now their capacity to run; eighty restless horses at the starting gate. Still they would not let the Mothers down by opening their mouths. All they needed from the accident was the reminder of all that powered their bodies; how observation, passion, strength and a sense of alertness should not be closed down just because they chose not to speak; that they should in fact demonstrate more of those qualities.

It showed in their posture as they returned to their places

once the vehicles were removed; how they no longer sat in misshapen circles but in row formations that underlined the steps; to Teddy's eyes, an organic shift that occurred without mass conference. Their eye contact with their neighbour appeared stronger than before. They still fidgeted, but less so. They did not sleep; instead, they mimicked the Mothers, each facing the doors of City Hall; a congregation awaiting their sermon, ready for the City to preach it.

'Is this what you call progress, kid? Sleepovers?'

'We have them by day, and the cops have them at night?'

'If it's supervision they need, we can assign social services. Chuck them all in a housing block in one of the outer boroughs.'

'Everyone's looking a bit too happy down there. Let them sit in the park if they want a festival.'

'Kid, I'd happily swap my days to be at a festival. Instead, I'm sweating hours at this desk, and going home to a family who ignore me. Let your folks down there know that there's a queue for the easy life.'

'Waiting their turn, boy. Make it clear to them.'

He continued to hold back. Gorged on words they could not reveal, Teddy sought to feed the Mothers in other ways. A Mexican food truck appeared at the end of the third week, followed by a woman who walked her cart uptown selling black bean and spinach soup. He twisted the arms of those who worked in the permit offices, promising one thing if they delivered another.

'It will read better if food is made available to them, rather than break up the police line anytime they want a sandwich. Easier to control. More helpful to manpower.'

'I'm inclined to leave things as they stand. From all reports it's a tea party every afternoon and evening. All the food they're bringing in and out. I read in the refuse report that there was a roast chicken carcass cleared from the bottom of the steps last weekend. Sounds grander than a night at the opera. These squatters are living well. Considering my wife is such a bad cook, I might as well join them.'

'No one there is living the high life, I assure you; least of all the Mothers at the centre of things. Water is what they're mostly getting. Or coffee. The police are already confiscating liquor at the line. There's no party going on when it's raining. No differentiation to call it anything other than a protest.'

'In which case, we have no responsibility to feed their bellies. Look at the dock workers' strike. They arrived at dawn and left no later than 6 p.m. They came out in larger numbers but observed their shift hours because they respected their fellow workers, who were obliged to enforce law for their own protection. They understood that those men and women had families they needed to return to each night. That the City needed its clear day/night infrastructure to run. That the streets would be cleaned while they slept, roadworks undertaken, sewers cleared and garbage collected.'

'And blockades built in their absence?'

'That was not in the hands of this department, son. Our work is tailored to an entirely different remit. There is no collusion.'

'I think you're forgetting yourself.'

'I see.'

'You see what?'

'How you play things, Teddy. They've trained you well, haven't they? The art of pulling rank. Your department are not masters of the universe, but I know that you're able to swallow me whole. For this, I apologise.'

'Look, can we afford for these people to get sick when there are news cameras around? Especially the older ones. If they are kept healthy and strong their minds will wander and they'll think of another way to make their point that doesn't bring about so much disruption.'

'Some hope. I've been around this block more than once. When protest groups realise they're being listened to – not responded to, that's something different – what they crave are bigger disruptions, more attention. Who would give up that rush willingly?'

'They will leave the square but it must be their decision, and not one made in illness. We want to avoid protesters being taken for hospital treatment. For this to be filmed as everything else is being filmed. The City does not need to see these people clogging up emergency rooms and pissing off overworked nurses just because we couldn't find an effective, low-key way to ensure these people got fed.'

'At our expense.'

'At their expense. The food will have to be paid for. We're just putting it in front of them. The vendor's pitch fee can increase from fifteen to twenty-five per cent in light of the extenuating circumstances. Who knows, some of the back-office workers might appreciate some Mexican food, too. Grant the permit.'

'And in return we get?'

'Resubmit the waterfront paper our sub-committee rejected last year.'

'And you have the ability to make this happen? I know what I've heard, of course. I am just yet to see it.'

'You see it now. Light conversations like this, where I'm just trading observations, is what they talk of. Approve the permits and I'll see that your guys get yours.'

The City has made a liar of him, knowing that their proposal will be buried or lost in an avalanche of similar griping; each sheet wet with tears from department co-workers shouting for perks that they were not entitled to. As the department head signed and stamped the permits, Teddy realised that he would go out of his way to make the man's life difficult so as not to acknowledge that he had ever had to walk into his office cap in hand. His career at City Hall had felt at times like a flit from one similar manoeuvre to another, uncomfortable with the vulnerability of the hustle; afraid of his sincerity being read, yet still determined to get his way.

That man's stock fell from the moment he signed those permits. He would have respected him more if he'd been shouted out of the office. Instead, he'd allowed himself to be softened by personal greed: further discretion in the granting and refusal of permits; a re-evaluation of proposed reductions in his department's budget. Teddy was prepared to block them all, undermine the man where he should be supported, to be obtuse until a point of no-confidence was reached. Teddy's personal power within the organisation was negligible, at times it felt non-existent, but his will was strong, confident in his ability to persuade.

Watching the children chow down on tacos, the police also, satisfied him as though it had come from his own pocket. He bought chilli and quesadillas for the Mothers, entailing three separate trips to carry all the food. Before, his pocketbook was never filled to the extent that he could act out so extravagantly; covering late rents and paying utilities was the most he'd managed for them, and only because he'd scrimped and gone without in other areas.

He ate lunch at his desk and avoided after-work social-ising. It had been two years since he'd bought an item of clothing for himself; five years since a vacation, a Memorial Day weekend in Miami, cut short after one of the children was arrested following a bar fight. His apartment, small as it was, was simply furnished, mostly with donations and found objects, a walnut desk chair pulled from a skip in Chelsea and carried twenty-five blocks uptown; a dining table and sofa from a downstairs neighbour on the morning of her eviction, freely dispossessing herself within the apartment building rather than see the objects she loved thrown on to the street. He saved every penny he earned, knowing that he would be called upon for it, an unforeseen emergency where fifty or five hundred dollars could make a difference.

Fear of debt kept him at his desk for six days straight; fear of helplessness was often the barrier to a restful night's sleep; as a child remembering his mother awaiting a thirty-dollar cheque in the mail from his grandparents that never arrived; how destiny could hinge on a cheque for thirty dollars. The ability to cover costs was freedom. Work was freedom, without it he would be no better than the Mothers, anxious to care – to change – but so often lacking the simple means. In their prime, there had been money in the balls and from the attention that came with it, but they were feast or famine queens, now enduring decades of drought.

He left five hundred dollars with the owner of the Mexican food truck and a couple of hundred at the coffee cart, asking to be informed when the tab ran low. (The truck was later switched to Vietnamese for variety and to ensure that no one complained.) He entrusted three of the children to supervise meal duty; back and forth up those steps with trays, ensuring all were fed, watered and cleared up after. They too had dollars stuffed into their pockets; secrets held from the Mothers, how he was subsidising their right to protest; how he would not allow them to rot among cheeseburger wrappers and putrefying fruit.

If they were well nourished they would be strong. If money was taken out of the equation, they could focus on what was necessary: their leadership; their spiritual work. His contribution came from silence also, a desire to remain in shadow. There was no part of his life where that wasn't so.

5.

His office was situated far in the recesses of City Hall so he was unable to watch over them during the day as he would have liked. On the upper floor was a corridor whose sweep took in a panel of front windows, but his excuses to be in that part of the building were flimsy and he was conscious of his attention to detail being read differently. Those who cared and were identified as such were demonised and robbed of any actual effectiveness they may have had.

He was expected to give a full account, which involved periods of intensive study, so whilst he could spend half an hour simply standing before the windows, able to see the Mothers, sphinx-like and magisterial in their poses, any longer invited comments of time-wasting or worse, a lecture from those who had trained him, needing to be taken in good grace before he lost his temper and smacked down their patronising tones.

'Easier to hide behind a window than it is to be out there,

isn't it, son? Your blood pressure isn't up for it. Here, you can stay in control of your breathing and vital signs. You've figured that it's not easy to be outside. Thinking on your feet. Having an answer for everything. The need to stay awake so as not to miss anything. Is it getting to you? The relentless beat; your head and heart pounding their own rhythms. Their needs over yours.'

'I'm just the same.'

'You may feel the same but your body will tell things differently. Have you noticed any difficulty in unwinding? In your bowel movements? How often did indigestion flare-up previously and is it lesser or greater now? I never had a migraine until I started to work in the field. First weekend of leave I got the bastard of all migraines, pulling my head apart. These are no coincidences, son, only your body demonstrating what you are otherwise afraid to say.'

'I'm in tune with my body, sir. I'm looking after myself.'

'If that's the case, you would be outside, not hiding behind the window.'

'I've been told I need to be here at least two days a week. That's what I'm doing, man.'

'Fuck those two days, son. They offer you that to see whether or not your ball sac has shrivelled from the stress of the field. It's a get-out clause for those who can't handle it. Two days become three and then five, writing an overlong report that the proofreader will hate you for and that no one will read.'

'Is that what happened to you? A five-day week of writing

reports, because you're never sent anywhere these days. All I see is you stalking me and writing reports.'

City Hall was ladders and trapdoors; stepping into any office his potential downfall. This was the culture and expectation to which he'd been trained. A history of personal success swallowed up by more spectacular failures; how effecting positive change begat greed and the black star that shone over those who would not concede power. He marvelled at those legends, those who thought they were bigger than the city they'd been called upon to serve.

A man builds a swimming pool in a poor neighbourhood and is spurred on by that success to build another. Between constructing a third pool and the revolution of a city-wide scheme, his motivation shifts. The need for children to be able to exercise freely and the pride a municipal pool can give to communities become a lesser purpose. Anecdotal stories of ghetto happiness are all well and good, but they cannot compete with the story of one man's personal feat: what one man could provide for the city through sheer determination and the accumulation of power. Committees that must be infiltrated and then conquered, housing boards to be overthrown, newspapermen to pally with and subsequently make afraid. It is a question of degrees, how one success generates another, and the tipping point where personal power is prized over the object.

Teddy is vigilant, acknowledges his powerlessness; the lightness his body bears on these grand steps. How the work of his hands leave no trace, his reports vanishing into the great unknown. Not for the first time he wonders why he was ever hired, his purpose through their eyes misty and undefined, until his eyes settle on what is happening below, feeding from the stubbornness of the Mothers who raised him; needing to be blessed by their plain speaking and their heart.

Watching as they eat tacos – his tacos – he wonders where his tipping point lies. What victories he has fought for comes from shadow; indigestion bubbling within the city's cavernous belly. Can long-term satisfaction be sustained from a round of similar action, small incremental moves which never disturb the overall fabric?

A vogue ball founded in an abandoned loft uptown; Houses being formed off the back of it; battles and walk-offs, and filming all of it. There are precedents from his youth to respect and adhere to. What he has outgrown, and somewhat despises, continues to resonate. College has enlightened him, yet still the achievements of the Mothers remain his backbone. How then to grow another, and still to serve both?

He waited tables and walked balls to pay for his college books. The history of sieges: in Leningrad they starved; in Warsaw, trapped like animals. He thinks of their city's history, of people who locked themselves inside the apartments for weeks; families barricading their buildings, entire blocks uniting in strength, closing their streets and homes to avoid their neighbourhoods being cleared. Battles begin and end with food.

The City and the Mothers should thank him equally, although that will never happen. For now he has to be satisfied with what he sees – stability and routine entering their outdoor tenancy. Two hundred has risen to two fifty now that there is food. Children he has seen from around, who flit in and out of the scene as time and funds allow; those he has not seen for years, grizzled beauties that still possess an element of their youthful magnetism; boys he had thought already buried by the city; dangerous boys, either in their mentality or in their activity, who left the table to sort business and never returned.

He sees four of these creatures once he is back outside, the banjee crew from his youth, who once slept on the other side of the apartment wall, years since he saw them last. He circles warily until he's sure that they're not a mirage; flesh and blood erupted from the concrete that previously entombed them; the city finally exhuming those bodies it had long coddled underground.

He remains as distant as he can be, retreating to the sidewalk, afraid to hear, smell, touch, and not yet ready to be in the presence of ghosts. With all that he has experienced, all that he knows, how it is possible to remain hidden for so long? Was it something in their mind that closed down, enabling hibernation, or his?

6.

'We understand that you can't speak. That these screams are all that you allow yourselves to give. We'd be lying if we said that we weren't relieved by the censorship of your welcome. The love we can see in your eyes, happiness in the wetness of your cheeks, but none of us were looking forward to the tongue-lashing heading our way once you'd seen us. Of course, we know it will emerge. We're prepared for it. But for now. This. The tightness with which you held us, in some cases, still holding us, is a wonderful thing. We're humbled you still think so much of our bedraggled asses. You have questions, lots of questions. We read it in your hands and the lines which have grown around your mouth. We've always told people how beautiful our Mothers were. Are. How some of that beauty was passed to us, even though we're not of the same blood. We know that time passes. We're not going to flatter you saying that you haven't aged a day as the city has left its mark across all our bodies. We have each been broken and rebuilt. Everything we've survived shows in the marks across our wrists, in our damaged voices, and list of daily medications. Yet we are still here. We cannot bow and take prayer with you because all that we've endured has killed any possibility of belief. God does not exist for our kind. Never has. We're better off with totems and idols. A Hummer or S-Class. The gold that hangs from our necks and ears. The rocks embedded in our teeth. God has never protected or helped us, bar keeping you safe. We can think of instances where divine intervention has spared us hardship or brought peace. Happy He has done so for you. It fills us with something we cannot describe to see your contentment, even in these circumstances. Tells us the true defender sitting atop His holy cloud is doing something right, even if He will not reveal himself to us in any meaningful way. In the deepest of our troubles there were nights when we begged for the existence of God. You cannot understand how deeply and widely we searched. The urgency. For we had run out of options and had no place to go. Jail; a grave; the river. That was our horizon. You know what it is when you've fooled with the wrong people. Made assumptions that only showed up your greed and naivety. We don't know the full stories of what happened when you were young, but presume that some of our experiences are shared. The invincibility of youth! All the trickery we thought we could get away with until we encountered folks who were well versed in those tricks; who recognised robbery when they saw it; identified the clumsy hands of amateurs who believed they were on the cusp of running things. In differing circumstance we might've gotten our way. Thinking of a business partner losing their sharpness, or a team too busy with other ventures to realise what was being lifted from them until it was too late. Those were important lessons. Never again were we ruled by our egos. Fear of losing our lives taught us well. We want you to understand that we did not disappear because we played off the wrong people. Our trouble, the years of it, only came later. Living as grown men but having no clue of responsibility: how to sustain a roof over our heads; how to fill our bellies. We were not the children to rise at seven for a full shift at the factory or office. We did not have the discipline or the brilliance that Teddy has. We weren't respectful of those rules. Didn't see ourselves in that world. Come now, with your sour pusses. Did you expect to find us behind the bank teller's glass cashing your cheques? Dispensing prescriptions at that pharmacy? We were barely able to hold down the jobs you found us: shifting lighting and stage blocks at the balls, running the coat check or tending bar. Across the ocean we'd be known as English eccentrics, intent on casting an alternative furrow. Here, we are the underclass, hidden from sight. We didn't group together to plot our escape. The falling away was a natural process, one you'd have recognised were you not so caught up in the demands of the balls. Can you not remember how we were losing interest? Our growing aggression? The walk-offs we would not show for? Did you never wake one morning and twig that you were no longer being indulged; that we could not be talked into competing in drag; that our femininity in some cases went beyond drag, so that the clothes themselves were of monstrous ugliness; the oppression of wearing those fashion labels; fitting into their narrow definition of form, when we needed to define ourselves in an image outside of our house mothers a decade or more older?

We couldn't wear those clothes and act the way you wanted us to act. Feeling like children trussed up for church; pulling at our collars, feet burning in shoes that were too tight. We dressed to please you and took pride in that. The Fiorucci cape we all fought over. Killing ourselves to prance and twirl in it. The Gucci belt with the butterfly clip. That fucking Gucci belt! How many murders were plotted when we couldn't get our hands on that thing? The shine and weight of the buckle. It spoke so much of having confidence in the world and in the wearer's abilities. Catastrophes did not befall those who wore a Gucci belt. They were never beaten, hungry or afraid. So yes, those clothes could dazzle us. We felt as safe and as entitled as those uptown muthafuckas when we wore the shit. We realised that we could be beautiful; how our bodies, the thickness of our hair, the softness of our skin and the clothes combined to make something bigger than ourselves. As separate parts each had flaws large enough to tear apart with our bare hands. For all our cockiness we were still so insecure about ourselves, but we understood through watching you how alchemy could be made. We were witnesses and in time became part of it, obsessing over the look we would push at balls. The preparation. Weeks of preparation! Through that time life was somehow lived, yet this took over everything. Soldiers readying for battle clean their gun and polish boots. They run ten miles, expelling yet withholding the energy they will need. They're drugged up to the eyeballs, fucking comfort women in conflict zones. No different to us: method and masculinity shared. It would be a misrepresentation to say that we were battle-scarred. Fatigued would be a better description. Restless, another. The day we chose to ditch the uniform – to dress in the way that we chose, simple and unhurried, when we finally remembered that clothes were clothes, not costume – was gradual in arriving, but its impact was immediate. We did not wish to dress up any more. Irreversible decision. Do you remember the first time you wore a kimono to the club or incorporated a fan into your vogue walk? How certain you were that things could never be the same once you'd interpreted the rush of feelings as akin to empowerment. That's how we felt in a Raiders baseball cap and white-boy jeans. The literal and metaphorical clarity that came when we started wearing our glasses again. We remained in the clutches of vanity, however, looking after our bodies. Pumping and moisturising our arms. Shaving what needed to remain bare. Keeping our bellies flat so we could still roll our T-shirts a little when the spirit took us. We wanted to fuck and still needed that to be evident when we were on the street. We desired to be seen outside of your gaze. Kids outside of the club: to sit in a bar or burger joint anywhere in the city and for people to think that we were all right by dint of being ourselves, rather than the clowns we had become. Don't look at us that way, like you don't know what we're talking about. As though it's the first time you've heard this. You stare as if we have blasphemed

in church. Speaking His name in vain. Do you remember
how angry you could be if we didn't prepare for the balls to
your timetable? How you would rage at those wearing the
wrong shoe or trying their hair a certain way? The children
expressly instructed to dress in uptown furs – Park Avenue
meets Swiss sanatorium realness – but simply did not, having
neither the means nor the wits to acquire them. There was
no incitement of theft but in rare instances when there could
be no doubt that the child dressed before you was in finery
well beyond their pocket or acquaintance, you were quick
to turn a blind eye so long as it was for the glory of the
House. Kids whose actual walk was sloppy, as if their clothing was all the substance they needed. Taking to the floor as
if half-asleep or overly aloof when what they needed was to
bring vitality. Those who vogue well do not move as if cast
in stone, nor are they as elastic and aerial as acrobats. Success
lies somewhere between the two, powered by intelligence
and instinct. If simple-mindedness lost us cachet at the balls,
and so disrespecting the House, you would cuss a storm,
involving Jesus, the saints and the wisdom of our birth parents in casting us aside. You would beat us backstage if your
anger rose to that extent, a slap or blow meted out in the
currency with which we were raised and learned to expect.
We saw this happen once, maybe twice. A coward on the
front line, punished by his General. A mother, publicly
shamed by her child. So you cannot look at us as if we're
speaking Cantonese. We grew up. Were ready to leave your

care. Listen to what we're saying. Sit down and open your
ears. Loosen your defensive postures; how your arms are
now so tightly crossed; the inward curl of your fingers. We're
here to support you, not to make trouble, but there are
things you must understand. That not all the absences you're
fighting for were enforced by others. If we walked freely,
then it's possible that others did the same. Many others.
Only they went further afield. Cross-country to the other
coast. A village bordering the desert. Another country, even.
Who's to say that this godforsaken country is the centre of
everything? There must be other places, where shared values
are greater, and it is easier to live. We found something good
here so long as you accept that we will always live like rats.
We work hard and pay our bills and taxes, yet still expect
the ground to shift beneath our feet. That feeling will never
leave us, marked long before you took us in. We could end
our days on a ranch surrounded by grandchildren playing in
the dust and still have that feeling. But it may be different
for the others. They travelled and made a life for themselves.'

7.

Teddy follows the boys uptown. By now the mothers are pacified and are curling into sleep. The supporters have packed
up their paraphernalia for the day – tradespeople with a
cause; cops, joked with and instructed. Same as during their
reunion, he keeps his distance, two-men deep on the steps,

one carriage further on the subway. To be covert and follow covertly are two distinct actions.

He realises that he has no interest in the latter and is not as careful as he would otherwise be. It matters little whether they are aware of their tail. He would be more amused if they were, willing to participate in a game understanding neither the rules nor the outcome. Curiosity leads him as much as anything; to see with his own eyes the pocket where it's possible to remain hidden; a black hole in plain sight. He listened to their argument carefully, waiting for inconsistencies or indulgences that would make liars of them; for whatever sense of brother/sisterhood they once shared was lightly weighed against the debt he owed to the Mothers. Their interests would come first. They would always be defended, even if they were wrong.

Two subway switches followed by a train out of the city, a suburban line that that would not have crossed his mind as interesting or productive for them. Were they all living there, or just one? Or had they caught on and were playing a trick of their own? Projects, freeway, and dense woodland all passed, and he remained as in the dark as the growing blackness outside. Only as they pulled into a small station, a farming town on the edge of the state line, did he understand that he was being played. That he had as much business being in peanut country as they did. His nickname used to taunt him as he pored over his school books now coming to bite him in the ass. They still had their brains, those boys, with memories stronger than his, he realised; less to do with the slowing of his cells, more from the habit of shutting down all that was no longer necessary. On the train platform, bare of any passengers except themselves, he holds up his hands.

'You got me, muthafuckas. You ran the chase well.'

'Mr Peanut Head got a brain after all. Who knew?'

They embraced warmly; kinship felt in the closeness of each hold, but they remained subdued until the return train reached the city; their carriage overtaken by a group of college kids escaping dorm life for a night, excitably and keenly drunk; their good-natured teasing and bitching over their less adventurous roommates muting all they wished to say.

Where they take him is where he expects, a fleapit bar at the furthermost tip of the city, last of the remaining businesses on the wrong side of the ring road, where ghost workers from the long-deserted factories freely roam. A dark, narrow space overlooking the looping freeway, passable only on foot, a pilgrimage only those with an alcohol dependency will make; a meeting place out of time, where they can be alone to console themselves.

'This your hangout?'

'Sometimes. Reminds us of the old days. The life you'd get around here. You looked like you needed a drink and this was the closest place we could think of. Ain't no guided tour, son. Just offering refreshment.'

Then –

'We heard about how much you do for them. We figured you'd be the first to run away.'

'Because of college?'

'Not just that. You had the look of someone who longed to be somewhere else. The first to leave the party.'

'First up in the morning, too.'

'Ha! That's a trophy you can keep, T.'

'You understand that you broke the silence when you were talking up a storm back there?'

'Man, are you crying already? If you were listening that hard, you would have picked up that they didn't say a word. Didn't encourage them to speak, either.'

'You said enough to make them want to speak.'

'Maybe. But we couldn't help that. You don't see your mother for ten years, you find you've got a lot of things to say.'

'It's not understanding the silence that bothers me. Didn't it register as you approached the steps from the subway? You would've heard about it somewhere, the news, or ... From just the five of them to now over two hundred joined in silence. Do you think those children needed to hear your life story? Just asking the question.'

'Are you a mother yourself now? You're sounding like one, for sure. Maybe college gave you the privilege to dictate how we should behave.'

'I've no authority over anyone.'

'What do you want, Teddy? Following us here to preach a sermon. We left to escape their preaching. Ain't nobody's disciples. We follow earthly desires. Fuck all to do with the divine.'

'Just wanted to draw your attention to what happened afterwards. How the children also started to speak, not just from boredom, but affirmation; as if you'd somehow given them permission to do the same. Talking amongst themselves and engaging with the news folks when they'd been previously told to keep their distance.'

'It's the sole right of educated people to monitor public behaviour, we expect. Didn't have you down as a law-maker, though it was probably inevitable.'

Their ability to cut directly to his vulnerabilities had not diminished over time. He felt great swathes of heat rise across his face and chest. They were unchanged: an air of maligned youth long retained; fast with the razor, but quick to bandage you afterwards. Frightened kids used to toughing it out; merciless with their bookworm brother, still fiercely protective of any outsider who tried the same.

Teddy could be as vicious as the rest of them, felt maliciousness run through his bones, yet whatever darkness that formed chains deep in his marrow was benign. He was not so sure the same applied to his brothers. Had their optimism been eaten away by their decimated neighbourhood, or was their inclination to teasing simply a reflex action, fired-up by memory.

They were being sharp because they were tired, he reasoned. But also because they felt that he expected it of them:

the closest they could get to dancing and blackface. Even through silence, the Mothers acted out their role on the steps as if by rote: delight, anger, consternation, tears. Now it was their turn, a mixture of sarcasm and rough-housing. He wondered about his responses when the time came; what the expectation would be.

'If you're on the steps, you are quiet. This is the rule. They abhor a ruckus or scene of any kind. Distracts from their message.'

'Bringing library conditions out on to the street. You must be in your element.'

They barked at each other in this way over several more beers, the group warming the drunker they became. Hands gripped shoulders, arms draping loosely around necks. They passed kisses from cheek to cheek, like Europeans at a wedding. My brothers. He was no longer self-conscious of his surroundings, filled with joy and sorrow at the years that had separated them. How he'd missed these muthafuckas, but even in his muddle knowing that this reunion could not be extended. Bar the Mothers, there was little happening in their lives now that they were able to share. Experience isolates you as you get older, he thought, not the other way around. A return to secrecy and imagined worlds; becoming increasingly closed.

One of the boys was talking about his landscaping business; another was cutting and styling wigs for Trans girls and cancer patients. There were marriages – the same two couples who first met at the balls; what television would call childhood sweethearts if the sight of their bearded, tattooed and jewelled femininity did not stick in their throats. He had nothing tangible to show for his decade: an empty apartment and a government pay check; how, outside of work, his life was as empty as the apartment he never got to spend enough time in. As he spoke, dullness crept across his tongue jumbling his words; a knot expertly twisting at the base of his stomach as a rarely acknowledged truth stuck in his throat, something the brothers mistakenly read as the over-effects of drink.

'Peanut Head still can't take his liquor! Four rounds in and he's floored.'

'It was the only way you could get him to walk the balls. You drank all of Amsterdam to get your Dutch courage, didn't you, Teddy? Not so innocent, were you, son? We all remember your dark shit.'

'My what? Yous laughing like that.'

'You don't need books to keep your marbles. We got our marbles.'

'What memories are you talking about? Sure, there were fights . . . '

' . . . where you always got pasted! Poor kid wasn't so quick on his feet. Thought too much about it. You stumbled. He's no natural, the Mothers used to say. Teach him some skills. And we tried. Remember those afternoons after school? When we took you to the park because you were too shy to use the gym?

But your concentration was always elsewhere. Eyes roaming towards the trees, as if you were looking for something.'

'I looked a fool.'

'You did. A regular Mona Lisa in boxing gloves. Only stubborn, and slow with your reflexes. You started walking differently after that, though. How you held yourself on the street.'

'Those lessons helped, believe it or not. Worked out that if I always stood straight, I'd be less afraid.'

'Good boy. See, we your teachers now.'

'But what's dark about that?'

'How about you getting arrested in Chanel? Some old bitch making off with bracelets and leaving you to cop it. The Mothers having to bail you out from the dungeon there.'

'Not arrested. Detained for a pair of lost earrings. It was a scam. You would've fallen for it just as easy.'

'What were you doing in Chanel in the first place? Boy feeling the drag a little too much? Less banjee queen, more queen?'

'I just ... found myself there. Got sweet-talked without realising. On the street I had eyes in the back of my head. We all did, right? Coming where we came from? In that shop I let my guard down, even though I knew I didn't belong there. That's not to say they didn't want me there, just ...'

'... you let yourself get played. You were a kid who looked suspicious whenever the Mothers offered you the last piece of chicken at the dinner table. So what was she, a magician?'

'Nope. Someone smarter than me.'

His curiosity outweighs his melancholy, or it does once he drinks the tumbler filled with water placed in his hand. Sitting amongst his brothers brings the feeling of total aloneness, but still wondering of an alternative life. What they may have gained from denying school books and living on the street; whether the exchange may have provided greater gifts. His brothers have lost their pinched look from earlier, their bodies relaxed, faces rosy from generosity at the bar and family love. What he shared with the Mothers now was more perfunctory: conversations about what they ate and whether they were taking their medications. He missed rough-housing and verbal sparring, the family kind where there were no consequences, not having to watch his back as he did at City Hall.

But then two of the brothers started squabbling over the check and he was jolted back to the Mothers' kitchen table, full house, a chaos different to the homes they'd left behind but recognisable in their essence; the noise and heat; arguments over the smallest things – crusty cheese not wrapped properly in the cool box, a sister using the last of the hot water, a coveted jacket stolen from another's bedroom. Not earth shattering, though deafening at the time. He misses these mirages: events that barely happened, if at all.

'Are you jonesin' for those days?'

All the longing that he has stored coming to the fore in his question; understanding that everything he now is comes from this family. His eyes become wet with nostalgia, his mouth tripping with promises he will later ignore and then forget entirely. The plans made across the bar table, sand-castles all, washed away by a swipe of the bartender's towel.

'They were all right, Teddy, but we don't need sheltering any more. Our birth mothers gave us their titties to suck, and we ain't jonesin' for that either.'

'And the children? The ones they're looking for?' Though he knows the answer even before they do: how their nostalgia was cut short; every one of them. There can be no explanation for what has driven him this far from the city he knows, needing the details they withheld from the Mothers on the square.

'They were wild, those girls. Restless. Never wanted to be at home. Wanting to upstage everyone at the balls. All the garlands. The most applause. Living for what they thought of as fame. It was fun to be along for their ride, if you sustain that level of acceleration.'

'You're speaking of them as if they were of the same type.'

'They were more similar than different, Teddy. The Mothers and their magnetic claws drew in a particular kind of kid. Fuck knows how you ended up among them. They were ruthless about the health of their Houses. Knew what they needed to keep growing. Those kids, pretty as they might be, but with ideas of their own, soon wriggled from their hold. North repels north, right? All they wanted were kids that they could mould.'

'We were all bright sparks. All had things we wanted to do.'

'But you have to admit that some of those kids were dumb. Born dumb and would stay dumb. Maybe the shit they went through in their childhoods cut short any further sense of wonder about the world. Parts of the brain shutting down just out of necessity, to survive. They made money from that thickness, the Mothers. The money won from slaying a ball category, any dancing they got asked to do on TV. None of that was passed on. Sure they dazzled them with trinkets and scraps the designers sent to them once the Houses started getting known. Clothes they neither liked nor could fit into. Crumbs off the table, son. They were paying us in dust.'

'We weren't doing so badly. Most of us pulled in jobs. I remember two of you working at the gas station on the inter-state, just outside the airport. Menthol cigarettes, corn chips and ozone. You reeked of it. We were of age but we weren't adults, then. Didn't understand that they had expenses to cover. The household. Utilities. All that. We shared, didn't we? Pooled what we had.'

'We wouldn't have been able to afford a sandwich if we hadn't pooled together. They had money, I'm sure. Just sit-ting on it. Unwilling to spend. Daddy Warbucks in make-up. A whole board of them.'

'They kept us covered when we needed it. Remember when Sherry hurt herself?'

'You say it so daintily. Gurl cut her wrist in the bathroom and got found before she started the other one.'

'We were punks with no person legally responsible for us. No healthcare company would've taken us on even if we filled all they paperwork they asked us to complete. Everything was taken care of because the money was there. They didn't hesitate.'

'If you're facing a death on your hands, in your home, and you can find a way to pay your way out of it, you bow to the inevitable.'

'That's unfair. What they did with Sherry, talking to her, keeping her alert until the ambulance came. How they cleaned up the blood and calmed us down. What was that song they were singing, about little miracles happening everyday? Always think of that night when I hear it. Holding on to Sherry as one of them bound her wrist and arm. The sweetness of those voices even though they must've been filled with terror and Lord knows what else.'

'Fear of being arrested and slung into jail. Fear that they'd be found out as exploiting minors. Are you really going to forget the nonsense they got themselves into? Their mania for taking our money? They were our bosses. Gang masters in drags.'

'But you remember the song?'

'Two of them harmonising like they were singing doo-wops on the stoop. Hiding in our bedroom, hearing Sherry screaming, and their singing growing over her voice. Pacifying her. Ten minutes before, one Mother had been set to punching walls over a lost patent shoe. Now there was only tenderness, cradling their baby.'

'My third week in the apartment. Thought I'd escaped all that.'

'It was no Disney castle, Teddy, but it was safe.'

'I thought about going back on to the street after they left with the ambulance. Felt like it'd be quieter outside.'

'You were mad that night too, Teddy. Wanting to hit the Mothers for keeping you from Sherry. Remember?'

'Us holding you back. You were a strong muthafucka in those days. Took all four of us to pin you down.'

'I just felt I should be there. That she wanted me there.'

'Man, she was so out of it, she didn't know nothing. Could've been the President and First Lady dragging her round and she wouldn't have a clue.'

'They spared you, you know. The Mothers. What were you then, sixteen? You barely knew her. No kid needed to see that amount of blood. The state of the bathroom when they found her.'

'It was beautiful how they sang to her, but being on the other side of the door . . . '

'You a medic now?'

'Thought she'd respond to my voice or feel my hand holding hers.'

'You were sweet for her, Teddy.'

'She looked tough but was someone who needed looking after. I was just the one who was around most, is all.'

'You're still sweet! So why do you stay in the city when you could beat a path to the other coast? That's where you found her, right?'

'You heard? How?'

'The Mothers got mouths, son. You tell them something and over time it filters down to us. We still talk to folks.'

'I found her records, if that counts as the same thing. Where she lives and pays her taxes.'

'Good enough for us. Gurl got her life. Respect. Get yours, too.'

'There's too much in this city for me to leave behind.'

'The old people?'

'They need looking after, too.'

'Even if it makes you unhappy? You've been on edge all night, Teddy, ever since we first spotted you. That's no way to live.'

'Who gets any choice in how they live? We just make the best of it.'

'This is the Mothers' fault. Living how they choose whilst they drain yours. We see that now.'

'And for this you hate them.'

'We don't hate nobody, Teddy. Least of all, them. But false sainthood is a dangerous thing. We can't be part of it, not when we know what they're looking for ain't even real.'

'None of us know that for sure. It's not certainty that keeps them on those steps, but uncertainty. In many ways they want to be proved wrong. To have other visits similar to yours.'

'They'll all come crawling out now once they see the attention we get. Them children not even part of the scene, that none of us barely know. People who weren't family; who were never family. The more the news guys get interested in what's going on down there, the more they'll pay for stories. These children drip for money. Hundred dollars for every word that comes out of their mouth. Two hundred for every untruth.'

The brothers are bemused by the situation, but hungry, too. Teddy recognises the familiar twitch across their eyebrows, wondering whether they had been too early with their reunion; if a further wait of a week or month would have proved more fruitful. Gardening equipment to pay for; a down-payment on a second-floor walk-up on the wrong side of the river – they were all a slave to expenses, eager for a reprieve.

If this is what's important to you, let me deal with it, he thinks. I can write a cheque, erase City debts; whatever it is you need. You compromise your power by selling your stories; all the sway you hold nullified by a pocketful of stained banknotes. But if money takes the stress out of the equation; if cash is all you need to enable you to return to the square and sit with the Mothers, keeping a civil tongue in your head, then give me your bank details.

But their quizzical expressions lapse and he realises that he has misjudged them. Sure they are wistful, same as when hearing of a man winning a lottery from a ticket at their local kiosk, but their wonder is no more fleeting than that. For all their disagreements there is loyalty – to their history – but in that moment, he realises, to him. They respect him. His viewpoint matters.

8.

His reports are shorter when they should be otherwise, tired now of the hectoring that comes out of hours from department heads who cannot sleep.

'You making progress, son? We see little evidence of it from our end.'

'The square smells like a fucking taco joint. This your idea of how to run ops?'

'Move things along to where they should be moving. If the weather turns and they're sleeping on the steps like a row of wet slugs . . . '

'It won't play well, son. Even if they're in the wrong, people at home respond to their humanitarian instincts.'

'The City should not be made to appear liable when we are doing our best to keep them safe from harm.'

'That's what we want them to think, at least. Shut this down, and soon.'

The satisfaction then, of sending reports this terse; almost malicious in what is recorded and what he keeps for himself: Lost newcomers at the state line. No leads. Worried for copycats and a trail of erroneous information. To share anything more than that would be to sully the peace brokered in the upstate bar: a promise that they would visit the Mothers more often once it was over, if only to pass through and make their existence real. No appointment or ceremony needed, just a knock at the door and a smile on their face. The Mothers lived too keenly amongst ghosts. They needed to be led away from that room into one where no dust settled.

It was the longest time that he had sat with his brothers. He had no recollection of ever having talked so much or so deeply. They would all talk a different way the next morning after their hangovers subsided, but he already missed their seriousness, produced by both the alcohol and the events of the day. They had been ready to finally reflect and much time would pass before they were in a similar situation again. He knew this as he left; that he would avoid any interim advances and do his best to maintain a clear distance. Still, he honoured them by keeping his report to those three lines. Fraternal love could not be honestly transcribed, too clean for the City's muddy hands.

He slept off the worst excesses of the beer for a few hours, and then walked the streets before dawn, shying away from the centre of things because he wanted to be distant from their orbit. He should meet no person or read no sign that could update him. This is what he wishes to feel; his feet pounding concrete and asphalt in clear, ringing steps; night's last breath stinging his cheeks and fingertips. He wants desertion: streets largely free of traffic, enabling him to walk blocks in the middle of the lanes if the fancy takes him; company to be had in streetlights, neon and traffic signs; guided from one lit lobby to another, the doorman asleep on the job and no one else to be found.

He pushes his shoulders back as he walks, unburdening hidden weight on to the empty sidewalk as he moves, dropping from the kerb and flowing into gutters. To walk through any part of the city without being challenged is what he thinks of; all the doors that remain closed to him; those who bar his way. Even with his remit there continues to be places where he cannot go, but now their boundaries seem temporarily negated by night's brief dalliance with dawn. Who is to say where he should be? Who is awake to report him?

He is drunk with purpose but not power. There's very little he can do at this time. Nothing of any note. He can stand on the steps of houses belonging to those he despises while they sleep, but is unable to move beyond that; his head just below a window sill, ascertaining where and how they rest.

The home in that moment seems a juxtaposition of both the impenetrable and the vulnerable; sitting ducks snoring into their pillows, behind cement walls. Oh, the surprise he could make. The damage he could do. Every bastard has to sleep, even those with the strength to ignore or belittle him; privileged liberals he had to deal with at college; those officers at City Hall whose rubber stamps remain out of his reach.

His birth mother slept between hours-long rages that decimated the apartment. His sister and himself were raw from
it; also as worn down as she was; their faces and arms tight
from having to defend themselves, the bloody indentations
of fingernails as they balled their fists deep into their palms.
His sister, too, would fall asleep once they realised that it
was safe to do so, yet he could not, intent on watching his
unconscious mother, his mind racing with all the revenge he
would inflict while she remained prostrate.

Once she beat their palms with a wooden spoon until
the skin cracked, and possibly bones. Punishment for taking
something that was never theirs in the first place: an apple
slowly wrinkling in the refrigerator; pillaged from necessity,
after an hour's debate, because they hadn't eaten that day
and filling their bellies with something other than coffee
won out over her raging. The apple had been in there for
weeks. It was possible that she wouldn't notice; that the
anger they foresaw, which prohibited them from so much,
was purely imaginary. But they were not so lucky, caught
in the act and forced to eat every part of the fruit from its
putrefying flesh buried under the waxy skin, to the stalk,
core and pips; the fetid acidity of every mouthful burning
their tender wind-filled stomachs. An amuse-bouche for the
whooping that came afterwards.

He stared at his mother's chubby hands, marvelling at
how the pallid fingers held such cruelty, blind to all bar its
own muddled logic.

'Let no one make a fool of you, boy, unless a fool is what you want to be.'

Why then, did those rules not apply here? How reflexes – instinct – could be learned, only to be locked away, when she was the biggest bully of all. Her hand should sting with the same intensity. Her shoulders and back should writhe with it. He considers beating her with the same spoon but knows that his strength is nothing to hers. He is seven years old and built like a will-o'-the-wisp. He will be no more irritating than a gnat bite, and only marked out for worse if he disturbs her rest. He looks to match the immediacy of the pain he feels; wishing lightning to strike from his eyes; for a laser's fine line to bleed into her flesh.

He thinks of what they have, an arsenal of punishment in kitchen cupboards and drawers, but he has little skill or aptitude to wield a knife or meat prong. Instead, he imagines being tall enough to see the top of the stove; fingers reaching to fill the kettle and heat it on the back burner; turning the flame off just before it starts to whistle, still conscientious not to wake her; holding the kettle with both hands, steadying himself for he and the kettle shake with nerves and weight respectively; walking the hallway to her bedroom determined and petrified, but the desire to see her in pain, to understand that power now finally lies elsewhere governs him.

He cannot reflect until he's done what he needs to do, again wishing to study her but aware that he must not allow the water to cool; how every degree is precious. One hundred degrees to match one hundred licks – eye for an eye. He sees his face in hers as he gets closer to the bed and wonders whether he too will meet a similar punishment inflicted by his child many years from now.

He cannot imagine either yet already understands that he has a similar anger bottled inside which may never be shared; the same small mouth crowned with thick rosebud lips. Will his mouth stretch and grimace to the same infinite reaches as hers? Will he maim and wound so readily? But in his dreams there he was, waiting – as he does under this window sill now – water falling in sploshes before settling into a long, slow stream; washing sins from troubled hands. Washing them clean.

If pushed, he will push back. Some lessons never leave him. His birth mother left him her mouth and her ideas on how to survive, nothing more. When the brothers once humiliated him at one of the balls, having the vogue caller cut his walk to shreds – his second walk: banjee frat boy realness, heavy in an approximation of Ralph Lauren varsity drag, but somehow still as naked as they came, sick from every pose he made, sensitive to the point of passing out the way the caller teased out his effeminacy before the crowd. Five minutes of being read without mercy: a mule tied to an abandoned post and pelted with stones.

When he discovered that it was all for the brothers' merriment, he pissed on their clothes while they slept; YSL embroidered hems soaking up pools of urine, staining the crotch of a Halston jumpsuit, tarnishing the patent of forest-green Chanel pumps. It didn't matter whether he was discovered or not, the act of one slight replacing another was important – an imbalance redressed; a further aid to restful sleep.

He recognises the pattern as he continues to walk downtown, his intent muddied but still looking for scores to settle. He would never shake his mother's touch. For the moment, he's square with the brothers. He loves them. The Mothers continue to frustrate but their attention is a constant that each party needs. His gripes are outside of family: enemies to the home. Those walking the corridors of City Hall who have no belief in him; wishing him to fail. He could channel his disappointment in his reports, partly does so already, but there is greater satisfaction in a more physical outcome; striking when they are tender and when he is clear-headed enough to administer it.

He thinks of a man, Don Meyer, who once occupied an office across the hall until he was carted off, gone half-crazy writing from the same desk and chair for thirty years. The same reports produced from inside the same four walls; boredom seeping from behind the frosted door; his body, too, absorbing and then oozing frustration; a sponge that would never completely dry. He began to compile reports on all those he hated; dossiers held deep in the archives. They included alternative minutes typed for the meetings he attended; the real view rather than the party line.

Stumbling on one of these reports in a dust bank of paperwork was the start of a period of minor obsession for Teddy,
reading everything he could get his hands on; a two-month
stretch between operations when he was confined to the
office. The beauty was in the nondescript detail, how the
reports were in the same formal style as the rest – typed with
the same ribbon and using the official letterhead. Often, the
opening paragraphs made it hard to distinguish whether they
were a bogus report at all, until he read on and found Meyer's
dissent lodged further down the page.

Isaac Sheinman rejected the latest raft of zoning proposals
due to procedural error and not because he's prepared to
choke on his own greed once the development funders
are allowed to greenlight plans to 'improve' central areas
in his precinct.

The education board vetoed proposals to extend the
music programme to community colleges, citing a conflict
of interest with service providers. These philistine cocksuckers who wouldn't know a trombone from a sausage
machine should have been thrown out of the chamber for
their sheer arrogance. I would have rolled up my sleeves
if I had the guts.

When the finance committee say that there is no
money left, they are tacitly admitting to the grotesque
Christmas parties they lavished on their departments.
Whisky-soaked grouse for people who'd never eaten

anything more extravagant than a broiled chicken. Gold-plated perfume spritzers for the ladies; chrome-capped lighters for the men. One secretary was overheard calling Dolly Parton's agent to enquire her fee. A library branch had to withhold buying books for a semester because Santa's stocking was dropped closer to home.

After reading these, Teddy's instinct was to mirror Meyer's spirit, soulmates two decades apart, but he lacked the mettle to take the initial jump, blaming his inertia on not feeling strongly enough about a current problem to intervene one way or another. The City had done its work well: for all his dissatisfaction he remained a company man. His reports contained errors to tax them, street lingo that would purposely read like the brainteaser found in Christmas crackers, rather than adding erroneous facts which would be easier to discover and then lay blame. Living vicariously through Meyer, his voice steering him through one council chamber meeting after another; motivating him through endless rounds of training, and helping him to hold his tongue when younger, less able members of his department eased their way to promotion above him.

Meyer had seen and withstood all, keeping his counsel against decades of bullshit and amateurism; the mendaciousness of bull-necked men, greedy for power. Holding his nose to keep their stink at bay. He had been a bureaucratic man rather than one from the street so never engaged in operations similar to Teddy. There was no way of knowing whether this was thwarted ambition or if he was simply pre-occupied elsewhere. It was all guesswork on his part. Still, he slavishly followed.

He talks to the garbage workers clearing the avenue outside the subway. Eyes and ears of the city, where every grubby secret passes through their hands. Those he works with and for have no understanding of what it means to dirty your hands, the backbone it takes to scrape shit off the sidewalk block after block; the stench of rotting garbage covering the skin on your face like a permanent film; the gases that fill your nostril and lodge in the crevices of your decaying teeth.

There is messiness to fieldwork – violence and unpredictability in some instances attest to that – but it's a controlled experiment; narcotics for thrill-seekers certain of their place in the world. There is not this: the grind and dirt, the sheer willpower needed to clear the city's waste day after day.

As with everywhere in life, there are bad apples among the crew. They are earning their living, will take what they can find: stolen electrical goods covered in a dumpster, paste jewellery thrown into a fast food chain's backyard trash. They will have the trucks ride them home rather than take the subway; one man driving to Coney Island with his kids before dawn to show them morning breaking across the surf and to pick up boxes of peppermint-scented taffy still warm from the pan.

Crews indulged their personal agendas and their

rivalries, formally excised through a monthly meet-up at the bowling alley, but unofficially aired at the race track and its parking lot afterwards. Teddy worked the garbage route whilst at college, learning there the importance of grievances between men. Brotherhood was important too, but this was the first time he understood that grudges and the conflicts which stemmed from them were an intrinsic part of life.

Happiness was poor nourishment. It passed too quickly through his guts. Sourness, its gristle knotted through his teeth, was where he would learn. They were defined and governed by work. This is what differentiated these men from his family.

There was space to talk on the rounds but little opportunity to daydream. They rode, jumped, ran, threw trash into the compactor, rode, jumped, and ran again. They eyed pussy – always on heat for pussy, always out of their league – never reciprocated; the truck's cabin filled with the combined heat of sweat, testosterone and shit; horny bastards scraping shit and animal carcass. Noses chapped to the pink from the cold, their view of the city framed by the truck's windscreen; avenue after avenue wiped clean, their feet below the kerb, treading where others would not.

He understood that you could have dog shit wedged under your fingernails and caught in your hair, and still be cleaner than the cologne-drenched automatons that ran City Hall. The distinction was true, in the main. The crews were entitled to all that the labour laws allowed and they expected no more than that. They felt the City owed them nothing else bar their wage and working conditions that did not make fools of them. The foundations of these blocks and bridges were in their blood: what they saw and used was there to be enjoyed, not possessed.

'Seen anything?'

'Nothing you need. A woman locked outside her building pissed into her evening purse. It's too far to the sidewalk, for some.'

'Uptown or downtown?'

'Uptown, like you needed to ask. That's where all the animals live now. Her aim was lousy. Either that or she needs a bigger purse.'

'You're no better after one too many beers. I still remember the night of the championship. Walking around the bar with your pants around your ankles.'

'I was drunk but I always kept myself clean. Sharp shooter.'

'Passed City Hall yet?'

'Nope. Running late. Truck's been playing up. Someone dismantled a washing machine and threw it into the trash. Fucked the compactor for a good half-hour. Animals, I tell you.'

'I hear it's going to be quiet down there. Everyone left after nightfall.'

'All except your surrogate parents.'

'They're in for the long haul. What are those stones they

have in England that the druids worshipped? They're like that. Grey from a lack of vegetables, and immovable.'

'Bet they're loving that, your bosses.'

'Put it this way: both parties are hoping for a swift resolution.'

'So they're turning you into a politician now, on top of everything else.'

'City Hall-speak rubs off on me. Makes me sound like a dick, right?'

'Bosses want their pound of flesh. You're not the only one who's had experience of that. Personally, I'd tell 'em to shove it, but then, I like a quiet life. Work, pay bills, drink, fuck, catch the game once in a while. No shame in that.'

'I get bored quickly. Something in this spaghetti heap interests me.'

'You saying you can't have an imagination on the garbage detail?'

'Hardly that. I-I-I . . . '

'Relax, Teddy. I'm fucking with you. You talk funny these days, but you're still a good boy. Give us the time of day, unlike those other bastards.'

'I'm hanging around for a while. If you see stuff around City Hall that looks out of the ordinary, let me know. Never sure that the police tell me everything.'

'Lazy asses know how to cover their tracks, that's why. First thing they do is clear the blood before they call into their precinct.'

'It's not like that any more. They cleaned up their act.'

'You say to-mah-toe . . . '

'Funny! They had no choice. Play it by the book or lose your job and pension. The City was ready to cut back.'

'Should've done it anyway. Once the badge is back in the drawer they're ordinary men with heartburn and pot bellies like the rest of us.'

'That so?'

'A badge doesn't make you God, kid. There are too many gods to fear in this town.'

'Armies were once revered like gods, not just their leaders. There are plays and stories about it.'

'Don't lose yourself in books, son, or daydream about these flesh-and-blood bastards.'

'My studying days are long gone.'

'Good. Keep it that way. Here, let me show you something we fished out last night. Not sure whether to hold on to it or hand it in.'

'That glove box still your treasure chest?'

'Someone has to keep the old traditions going. First day on the job our crew boss says to me, "Any good shit you find goes straight into the glove box. Anything you see, box it, and we share it out at the end of the shift."'

'"Don't be hiding stuff in your drawers because no one likes a hoarder."'

'See. You never forget the important stuff life teaches you. I meant it, earlier. You're a good boy. Sailor's honour.'

'Good teachers.'

'Yeah, that too. Now take a look here.'

'It's empty.'

'I told the guys not to put anything in there tonight. The less they know about it, the better.'

'Who's hoarding now?'

'Not the kind of gear you want to leave on the street. This was in a doorway. A fucking doorway from those nearly finished apartments across from that church of yours. We still see you going in there in your smart suit. Your face already in another world before you've even crossed the threshold.'

'I never see you there.'

'Times when it's appropriate to open your trap, and there's times where it ain't. I got manners.'

'Discretion. Appreciate it.'

'Sailor's honour. Like I said.'

'Well, it's not loaded, which is a good thing. But you still can't hold on to this.'

'I know that. We've found guns before. I'm a kid fresh off the boat, now?'

'There's no reason to hold on to this. You should've handed it in yesterday. Might already be a search on it.'

'Needle in a haystack. How many gods did you say there were in this city? What's a superhero without their strength?'

'Back to pot bellies.'

'Hey! I'm cutting down. Eating healthy.'

'You're looking good. I should've said it before.'

'I'm with those Mothers of yours. It's never too late to pay a man a compliment. I never said anything about holding on to this, by the way. It's aggravation that I don't need. My dick's too big for it to fit into my trouser pocket anyway.'

'Drop it in at the end of your shift. Concentrate on finding the good stuff.'

'There's new bastards running things now. I wouldn't trust them to keep it for themselves. Ten grand went missing last month. Packed in a holdall we found in the park. Too big to keep for yourself, that kind of money. And new notes, too. So we handed it in, filled out the forms in triplicate, but somewhere between completing the paperwork at the depot and the holdall reaching the precinct, the money vanished.'

'You should've told me about this before. A corrupt office I can help with.'

'And risk getting my shifts cut? Ain't stupid.'

'You become the better man.'

'If it happens once, maybe. But when you see it repeatedly. I'm the fat man swimming Coney Island beach getting cramp, surrounded by strong swimmers.'

'Never means that you need to join them. Don't you think that City Hall is populated with these assholes too? Buildings going up that should never have been greenlighted. Cases physically disappearing from desks and erased from board minutes when things become difficult. None of these things can be solved with a gun. We educated ourselves to seek alternatives. We didn't all come from this, but we can do better.'

'Only way to fix things – the cross or the gun.'

'Money, too.'

'Nah, Teddy. Not everyone can be fixed by money. Spent my life on the street and seen enough things I shouldn't have. Think of all the people quietly trying to resolve their private affairs in a back alley, only to be interrupted by a man pulling up in a dumpster truck. The things you see in the headlights: a handshake or a hand around the throat. It might be the actual moment you see or the seconds before or after it. You are seen and you are found. We don't wear badges but the trucks are easy to trace. Takes one call. How can you be silenced if you don't take their money? The cross or the gun. It will always come back to those two things. Your Mothers, sleeping so soundly outside City Hall. They worship and fear the cross, you've told me that much. We've seen them leaving mass, the one that takes place at dawn so that they won't have to mix with the larger congregation. Interesting that you don't pray at the same church, not that it's any of my business, but that struck.'

'Keep talking and I may find use for the gun myself.'

'They can believe what they like but the cross won't protect them as they sleep. They're watched over by gods, that's certain, but not the God they need.'

'They sleep in the safest place. Their homes, another matter. Out here . . .'

'The City'll lose patience. Move them somewhere quieter. You can have your right to protest so long as you don't hold up the business of any other bastard. You live in a world of laws, yes? How many of those are being fucked by your Mothers warming their asses on those steps? How much money is the City spending or losing on this? 'Cos they'll reach a point where the balance sheet hangs over their heads. Their fate decided by profit and loss, like every other working man in the city.'

'The more noise made, silent or otherwise, will trigger due process. That, along with other ideas being worked on, inside and out.'

'Hard currency can't be fought. Our dollar bills are the mighty avenger. Nothing finer. Judgement comes from the thickness of the paper wedged into your billfold, not what a courthouse or police room hand down.'

'You can be cynical, sometimes.'

'I clean up the city's shit. This is what it makes me. You're hardly the idealist, either. I can read it in your face. This truck cut us from the same cloth. I've learned to mind my business. You, though ...'

'Keeping an eye out for my Mothers, is all. It's what's expected of children.'

Teddy leaves the truck to its work and walks the five blocks towards City Hall, aware that the Mothers need a further degree of protection, but unsure as to the best means. All he knows is that a gun has no place there; it doesn't belong amongst their holy things. Yet it sits heavily in his jacket pocket as he moves; guilt in its physical form, weighted across his chest. Redemption in its physical form, too. Confidence. Like the cross, many damnations, but also, many blessings.

The City would have issued a gun if he'd only asked, but its every minute of handling would've needed to be accounted for, additional reports he did not have the heart to write. Many of his colleagues in the field would never have left the confines of City Hall without similar protection; the only object to give confidence that matched their belief of the job. His belief was all he needed; he feared neither the street nor the snake pit that lay beneath City Hall's polished marble floors; only a dulling of his brain and the rendering of any knowledge which would make him impotent.

It was no longer possible to effect change using his mind and aptitude – the option was to point a gun in the direction of enquiry and see where it led. He could see the Mothers receiving answers to their direct questions if only they had collateral, the bulk that comes from gun metal. But he did not want to fall into the trap of former colleagues who became hooked on its easy means of persuasion; how it blighted out nuance and reduced the world into decision-making that was either black or white. He was neither a frustrated investigator nor a homicide detective. Policy drives him: change that could not be effected or envisaged from the chaos of his upbringing, nor those of the children who cannot be found.

Their place in the minds of the Mothers is greater – he was a good friend when they were around to be friends with – so carries neither the weight nor the sorrow of the protest's instigators. However, their energy and sense of injustice can be harnessed to suit both parties.

This sounds so logical when laid out squarely, but he knows that his personal limitations will let him down. He will put the Mothers before himself, as much as he doesn't wish to; how an obligation to them, neither asked for nor contracted, stops him from being his own man. He should be standing on his balcony by rights, still drunk and watching the sunrise. Instead, he walks through the rescinding dark with confidence and redemption lodged in his pocket.

Traffic moves, but there is little activity in the block leading to City Hall. The wilderness of the final hour before morning truly breaks. Many nights he has been tempted to sleep over with the Mothers, curious as to their community once they are finally left alone; wishing to become party to the last act of privacy, wondering what, if anything, may be kept from him. They have never asked, and so far he's never offered, knowing that other agencies – the police – are best left to monitor that business.

The gun does not give him agency, but he understands that he must be bolder, his presence in the square felt more deeply, especially at night when they are reduced to their core. He should not be afraid to direct them more strongly, to prevent their silence from merely amplifying the sadness of middle-age. People have long sat outside banks, oil companies and government buildings. The successes and failures of all needed to be learned from. The protests of their past too, when they were unafraid to use fire to stand up for their people. He must also explain what he is doing, how he is pulling apart the barriers inside City Hall, piece by piece. How they must be patient and trust in his ability. Most importantly, they need to keep going, believing in their strength and their community. Without those, the sum of their efforts will fall apart.

He's afraid to tell them these things, like all children who still believe in the heroism of their parents. He recognises their flaws, preferring to be distant rather than acknowledge them. How to tell those who protected him when he sorely needed protecting, that their pride and weakness will be used against them if they do not keep their wits? Their circulation is not what it was; their urgency reduced to a dull point. They bruise easily and cry more often. They are silent mascots for a movement they don't understand; their complexions becoming greyer by the day; slowly turning to monument. The movement is theirs if they do not weaken and allow themselves to be distracted by the children and their short attention spans. If they are lions in stone, let them roar at precisely the moment when their voices should be heard. Roar, so that their presence is felt across ten blocks. Tear these muthafuckas to pieces. Devour all liars and naysayers. Leave no trace of their inaction and contempt.

Yes, the gun gives him agency; reminds that he has a voice of his own. He should say these things once and let them act upon it, or not. There remains urgency in his work and he should not be overly distracted either. Harmony can emerge from areas of conflict and uncertainty. It's simply a question of application. If they listen, he can help. Truly, if they listen. He should speak with the gun in his hand, giving him the authority of what – a politician, dime-store preacher, or a teenager holding up a bottle shop? He recognises that he must be all of these things; how there is truth and falsity in every aspect.

He studied hard to move beyond the future of the kid with the gun. Acting it out now is a luxury, no different to his bosses on their weekend hunting expeditions, or a guy letting off steam at the shooting range. This is merely a role he is playing. If he is stopped he can explain that. He is play-acting with an unlicensed firearm. He is indulging all that he has long denied. Heady avenger. Master of the city. He could run the square if he wanted, every answer he seeks directed into the barrel of the gun.

He thinks of his brothers and wonders whether their ease with life stems from a similar metallic confidence; how the short cut may be more satisfactory than the long game – for it is just that: an endless game where he follows and turns with no hope of outright championship. Every victory is merely an increment, a further nudge towards progress hidden deep into the horizon. Fuck his pigeon steps; his slow backward bowing out of every council chamber; plotting to outsmart those whose legitimacy is already set in the statute books; who need no defence because the book is all they need. The bluster he could cut through just by wielding his gun. The short cuts he would take, tearing through one chamber to the next; rocky off-road tracks that were the fastest route into town.

He thought of the countryside off the far-east coast and the barren plains of the west, the dust clouds expelling from the speed of his vehicle. Joyriding with his brothers. The freedom to fly. How time could be found for those on the upper floors of City Hall who were previously unable to schedule an appointment with him. Meetings suddenly opening up; the good coffee and an unencumbered view of the cityscape. He wished neither to belong on those levels nor to be feared, simply for his presence to be acknowledged and his questions given merit. He would scare them senseless if he did not get his way, but frank discussion and civility were preferred. It was how they'd trained him after all, because for all the thuggishness of the gun, he remained one of them, irrevocably so.

He walks quicker with the gun. He clears blocks quicker than he realises; a sprinter whose feet remain on the ground. He understands the foolishness of what he is about to do, but his desire to show off in front of the Mothers is stronger. Look what I can be, what I can become, he wants to tell them. I lived on hamburger rolls and salami to get through college. I danced on bar tops and shook my junk. I walked balls in lace underwear and a fan if there was a chance of winning a hundred bucks. But all I needed was the gun. All I need is the gun in my hand to wipe your tears, not the education to write letters and lobby those with deaf ears. We needed none of that. Self-respect and a gun was the route, was always the route.

How did we think we could achieve by other means when the way was signposted so clearly; when we were told that this was the future set out for us, as determined by our origins? Who were we to go against that and look for another way? Foolishness of a high order; yet he remains intoxicated by the freeze of metal against his thigh. In this moment he is prepared to exchange all the knowledge he has accrued for simple binary power; a bullet for every lie; metal that strikes through bullshit; that can definitively end things, as much for the Mothers as for himself. The thrill is purely his, but he wishes them to sleep soundly, and find a place where they can ease into a gentler age.

In the square he finds them hunched in familiar positions of repose; a whale pod beached on concrete and slowly turning in on themselves as their bodies reduce to vital functions. Four police snore inharmoniously in their squad cars. He crosses them gingerly, a babysitter mindful of waking a room of dreaming infants. Protection or no, he marvels at how it is possible for a group of people to curl up and sleep in the middle of the city night after night; how an unspoken negotiation has been reached between the Mothers and the City as a whole: that what is public during the day belongs to them after dark; the square becoming a private room that must not be trespassed or spied upon.

They sleep as they would do in their homes, fart and scratch themselves with no self-consciousness. Their faces freeze in silent argument when one has taken exception to another, moodily turning their backs, or pelting the offending party with scraps of stale food. There is more of this behaviour than not, once the children and other supporters have dispersed. The night police are also in their private zone, most often listening to sport on the radio at low volumes, and talking about women, either their own or those that they covet. With no permits or approval, he stands in an apartment block without walls, its boundaries clear and its occupants oblivious to each other. A structure resulting from both necessity and the passing of time; the Mothers a line of red-bricks, slowly weathered by age. Agreement has somehow been reached, and without his hand, enabling them to sleep without fear.

Which dark corner was he turning over whilst this happened in broad daylight behind him? What other accords have been made of which he is not aware? It feels like a citywide consultation, with opinions canvassed from block to block. Somehow, between those who do not understand the fuss and those who believe in their right to fuss, they are accepted and left alone, no more out of place than a group of bargain hunters sleeping outside a department store the night before a big sale.

They are as faded to daily life as the army of homeless or a group of persistent teenagers waiting outside a hotel for a glimpse of an idolised pop star. They are seen but not; tolerated, so long as there is no discord relating to their own lives; an indifference that keeps them safe. He understands that he is not needed, that it has probably been that way for longer than he realises.

Through his tiredness he racks his brain, trying to recall when the sea change occurred, if there was anything in their voice or manner that should have alerted him to their new-found security; how they were merely fatigued now and no longer drawn with worry.

The realisation should make his walk lighter, but he instantly feels burdened, unsure what he should be doing with his time, knowing his weakness in simply being there, chasing them so. He should turn back towards his apartment, and the unmade bed that awaits him there; to collapse into a stupor that is deliciously, privately his. He can allow himself the weakness of dreams, a state he has previously deemed selfish, for those without obligation or of a lesser mind.

How beautiful it must be to sleep and dream, to find yourself in a world where there is only pleasure and an affirmation of your gifts. To even be thinking of it now strikes him as a dream in itself, a new-dawn dream, and he shakes his head, as if to chide himself for abandoning such an easy escape. Going to the balls for the first time, a three-year dream before slowly removing himself, taking pleasure in a tougher, more untrustworthy world, gave him the same feeling: identical sensations of lightness, then fear.

This is the dream world, how he lives now, learning that power lies in his hands if he has the will to act upon it. Power does not come from the dependency upon others. It is simply a question of resolve. It no longer matters whether the Mothers need him as much as before; whether they've outgrown their wet nurse and established a confidence and routine of their own. So long as they're handicapped by silence, emboldened but still chained, he remains in their service. He serves by leaving the gun in his hand; how he will place it under the head of one of the sleeping Mothers. Protection shared, strength doubled.

He thinks again of what lacks in their campaign: weight; how three kilos resting in their palm would rouse everyone from their stupor. Tired now; wanting to send a signal. The Mothers with sharper questions, City Hall with a clear, detailed response. The gun makes things clearer than he can ordinarily allow himself to be, a coward hiding behind regulation and suits; scared to reveal what he knows. Now there is no need for his reports or his worrying, he realises, for he can give them tools to enable progress without their middleman; for each party to see the other's sweat. Have the hard discussion away from his diplomacy. Let them get on with it!

He wishes to gift them, the way they had surprised him and the children with gifts at Christmas and birthdays. His first birthday once he'd made the decision to leave his mother (his sister now gone); that he would not survive another year if he stayed in that apartment with its attendant chaos and fear; wondering whether to mention the upcoming age, sixteen, withholding expectation because nothing could come out of it, because he had only slept on the sofa for three weeks and nobody knew him from the man in the moon.

There was no connection, loyalty or obligation for them to mark the date in any way, bar the sincere but distant congratulations you give when a stranger that you serve in the store shares their happy news. He was as familiar as a store clerk or gas pump boy, where you wished congratulations with all the sincerity in the world, only to forget it in the following moment.

Was it better to have those ten seconds of purely felt generosity or better to leave the day unmarked by not mentioning it? Which would nourish him better? In any event, he told them, because he was still at the age when a birthday was a marker for optimism rather than regret, and he was sufficiently relaxed to let down his guard.

'Child, you're not going to eat your cereal? Are the standards of this hotel no longer meeting your ideals?'

'I was going to make pancakes for everyone. Bought a carton of eggs last night. It's what we always eat on my birthday.'

There was little they could do in the moment bar the well

wishes he was expecting, simultaneously heartfelt, awkward and distant. He was homesick for his mother but knew that the attention he craved from her was a mirage from much younger years. She would not remember the date now, would have to be roughly woken from her haze to even be reminded. So the greetings from these new Mothers was as good as it was going to get. Boy better recognise.

Having been taken unawares, they had the day to cobble together a more meaningful reception when he returned home from school; a party of sorts that had elements of both the child and the adult: bubble-gum ice cream and root beer floats (the merest hint of rum in the root beer), cigarettes, and his pick of the turntable. A faux silk scarf with a bucking horse motif from the children, lifted by Sherry from a market cart outside the subway, and a leather notebook from the Mothers.

'So you can make notes from all those books you have your head in. Maybe write one yourself.'

The perfection of the gesture, how little had matched it since, too concentrated was he on looking for the reason behind everything. The sincerity of leaving a gift under their heads was a desire to replicate that moment as simply and honestly as he could. He would leave no note, just the gun wrapped in his scarf, which they would be sure to recognise. He could explain more fully later what was driving him to act so, but for now only the near-silent gesture was on his mind.

If he had children of his own this would be a Santa Claus moment; perhaps this would be his only chance at the role, a thought that wearied him, not willing to think of the future other than what was happening now. His head was filled with magnanimity as he turned the corner of City Hall, equating power and philanthropy as one; how he wanted to be known for the aggressive creation of good things; clearing the table with a flick of the whip; that those who did not understand suffering would be made to suffer if it was for the greater good; how power could be accrued just by benefiting the voiceless.

Do you understand what I've given you by holding back? he thinks. Your freedom to wear black, to pray, and to mourn. The luxury of your piousness; how the hours stretch before you, as carefree as millionaires, who have cut themselves free of domestic ties. Do you recognise how selfish you have become after being absolved from blame; because you could not be held accountable for misdeeds that took place under your roofs if they were out of sight, and if the children insisted on hiding from you what you did not need to know? How you prided yourself on being all-seeing and all-knowing, but in reality you were no better than the man with the white stick who begs outside the subway. He, at least, is industrious – what do you have? You shy away from guilt and look elsewhere; denying its presence in your homes. So why not let me have my freedom now?

Easier to point the finger at my deficiencies, the sloppiness of my attentions, how I stretch myself too thinly in an attempt to please everyone. You are proud of the career I've carved for myself yet you remain frustrated by it, resenting its conflicting demands on my time. In asking me to bus you to church, to dry clean your best clothes for certain masses, you understand how it impedes my life outside of City Hall, but you cannot acknowledge it directly. I am here because I want to be here. This is what's expected. We are here in good times because we have got through the bad. Children no longer disappear and for this we must be thankful.

We have cried and grieved; plotted and fought. Through both missteps and success we find ourselves back on the front line, held up by the weight of what we believe. It does not matter whether we are good people, only the goodness of our intentions. In your mind you sleep like angels on those steps, emboldened by the Divine. You do not see how the cops champ at the bit for the liberty to rain their batons upon your prostrate flesh; their desire to beat your stubbornness from you. Their ache to rip those kimonos to shreds, to set your wigs alight, whether still worn or not. They be jonesin' to see you hurt, brah, all the more so by their hand; longing for your puzzlement and retreat, your blood and piss marking the spots you once so tightly held.

Your ability to sit so still, to hold your voices, comes from moving heaven and earth; the logistics of twenty-four-hour protection and sanitation, the delivery of food and the management of news folks. How the children's expectations must be managed, their participation strong-armed, and their behaviour monitored. Do you think that this all happens naturally, that this circus has evolved just from you turning up to take your seat on the hall steps? You're crazier muthafuckas than me if you believe that to be the case. I'm not bitter, he thinks, just telling it like it is.

You, who believe so strongly in your First Amendment rights, deny me the ability to speak my mind. He's flooded with the injustice of this as he looks out across the city; twenty million sleeping in the knowledge that they have the ability to speak their truth. His, he can only hide.

Not every battle needed to be fought with a gun, but let it just be this once, to remind all of where he came from, and where he could fall. He was deaf to the silence that greeted him, so consumed was he by internal noise; that his footsteps must be soft, his movements gentle so as not to disturb his charges. Babies sleeping the night before Christmas, dreaming of candy and gifts, and goodwill to their people, just for this one day.

THIS BRUTAL HOUSE

1.

Three nights in a prison cell until they decide what to do with us. We tell ourselves that it can be no longer than three days, for reasons of hygiene as well as legality. Seven packed into one cell – five of us entering the home of two grizzled old-timers. They think they insult us by throwing us into the first cell they find; that the time spent separating us is not worth their effort, but we are grateful for their nastiness and contempt for procedure. The sweat and stink of seven: four bunks and a toilet with no partition. Shit, spunk, industrial bleach: all were in and exhaled. We are seasoned enough to understand that this is merely the antechamber, left to stew before we are either swallowed into the belly of the building or shipped off elsewhere. Our companions are in a stupor of their own, cowed by the situation and the size and strength of us.

'Y'all private army muthafuckas got yourselves arrested?'

'Yous a terrorist group or some such? Too old to be gang members.'

'They tell us that terrorists are no different from your neighbour. These muthafuckas come from another planet.'

'Why you standing so tall? Almost tiptoes. You ballerinas?'

'Private army of ballerinas ready to take our law-makers down. If that ain't terrorism, I don't know what is.'

'All I know is that these cats are strange. Y'all better stay out of my way. I'm army-trained too, bitches. They drilled us to act crazy after the things we seen.'

We cannot bring ourselves to speak. Any state other than this is unnatural to our thinking. When the protest first began we vowed that we would no longer speak until our questions were answered; that silence was our only option until there was no need for the movement. We did not envision a time when speaking would become anathema; how words needed to be pulled from our throats, buried as they are; our vocal cords shrinking, vocabularies disintegrating into our guts. Silence, through faith, has enriched us. It allows us to communicate everything we feel and know – and fear – without bullshit. It separates us from the sewer rats that hold our chains. We cannot be broken in this cell. We can feel our blood pressure rise from the claustrophobia yes; how the thickness of the stench, almost as solid as the shit that's flushed away, makes us wretch into our pillows or the shoulders of others. We hear the din encroaching through the stone walls, the monster that is the main prison screaming to be fed with unfamiliar flesh; we feel the stickiness of the bunk rails and the colony of germs creeping upon our skin; we sweat in the heat and shiver through the cold, the synthetic blankets bobbly and thin from use, perforated with burns from illegal cigarettes. We will take all that they can serve in this period of indecision, seeing it as either a holiday or a honeymoon from what comes next.

There was no reason for us to hold a gun. We had never even discussed firearms because of the belief shared that silence was our weapon. Our backs are already battle-scarred from protests past; the voices of our younger selves hoarse from shouting the language of violence. Five apostles sitting atop City Hall steps day after day; the strength of our line, the amplification of our silence. A gun only polluted that, reduced us to street hoods emerging from our ghettoes. The police are a fine example: at first bemused by us, but gradually respectful, because our deportment and intent couldn't be negated or questioned. They would do the same for their children if there was no other way. There was no need for a gun. Our intelligence was greater than that. We could not understand why it was under our heads, how its muzzle poked against the pillow and iced our cheeks. The weightiness of it in our hands.

We had forgotten the weight and the indentation left on our open palms; creases on the soft parts of our hands reminding us of when protest turned to riot, or other more personal times, when we took in troubled guests who should never have been sheltered. We were disbelieving as it passed between us, a chain of incredulity back and forth, still unable to comprehend how it had appeared – whether the Tooth Fairy had turned hood, or if we'd been marked by a darkly intentioned well-wisher. For all the bewilderment, and abhorrence, we were hypnotised by it, standing as five little moons pulled into its orbit. Two of us had fired bullets from an identical weapon in forgotten pasts now exhumed; the motion and sound, how the shoulder tore backwards from the force of the shot; the wounds of our intended, which spurted and grew before our eyes; the damage and thrill. We were younger with the gun in our hands, but also wiser and more afraid; aware of our vulnerability, seeing ourselves as others see us – either as old men, too subdued to throw a punch, or as leaders of a campaign that required kick-starting; either way, as fools, lost in the depth of their minds.

By nature we are crowd-pleasers, craving the approval of our own, wishing the children to be schooled in our ways, independent, but cut from our cloth. How else can any of the old ways survive? Would possession of a gun wrapped in a tatty cloth keep the children closer to us? Was this what they wanted to see, a siege becoming a storm? A conjecture we would not see realised once an armed squad surrounded us; the gun falling from our hands. Our ears were deaf to the creep of police boots up the steps, our peripheral vision closed to encroaching movement, blinded by the death machine we held. We were no strangers to kissing concrete, sleeping on our bellies for part of the night, but the hands that pushed us down were more forceful than we would've liked; another sense memory returning to the fore, the cacophony of barked instruction and force from multiple police officers working to drain strength and thought.

We could take any incident from the last four decades and recall a matching scent; how fear and righteousness combine with a metallic blood tang. We lay in a row on the steps' upper gradient, spread-eagled, feet kicked from beneath us; a feeling that we should roll towards the sidewalk if we did not reach for the top step with our fingertips. They worked well to disorientate us, screaming to stay silent when we were yet to utter a word; hands patting us down once, twice, cracking like thunderclaps on our backs and thighs. Voices we'd previously understood to be kind now returning to their default: a snarl loaded with abuse and pent-up contempt. We were surrounded by ill-abusers, reduced to scheming ghetto faggots because of what had been left under our heads. To have your prejudices justified in defiance of changing winds is to ride with the righteous. Their voices rang as they prodded and restrained us, as joyful as if they were in church; connecting with their maker as they sang from the pews. They were victims of a confidence trick, lulled into a false sense of security.

How could a protest morph into anything else but this expected outcome? Those scrabbling a living in the margins, their ignorance and socio-economic status festering to an inevitable rot, would never ascend to the levels of decent common sense. They would always be ruled by ghetto ethics and the laws of the street, and here was a crew who were no different from the rest. Their window dressing was novel, but they still could not help but revert when the path was closed to them. Each roll down the steps was acknowledgement for every lousy donut they'd delivered; the same benevolence they'd show to a neighbour or a distant aunt living on her own. Every shout was for the coffee they'd brought, always piping hot, wasted now in its hydration of those ungrateful, extremist mouths. There were scant kicks, rained upon places where their touch would only leave a minor trace: caressing cheeks of pudding face, and in the soft bulge of muffin tops. They had been suckered to the point where they were spending their own loose change on these two-faced militants.

The young people they carried on with, you could see from a mile away that they were trouble, disturbed from the roots of their unwashed hair to their painted toes, but the old folks carried themselves differently. They were different, weren't they? They had decency there. You could see in their eyes the honesty in what they were doing; how their chests were puffed out with motivation following their visits to church. All that promise, to then fall back upon a gun? Their treatment was justified; every cut, bruise, crunched nail or bone was a response to the immediate danger the force found itself in. Protecting themselves and their reputations.

'You boys got yourselves tore up! We saw you from the rec yard, coming out of the van like a band of Robinson

Crusoes. It's easier to go quietly. That's shit you gots to learn. Between the cuffs going round your hands and your feet touching prison soil, no one cares whether you live or die. In the name of self-protection and a future for yourself, you rein that shit in.'

'Listen, you can't tell these folks nothing. Look how they got their mouths twisted. They have no care for anything you say. They think they got this. Busted eye and lips. One muthafucka walking with a limp and they think that they got this.'

'What they got is a period of indeterminate incarceration.'

'That and a whopped ass.'

'Ha! You must've really pissed someone off, boys. Bet you never thought keeping your mouths shut would get you in this much trouble.'

'What kind of world do these naïve fish live in? Prison ain't no doll's house. There's no candelabra on the dinner table, you understand.'

'Not counting the candles they smuggled up their asses. Muthafuckas looking at us like we're crazy. We're not the ones with cut lips and purple fingers, crying our eyes out. Y'all need a reality check.'

Everywhere we go, we are judged. The prison cell is no different from the grocery store for the assumptions spoken and otherwise. Some of these we address directly, other times stored but we feel no shame in taking this time for ourselves. These sorry-ass cellmates can speak their trash until the stench of shit knocks them dead. (How anyone is capable of speaking in the thickness of this atmosphere is beyond us; almost forcing us to close our eyes, such is its weight.) There is no reason to speak for words are of no consequence here. We have no case to answer, no plea to make. If the children have any of the intelligence we have long-attributed to them, they will find a way to have us released within seventy-two hours. Teddy. He must have been called by now; must be waiting outside or tearing up hell across phone lines. Bloodying lips and noses in the back rooms of City Hall. Seventy-two hours is all that we can give ourselves, the longest we can keep despair at bay. After that.

The excesses of the strip search took us back to darker times, when we were no longer in control of our bodies or bodily functions; a reminder that the state owned every inch of our flesh, inside and out. We could strip down to the barest of underwear at the balls, proud of how our bodies looked and moved; how we could serve and slay, without a single eye leaving us as we strutted and posed. Voguing was never a seduction dance unless your idea of seduction was a peacock of fine posture who threw one pose after another, some alluding to editorial spreads from fashion magazines, others gymnastic in their composition. Clothed or no, we were never self-conscious of our bodies, lean from exercise, youth, the limited availability of food, or a mixture of all these things. Even on City Hall steps, older, thicker, we thought nothing of changing clothes if it was warm enough and there was no other place to do it. A dancer's mentality of rolling with your situation rather than how it was observed: militants who had lost all sense of standards. The cuffs should've been the reminder, but that journey from the police truck to the prison walls remains a blank, wiped out from shock and effort, needing to withdraw, if only to recharge and regain our wits.

The first removal of the cuffs at the prison was a false relief until we understood that we were expected to strip and have every cavity examined. The pride in our bodies withered to something childlike and fearful, suddenly self-conscious of being naked in front of each other, our humiliation reduced to individual ones; collective power temporarily frozen. Our willingness or otherwise as we opened our mouths and spread our legs; the guttural sounds lodged in our throats as their greased, gloved fingers explored. Our mouths belonged to them. Our hands, intestines and rectum. We had no free will over any of these things because the gun had taken it away. For weeks we had demanded that the City take over. Now they had.

We were indifferent to the prison overalls, appreciated in some quarters for being clean and dry; and those who handed out our kit were not bastards; hardened, yes, stern in their greeting, but not sadistic in their tasks, like we had experienced in younger days. The welcome was as good as it got. The welcome was the demonstration of their evolved selves, dictated by legislature, and informed by past institutional failures of which we may have been part. This was the red carpet, this brightly clinical and plastic holding area; the closest we would get to being in public view.

Seventy-two hours: that is the longest they can hold us for. We cling on to this like it's scripture; the only Holy law we can live by if it quells our panic and keeps us from going crazy in the cell; less to do with outbursts, more the fear of darkness numbing our senses and losing our minds with only our brothers as witness. We have seen grown men who ran the street lose their senses within hours of being held within these confines; even flanked by their soldiers, their strength diminished with every step that took them further inside. A man's outside status continues to be held here if he has the structure and mythology to hand, but even these cannot protect from a weakness of mind induced by airlessness and claustrophobia. Kids who ran blocks like fiefdoms, with organisational capacities the City yearned for, no strangers to brief periods of incarceration, defeated by the short distances between their cell walls, their body attacking itself through fear, their mind sealing itself from further harm by shutting down.

The cloying sweetness of a shit-smeared toilet pan keeps us alert; every dry cough to clear the fug lodged in our throats is a jump-start; a reflex action jolting our chests forward and triggering our hearts to beat faster, pumping more blood and stale oxygen around our bodies, so that our toes wriggle inside our boots independent of thought, and our heads fizz with energy and ideas. We are despairing yet we are conscious! Our bodies, knowing better than ourselves, refusing to go quietly and shut down. We are fighters, from our bones. Also we are gossips, kept alive by our cellmates' gripes and stories; moaning about the food, the brightness of the overhead lighting, and the itchiness of the regulation overalls. They complain of allergic reactions to the dust mites buried in the nylon-fibre mattresses, and the slow pace of bureaucracy that keeps them locked up.

'There are people whose livelihoods depend on us rotting in here. Clerical staff who type the reports and what have you. The lawyers who keep the courthouse running. If there were no cases, they'd have no jobs. If cases were processed twice as fast as they are now, they'd be twice as poor, and no better than us.'

'My taxes paid for my lawyer's shoes and calfskin brief-case. These public defenders got taste, boy. Fight corruption in their eight-hundred-dollar shoes.'

'Fuck the shoes, man. It's the flow of money we need to get to. Under our feet right now is a sea of money flowing back and forth from the city to here, and lining the pockets of those bastards. Everyone is getting paid but us.'

'Even though without us they wouldn't be here?'

'It's what I'm saying. They get bank. We get penitentiary.'

'Do you folks understand that sitting there all nice and sweet, like mutes in uniform, gets you nowhere? Meanwhile, the lawyer that's been recommended to you is getting paid;

the suppliers providing your food and clothing are getting paid. The clerk in the courthouse typing up the bullshit file that got you sent here in the first place is getting paid. Most of all, the governor, charging the City for every night you spend in this shitty hotel.'

'We've been in and out of this system for so long, it shifts your focus on to the things they don't want you to see.'

'Who gives a fuck about rehabilitation? Least of all them. If you're compliant and do your time, you have the space to think about their time and how it's paid for.'

'That and not getting caught in the first place.'

'Yes, muthafucka. That too. If I wasn't so fat they wouldn't have been able to outrun me. I'll be as skinny as you silent shadows by the time they let me out. See if they catch me after that.'

'Skinny-ass bitches, looking pretty for their mug shots. That your rehabilitation plan? There's worse ways to get outta here.'

'I aspire, man. Blessings. Blessings.'

They photographed us once we had changed, when it was ascertained that we would not aid their processing any further. We had nodded in confirmation of our names, withstood the humiliation of being naked in their presence, our cavities being searched no more gently than a museum guard pushing his hands through a line of bags at the entrance queue. They had taken our shoes and jewellery, all the visual pieces that helped us to define who we were; our fingerprints were taken with great care, they held and pressed each digit over the inkpad as if our hands were precious stones, something tangible they could store away and rely on in hard times; ditto the mouth swabs, and the strands of hair pulled from the tops of our heads.

We were raised in a country whose very foundations lay upon the notion of processing; generations of men whose tread upon this soil was analysed and assessed for risk; liberated from their valuables, and proscribed names to fit into the culture. All for the honour of living upon this blessed land, where exploitation – whether through employment, housing or life expectancy – was simply an honest opportunity that had failed to be realised, through either laziness or ineptitude. We stood in lines all our lives, waiting for our food stamps, to enrol into community college, to plead with our housing boards, to see lawyers or organisations that may have shown even the slightest interest in our case. We stood in lines and waited our turn. We answered every question presented to us. We complied with every rule, so as not to jeopardise our chances, lying only when necessary, when only an adequate lie would further our cause.

We had been processed until we became carbon copies of ourselves, the ridges of our fingerprints reduced to the delicacy of spider's web; losing syllables in the nodding or utterance of our names, as if each affirmation also shrunk an unacknowledged part of us; every new case file becoming a fiction of the one that preceded it. These are the gaps that create mythology, and if we had that need, the burning pain that can only be extinguished by being recognised as notorious, we would have acted upon it. We remain ourselves but we are tired of our participation in the charade of providing answers demanded of us, of being lined-up like cattle at market or slaves at auction; the implicit expectation of obedience, of which we have now had our fill. We have been patient and given our fair share, and for this we are incarcerated. For this, they take away our clothes and photograph us.

How dare these muthafuckas! How dare they even try! We want no record of us being in this institution, essentially to disappear within these walls, so that our presence only registers as an apparition that flickers and creates unease; our silence to haunt them as they walk these corridors; our faces faded to line drawings when they open our case files. We have scant knowledge of the law, but we know about flash bulbs, understanding how shadow can be created or erased from a face by a head tilt or the slightest deviation in posture. We've learned that widening the eyes rolls our brows and cheeks upwards, that closing our mouths but slackening our jaws contours us further. In posing so, our photographs give the least of ourselves, shrinking body mass, details of our skin and eyes negated by the flash bulb's glare. We are eyes and the numbers dictated by the card held in our hands.

Other than that, we give them nothing. Each time they refer to the file, there will be less to see, the photographic paper itself deteriorating, the typescript that accompanies it, scant; a lack of detail to make them doubt their own ability – to take notes and follow procedure; of their presence when the intake occurred, a lack of corroboration impressing a haziness upon them: prisoners appearing from nowhere, who have tales to tell. There is no power we can wield here, other than the weight we place in small gestures that will bite them later. It's all we can hope for.

'We've seen you on TV, man. They all know who you are. Bunch of queers starting another movement. The brahs who got City Hall on their knees, trapped in their building like rats. Seeing too much of our skin tone outside their door and shitting their pants. You've no idea how it warms our hearts to see this. You're doing what we never had the balls to do. Oh, we've been angry, you understand, but somehow we've lacked the organisation, the will, or the sheer manpower needed to amass. There were movements before, but none relevant to us now. We could never agree on the cause, having too many grievances to be reduced to one. There was never a moment when we felt it was possible, waiting for someone else to drive it through. This is queer shit you have going on, so we cannot stand outside City Hall and support you, but know that it warms our hearts to see you following your path. You'll have paper coming your way. Change too, if you hold out long enough for it. But first, they're going to give you money. They'll pay you to make this go away. The mess that you're making on their front lawn. All they see are dog turds shrivelling and trod into the grass. They can't hear themselves for the noise, not to mention the smell. People of your class and hue stinking out their building so that they have to keep the windows closed. You're stopping good people from crossing their threshold; citizens who have always followed the rules but are now denied the help and assistance they require because they are too intimidated to cross your line. Imagine how quiet it must be in the corridors of City Hall. Their business grinding to a halt: no births or deaths registered, no weddings taking place. Whole departments scratching their asses because they have no people to face; no one to aid, placate, argue with or restrain. If you think about the business of City Hall, for it is a running business as well as Church and Father, how their business is people, depending on a quantity of footfall to pass through their doors, no different from a department store. If you measure the health of their business by footfall, you can see that they're in poor shape. Not only are their operations stagnating through lack of access, they are paying whole departments of staff to do nothing. They are subsidising a strike for which no motion has been passed, and remaining fully staffed while it happens. They may fear your silence, but a loss of money and rolling malcontent within their building frightens them more. Believe me; they'll be coming down here with cash-stuffed bags to make this go away. Order must always reign over chaos. I can see that you're tired, but this is not the time to rest. You must be more alert here than you were out there. You must plan and gather strength. Send messages to those outside who support you. Like I said, I cannot lend my hand to queer shit, but you are making a difference to all brothers. You have them afraid. It warms my heart to see it.'

His speech exhausts us, but we in turn feel less afraid. We are respected here. We've been shown respect. If a small percentage of this sentiment permeates through the institution, all will be well. We can find a place for ourselves and live in relative security so long as we mind our business and resist the temptation to speak our minds. The lining of our guts continue to spasm of their own making, but we slowly relax into our bunks, loosening the straps on our shoes.

We should submit: allow the bed mites to bite, let the skin on our backs and elbows erupt and swell; bouquets of urticaria springing from one to another. We need to breathe deeply, for the stench will never dissipate. We cannot separate from gases and stench for the time we are here. Without oxygen we have no clarity and lose our ability to organise. We need oxygen to ward off lethargy and negative feeling. We cannot reach if we do not breathe the wisdom of our new brother; the education he brings.

We dream of freedom in our sleep; attacking all who oppress us. We rampage through the square and smash their faces to pulp. We slay the unfaithful and gorge on tacos until our stomachs are fit to burst. We've hit the children before, when we've had just cause. We know their tender spots; the places to break or merely bruise. We beat them mid-speech, forcing them into headlocks until they speak our names; burning their tents and possessions until we have a purity of line and form; a row of children crouched in prayer, cross-legged and rapt as they listen to their elders. In most cases we were brought up through a web of argument and fist. As much as we run, it never leaves us.

'Sleep, children. Accept that you have entered into your fate. Close your eyes, queer babies, and dream of your revolution. Dream of those you've beaten to the punch. Those you've left behind who will never reach your goal. Pray to your maker to find strength. Pray to find your children.'

2.

'They're exhausted.'

'Still need to wake these bitches up. No special treatment here.'

'Frightened. They got sentenced yesterday.'

'Aren't we all? Meat a' scared a' screws. Screws a' scared a' meat. Vicious cycle.'

'Except we hold the keys. Get to leave.'

'We ain't the ones sent down. They sleep in the big house, they follow the rules. Three months pass by quick.'

'C'mon. An extra quarter-hour while we open up the other cells won't be hurting no one. They'll be grateful for it.'

'You soft bastard. OK, fine.'

'They'll acclimatise best they can. Quicker, if we help in small ways.'

'We're letting 'em pray 'cos Teddy asked for it. What more do they need?'

'You're a jerk sometimes. I stood before the priest at your boy's christening, and you're mocking their right to prayer?'

''Cept, they've stopped seeing the chaplain. Prefer to hide in there. Pity party protest boys. You think they're banging each other?'

'You're ridiculous, d'you know that? Let them adapt.'

'I think about all the sex I ain't having, even when it's queers. So what? You get a certain way with these cases.'

'Quit playin' the fool and get the rest of this wing opened up. You heard how quiet it was. Nothing from their cell all night.'

'Too scared to cry or make noise. They should all be this frightened.'

'It's not fear ... more like, faith. Give them their extra minutes. Let them be.'

3.

The children's protest has dwindled to a core of twenty people, the news folks had also moved on after a week with other stories demanding their attention; the music getting quieter, the gathering itself smaller and better behaved, more of an outdoor study group than a movement to topple judicial decisions.

'I'm telling you this,' says Teddy, 'because I know that you'll pull my ear until it's blue if you learn this from someone else once you get out. They can't agree about anything. Arguing like street bitches in front of the camera. Differences of opinion regarding who should speak and what they should say. Your names stopped being mentioned and they used the forum to air other grievances, small fry that the news folks had no interest in recording. I told them to expand further on their mistreatment by the police when they were barred from entering the square and everything before that, but they were woozy on detail and sounded unconvincing. I asked them to roll up their sleeves so that the cameras could pick up on any bruising that they may have received, but they were marked in parts from physical squabbles with each other, so no one injury was clear. They don't make things easy for themselves with this nonsense. Their passion is authentic, their credibility, not. Look, you'll be out sooner than you think with good behaviour. Just be patient and do your bird like good folks. Feed quietly from the trough. I can work on making things comfortable when you leave. There are things the City may do. Certain financial obligations to clear up this mess. It'll be easier for everyone if this mess goes away. It'll be up to you to decide whether the cushion they present is plump enough.'

Teddy's office talk. The garbage he spews from his desk. Is it easier for him to believe these things from a distance rather than tell it to our faces? How much truth does he escape by dangling a carrot between phone lines? Is there relief when we suddenly hang up before he's finished, or a further attack of nerves? We wonder whether this offer was Teddy's idea or formulated elsewhere: a criss-cross of negotiation between City chambers and a lawyer's boardroom.

Who gets to decide whether money can make this thing go away? It will not shorten our jail time, that is clear. Money is easier to produce than the information we asked for. Signing off cheques, cashing them, is a mechanical exercise, nothing strenuous in their obligation; simply a figure hidden on an obscure spreadsheet, later to be written-off.

We have not earned money for months, behind with our rents and bills. For all the magic Teddy has conjured, small pillows from his salary to ensure we are not slung out on to the street, that we are fed and warm, pales with what he is now offering. We are working a job by being in jail, for which our salary will be presented upon release; salarymen, like Teddy, with obligations that hover above our cheque. Money has been the root of disagreement between us. We've argued over a dime, ready to cut a bitch over monies owed or denied, but we needed no conference before we refused Teddy. It is the easiest decision we make, for money cannot compare to the luxury we have. We could be overfed billionaires yet still we would crave a pencil-thin mattress and the comfort of the dark.

Our silence cannot be bought because it remains our choice whether to speak. Freedom is power of choice. Even from the confines of our cell, we can be felt, buried, but somehow still visible below the earth; our body heat radiating through mud and clay. We wish to write letters but correspondence can be redacted, negating the impact of what we wish to say. We can access a computer but we do not wish to rant, knowing that our measure can only be revealed by the space for thought that using pen and paper gives us. It's how we were schooled; how we learned.

We think of the flow of mail to and from prison, how writing becomes an industry in itself, the way the notorious cement their mythology. We are none of these things, just ordinary people refusing to shut down over the same question: where are our children? In many ways, we do not wish to correspond with anybody, but how best to share what we know? We would write to the children but they're never home to receive letters; the notes we would leave around our apartments to remind them of their obligations regarding mess and dinner attendance, or simply to wish them a good day, either discarded or ignored; the cards or Post-its gathering dust and hair, becoming more a missive to ourselves as we spiralled in and out of gloom.

By writing we wish to encourage the children in their stand; for them to know that they are appreciated but in no way bound; how they should be free to protest in their way and over what they choose. We are footnotes in their manifesto, nothing more, and this we accept. But would they resent our letters, seeing them as intervention that was sour and bordered on the meddling; disqualified jockeys who keep to the track, busting their guts to find a way back into the race.

When is the time to retire, to hush your mouth and retreat? How does a man leave his firm after decades of service only to return back to it? Letters would be wasted on the children. They would not cherish us in the way we wished to be cherished. Our words would be half-read and, in most cases, not responded to. Teddy, also, would see our letters as foolishness, unless there was something contained therein which was admissible – on either side.

'We're talking on the phone, now you're writing letters, too? Do you not have better things to do with your time? Are there programmes within the prison that you wish to attend that I can petition for? Library. Laundry. Something that will occupy your minds and take you out of yourselves.'

Teddy wants our facts over feelings. He can act upon facts; delegate. He does not have the vocabulary to discuss anything outside of this. In many ways he does not want to know. His presence is a physical one, his help, tangible and constant. He will glance at the letters and never think of them again, wishing to reduce what we say into the rantings of a group of depressives, whose ardent faith had left them unhinged. We do have the tenacity to keep a diary and also fear it being destroyed by hooligans, in or out of uniform, before our release. We do not have the strength to create something so precious to watch it being torn apart or flushed away as punishment. The only person we can write to is the prison chaplain, whom we've barely seen, realising that our words will not be redacted if they stay within these walls. Stories that remain sealed by bar and brick. Also we can hold him to account, spit words on paper rather than in his face – which was our initial desire: to excise our abuse and tear his compliant face apart. That bitch can sell our letters afterwards and die from guilt. He should drink our venom as if it's the blood of Christ.

'Write us some letters, man. We'll pin them to the wall. My kids don't speak to me because of the reasons that got me here. Your boy here got kids from three different women. Doesn't know where the hell they are. Everything we got on these walls is old. We need fresh love. Something new.'

How to tell our cellmates that we are not capable of kindness, too intent are we on murdering by letter; cursing the chaplain to filth in a way that brings about his death. For every prayer he has recited we wish to offer an alternative; releasing curse after curse until there is balance in the universe. It demands something greater than a series of letters: a book of spells, by witches who are sick and tired of this shit and will not take it any more.

'Why is it you stopped praying? That chapel's a ratchet place so I can see how you could outgrow it. It's a prison cell as much as this one. How you get redeemed in a room with no air and no windows, I have no idea. You might as well set up an altar in a cave. But you stopped praying, man, in here, and we don't understand why that's happening. In other people there'd be something funny 'bout it. Like proof that their faith was never genuine in the first place, but not you cats. Muthafuckas are the real deal! Something in what you were doing made even our stringy hearts want to believe. So when we see you cutting prayers from your time it worries us. How you no longer stand together in your circle on waking and before bed. How you've stopped saying grace before your food. Our stretches are long, understand. We have very little before us. Nothing on the horizon. You stop saying your prayers and we have less to fill our day. One thing less to mock. One thing less to aspire to. How do you plan on using your time if you stop going to chapel? You sent the library guy away, so books ain't on your mind. You're leaving most of your food as well. We see it. We see it.'

We no longer eat for the need to cleanse. We feel the polluted blood of Christ passing through our veins on our rare visits to chapel; nourishing our cells with untruths, wishing only to flush it away. We want those blood cells to deteriorate and die – heretics all – and for new cells to be born, stronger and more powerful in their delivery. We are weaker without food, aware of the flatness in our stomachs and chests, hollowness emerging in our cheeks, drawing further attention to the darkness in our eyes; the ability to lie flat on our mattresses and pray in the dark, seeing the purity of intention only in the clandestine. Praying to what makes sense to us, our gospel, over the muck we have been fed. We can only return to chapel if prison staff are not present, and even then our formation will change; how we use the space; where exactly to stand. The Apostles started their work from the same position of uncertainty; prayers to be formed in their language; their darkness; their light; we will not allow ourselves to be distracted again.

'Listen to what we're saying. You folks are new but we're the old guard. We see what happens when people lose their way. They become dead in the face. Crumble to dust. You guys are hardly a bunch of comedians but you know how to speak without opening your mouths. Look how one of yous stopped wearing the earrings you always wear; the ones you bartered for a tube of half-used toothpaste your second day here. You wore those damn hoop earrings in the shower like you were cooling down from a day at the beach. Knowing how they caught the light and just how to tilt your head to accentuate them. Hooker at the traffic lights working those earrings into the ground. Made us laugh, but damn, you got props for that. But now you ain't wearing them. Already it lessens your face. Learn from history. What not to do. You are resilient muthafuckas. Show me that. If you truly fear God, then your beef with those in charge here means nothing. Don't hide, man. Go back to your chapel. Let them serve you. Have them reciting those prayers until they have no breath left. Let them bless you until the pins and needles in their fingers travel up their arm and chest. Allow them to give communion until they keel over and turn blue. We expect great things from you talkative bastards. You cannot let us down by hiding away.'

'The two of us are giving you bitches tough love. Your strength outranks theirs because what you bring is something to be feared. They only turned when they heard how you blessed that boy pissing blood in the bathroom. Oil slick on holy water. Repelling all that you are. We were blown that you're in the blessing game now. You're legit prophets now. We didn't see it coming, same as those who locked you up. Only difference is we ain't threatened by your powers. We dig what you do, from the smart-ass sidelines. They could never do as you do. They don't have the backbone, understand. Ain't fit to clean your shoes, but you must return and let them attend on you. We won't allow you to become invisible here. No, sir. That is in no one's interests. In more open wings, we'd be charging those in need for our pep talks. You ain't the only ones who're old hands with their magic. Come to our pep talk and leave the cell with a renewed sense of optimism, but also one of obligation to us. Favours to be called in at a time of our choosing, whether here or on the outside. Anything from a con changing their brand of cigarettes to one we stocked, to a job opening for a member of our families. Look at your faces. Don't worry, son, this ain't the same kind of deal. We were raised around faith for long enough to know when something is genuine. Your need for prayer comes from a place beyond vocation. You ain't careerists, like the folks in charge. There's no peace in their faces, only shiftiness. Why d'you think they talk so? We're only saying this so that you're clear when someone dissects it afterwards. That your cell brothers had no agenda other than goodwill and a desire that you should not crumble at the reality of what this place is. Go back to chapel and say your prayers. When you feel lifted, energised, you'll thank us for the hard time we're giving you now. What you pray to is of no concern to us. It could be a frog prince or celebrity hoe for all we care. What you have gives you strength, whether it comes from a crucifix or a light you already carry. A light you prefer to hide. It's what gives you power, and power, we recognise. You won't change your situation by refusing food. They'll only interpret that as sulking that you're no longer being treated like princesses. You could hang yourselves and they would say you were just crying out for attention. These motives they understand, crocodile tears that fall from their skin. When they open the chapel door and see you knelt in prayer, they do not understand the process is familiar, but what you absorb is unknown. They won't take that away from you. The privileges you've been granted are specific in their detail, and they'll not allow themselves to be accused of religious hatred, either by the authorities or by their own families. Instead, they'll create conditions that force you to give it up for yourselves, to prove to everyone that you had no faith in the first place. That it was as substantial as a dog whistle, not a bell. Them bells ringing in your head? Is this yanking your chain? If so, show us, by rising from your cots.

Get on your feet and pull on clothes that aren't pyjamas. Hook those earrings back into your lobes and rap on the door. Tell them it's time for evening prayers and that you're ready to go. Pray for your appetite to come back. Pray for your memories to return. That hustlers cannot be downed by overweight bullies with no imagination. Return to prayers. Makes these screws work for you until they're exhausted from your devotion, for nothing is possible without strength.'

Our knees bruise easily from the weight our bodies force them to bear as we kneel on the cell floor. It's three weeks since our last visit to chapel; our bodies losing all memory of what we ask them to do. Each rise and fall, every pose is studied and marked; a rehearsal for a more public display of faith, if we can get ourselves together. We are soothed in ways that we don't understand; something primal in our need for enlightenment which cannot be hidden or discouraged; the need for this particular brand of knowledge, which cannot be delivered from our cell brothers, for it must come from our hand; those we must help; those we can deliver. Only now we understand.

TEDDY'S CITY [iv]

Bridge & Tunnel

1.

He will not live by rules of divine judgement. Those days are over for him. His mistakes are paid for on this earth, not in a higher state that he can no longer imagine. For messing up his posting he's moved to a less demanding project with far greater supervision. This is a fair exchange. Without punishment you do not learn. His weakness in letting the protest on the square turn into a near gunfight; the carnival of the second protest, a movement with an anger and energy he recognised and almost understood; both had been addressed and sanctioned.

Now, from a grubby locker room at the edge of the highway where he observes mutinous airport workers, he is satisfied that he has been fairly dealt with. Each report sent on baggage handler dissent eased his overall debt. Nothing more complicated than submitting one name at a time. In completing the posting he would be square, able to walk through City Hall with purpose; confidence lighting his face. Those with longer memories he would avoid or learn to push aside.

His anguish on seeing the Mothers jailed – in his mind, an act that would only ever have seen them cautioned – dissipates on learning of their stubbornness; how they continue to make things difficult for themselves by observing silence. If at any point in court they'd opened their mouths, the City would have had a case to answer; one story against another; flimsy evidence malleable to a judge's differing beliefs. Dressed in the same clothes they were arrested in: joggers, wigs and shawls; nothing made them look serious or penitent. Only he knew that they had nothing to be penitent about: their drag was defiance; but they could have helped themselves by playing the game instead of their wilful ignorance of it; sitting on the bench, blank, as if they had no emotion left; leaving it for him to feel what they could not – bottomless fear, his insides in free-fall for the three days of the trial.

It was weeks after the verdict before he was able to land, grieving for the Mothers and for his mistake; wishing for physical punishment to be meted out: a heart attack from the stress, or a random beating in the street. He ached for his body to be maimed by another hand, picking up the roughest trade he could find for sex, gangster boys, whose queerness was blocked from their minds; starting traffic arguments for no reason other than to force a punitive measure.

He could think no further than that moment, a rupture

or blow that would cause him to double down, temporary paralysis that twisted his insides and stopped the blood flow; something to remind him that he was accountable; that divine intervention would flex its hand if the Mothers were unable. He longed obsessively for a highly visible action: to be beaten for wearing the wrong jeans, for his heart to seize at the top of a staircase. He could not take his payback in the dark like a coward, championing unexpected humiliation, understanding that only through this could he be free.

But putting all his energy into inciting chance action was faith of another kind, and he was through with faith. What he hoped for would not come: the instant gratification from a well-aimed punch. If he was struck down by anyone it was down to him being a prick and nothing to do with the Mothers. Only they could punish him, but how could they if they were not aware? This he was not brave enough for, unable to predict the outcome. In their current mind frame he could just as easily be forgiven as cast aside. His choice was to allow the memory to fade. The harder he worked at the airport, the easier it would become to see the man with the gun as a stranger; an amateur with dirt falling from his hands.

At the airport he monitored the productivity of those working on the ground, shifting bags on to trolleys with the other boys, listening to cleaners gripe their management complaints over a cigarette or in the safety of the restroom, sympathising and chipping in when required. During breaks he wrote down the names of complainants in his notebook, to be expanded upon in the reports he wrote each evening. He'd been downgraded to a rat in overalls, scarring his hands with toil. He felt the vertebrae in his lower back warping as he tugged suitcases filled to bursting, grunting with effort to keep up with the other men.

There was relief in work so linear, reminding him of his college years jobbing on the trash detail. His treatment at the City's hands differed from his colleagues. Those who drank at the club, who took boat trips with each other's wives, or prayed at the same church, had a softer descent. At City Hall he'd worked alongside men who stole, or bent the rules to make their lives more comfortable; falsifying building permits to enable them and their families to extend their houses; putting their children at the top of lists for schools for which they were not eligible; taking backhanders from developers wanting to bulldoze unprofitable buildings to make way for more lucrative apartments or stores. Those who did not have to study so hard to find their way to a desk. Those whose childhoods were not punctuated with uncertainty; whose desks were littered with pictures of happy families – whether an image or reality, this was something he could not produce; not one that they would recognise.

The minor digressions of these men were swept aside; only when there was the threat of accountability to an outside agency was action ever taken, and in most cases many simply stayed in their existing departments. He accepts that the rules are different. His origins make it so, yet at the same time he is grateful to avoid their treatment, becoming more alert and determined because of it. His salary is scaled down, making him hungry in both ways. He fills his hours at the airport. Bides his time.

During the week he sleeps at a cheap highway motel that borders the airport, returning to his apartment at weekends, where lawyers' letters and other business of the Mothers await him. Each Sunday he visits each Mother's apartment, cleaning and sorting through their mail. He could leave this to one of the children, but doesn't trust them not to fill the place like a flophouse, and to rifle through what is precious: rails of clothes no longer worn, and photographs of those no longer here.

Once the windows are opened, it takes several minutes for the stale air to no longer stifle him, often holding himself there until the smell passes, distracted by the street scene below. Each sidewalk is home; from every window he spies historic markings of elation or despair. He's quicker to put their houses in order than his apartment. If the Mothers were released that day they would find their places in a better state than they left them: dry, clean and dust free. Bar food in the ice box, each apartment is ready for them to lay their head; to recover and make sense of what they've been through.

He can bring no softness to what they're experiencing in jail – a set of T-shirts and washbags is poor insulation for what they find there. In many ways, it is the reason he has avoided visiting, hiding behind excuses of not wanting to upset them. It is he who will blanch at what he finds; their fragility enhanced by their surroundings; how jail time reduces them, haunted by their hollow eyes and inability to speak.

His fussing over their apartments: fresh flowers replaced in a vase on the coffee table before leaving, changing bed linen and light bulbs, can only be deciphered as compulsive behaviour in their absence; a pilgrim taking care of his shrine. Only on their return will his efforts be appreciated; how all that they long for has been anticipated and provided. His own apartment remains a shambles, rotting food and dirty laundry piling high. He has taken to buying shirts from an outlet near the airport rather than tackle the mountain of laundry, wastefully throws away socks and underwear rather than rinse them under the hotel sink; money he can ill afford on poorly stitched nylon boxers. His stomach flips between spasms and contractions from the lack of fresh food: finding burgers and subs the quickest to fill him up when hungry.

He looks at his co-workers eating fish and rice prepared by their loved ones, garish Tupperware lining every bench, and understands then how poorly qualified he is to judge them with his insides rotting from lack of care. Whose standards does he defend if he cannot even look after himself, looking for any distraction to avoid thinking about his personal deficit? The laziness and duplicity he reports upon each night, he mirrors in his private life. If those he betrayed saw how he lived, they would shake their heads, partly from pity, but mostly from bewilderment that a fool could be given dominion over their livelihoods; that their work – and loyalty – would be judged by a man who ate cold soup from a can.

The children drop by the motel some evenings to ask why he doesn't visit them; their hands idly passing over his things, appraising what to discard and what to keep. They come to nag and borrow money. Never leaving until their pockets are filled.

'You too uptown for tacos now? Has education priced you out of that market?'

Those who have no boundaries have difficulty under-standing when others are strictly governed between lines.

'I have work.'

'Don't blame your job, Teddy. We all got jobs that can be wriggled out of. Your problem is that you're not creative. You have the imagination of a pen-pusher. Can't see what's beyond your desk.'

He visits them, of course: late night, keeping his distance; seeing all that he needs to from the end of the street. He smells the fire that burns in the parking lot well before he turns the corner, smoke spiralling across blocks before being swallowed into night. They are quieter than he imagined, talking in groups, laughing, but without the confrontational note of before. There is little aggression to be had in a cluster of groups sitting in battered plastic chairs, smoking and eating food. Without the placards it's a hangout with benefits; spice, beer, company, the promise of sex. There are enough strangers in their circle to make it so. He recognises the body language in their flirtation dances, feels a pang that he is not so forward. How much of this protest is of their making, and how much is down to a correlation of circumstance? The restaurant and the parking lot has been a gift. They have not had to fight to physically define their space in the same way as the Mothers . . . yet.

That time will come, when they are stopped from pissing where they want, refused jobs or apartments for no other reason than pure dislike; when religious freedom denies their right to marriage. Where they looked at the Mothers' behaviour with incredulity, they will latterly understand the logic: how shit only changes when they don wigs and bear arms. Their good times will not last and everything they take for granted will be ripped from them if they do not fight, but he will make them ready. For now, he doesn't know whether he resents how carelessly they sit in their chairs, or if he wants to congratulate them on finding an easier way.

If a club party in plain sight makes its point, then who is he to judge? He should be crossing the street to order a round of tacos but cannot bring himself to move out of shadow; wanting to see that the children are safe without tripping over himself; botching his good intentions by turning parental and sermonising. He lacks the ease of the

Mothers, who always knew how to talk to them. Then, as now, he feels stranded between them – too old to be their sister, too young to earn their respect as a mother. In this undefined space he exists.

'Seriously. Come by the place and see us. We need to be brought into line from time to time. Ken would be pleased to see we've a responsible adult to mind our well-being.'

'You mean a contact to chase for all the things you break. He gives you his restaurant and you wreck the spot. How many broken plates and glasses?'

'That too. We don't want you left out. Not saying come sit in our filth every night, but find a way to be part of it. We miss you not being there.'

'You miss someone asking to turn the music down?'

'Just looking for someone to blame when it goes wrong. If you're not there, who do we have?'

He relaxes by watching night flights from his window, or from a bench in the motel car park if the weather is good; the lumbering fleet of DC-10s taking flight; the far end of the runway in tandem with the highway and motel. Night birds of another kind, flying to cities he's never been to, places of mythic status in his mind, both of his country and overseas. As a young man standing on the rooftop of one of the Mothers' apartment buildings, he'd let his aspirations be carried by those flights; his dreams crossing to the opposite coast; ever reaching, his hope travelling oceans. Now he guards the scant optimism he has left, not to be shared or expelled, almost unbelieving that he once had so much of it. What he now has to offer can only drag the plane back towards the tarmac, its frame unable to bear the weight of past foolishness.

'If things are getting stale here, you can travel. Your job could take you anywhere if you flattered the right people. We can take care of the Mothers.'

'It's not as easy as that. What's here is what I have. It can't be thrown into a holdall and shipped to another city.'

'Dazzle them with your education. Do whatever you have to. You look tired of it.'

'I'm tired from not getting enough sleep. Do you know how noisy those damn planes are?'

'It's a different kind of tiredness. Since the trial. Don't think that we fail to notice things 'cos we're running around in cut-off denims trying to be beautiful.'

They speak as children sending their parents away, only to wait anxiously at the door once the thrill of the first few nights has worn off. Willing mischief, but knowing that they'll tire of it. The freedom they wish for belongs to them alone, same as the Mothers; what he provides is a safety net, permanently tethered. His dreams of walking the streets of another city are real ones, but the fear of vertigo remains; how he'll be unable to set one foot in front of the other, unsure of what to do or how to spend his time. Something crumbles in the knowledge that you are no longer needed; he anticipates how previous certainties will fade; that he is not the type of man who can rebuild. Those who lose everything through war or catastrophe, who have the strength to begin again, new homes and families, entire identities rebuilt from carbon and ash. People have made this happen, he thinks. It's recorded. You can become another person simply by willing it to be, recalling his brothers and the possibilities of those who disappeared; whether they have the bravery he lacks; how they were able to move on because their reserves were greater. What he creates from himself only exists in this limited space: this city; these blocks. Maybe there is something to be said for a man who knows his limits, recognising how little effort his colleagues make to extend past their desks. Good life right there, if he wants it. Desk jockey and night flights. All those reports on the ones who have the temerity to extend.

'Two of the prison guards' kids got meningitis the day after they beat the Mothers. Had their families praying to their chicken-head gods for a week.'

'That I didn't hear.'

'Kids were in hospital, pumped with antibiotics, or whatever it is they give them. Two kids in different households across the city. The doctors couldn't explain it.'

'Aside from the prison connection?'

'Except there was no sickness there, only that beating. I'm telling you, they're too scared to fuck with them now, the Mothers. They're untouchable.'

His blood rises on hearing this but he says nothing to the

children, clear now that divine intervention reveals itself; bastard men remembering their fear of God.

When he emails the Mothers they mention nothing of this, only what they're up to; their daily routine now supplemented with an hour of washing dishes in the prison kitchen. He wonders whether it's in their nature to forgive; if their neglect in telling him this story is a reflection of their fear of magnanimity. He is too bull-headed for either, wanting to find out where the guards live and all the information he can get on their detail. His instinct is to tear them apart, to find a place and point where their vulnerabilities lie, to humiliate them the way he imagines the Mothers were humiliated; his contribution to addressing ignorance and the arrogance of muscle. He will burn those meatheads until they are husks, make them worry for their jobs and pensions. He wants to see them hosing sewers by the time he's done; ready to swing their necks from the bars they cowardly hide behind. But he will not do any of these things. His is a world of regulation and governance. If he does not believe in the power of these as instruments of change, why did he put himself through the trials of education? If the regulation books should be torn up, why is he not in the taco car park whooping it up over a round of warm margaritas? His faith is in these rules, untangling and reshaping them; to rewrite all that is archaic; to challenge what is unfair. Even on a losing streak he can make himself known by using his voice. So the prison guards got heavy – that can be addressed. He may lack both the testimony and the photographic evidence, but he has the sickness of their children and, as importantly, their superstition. This he can use: letterhead and the language of folklore to unravel all that they hold close until they fray to the barest twine; flayed to soft flesh like his own community who only wished to trust.

Every afternoon before we leave, Tasty bakes us a custard, the Mothers write. He holds some eggs aside and skims off the cream from those he says don't deserve it. They produce too much bile to handle dairy, he says. It tears them up inside. The custards, baked in coffee cups, are barely set, and sweet. Teddy boy, you would love it. The consistency is silky; the taste, eggy and rich. Sometimes the top will be dusted with nutmeg if he is allocated it, other times cinnamon dust from the bottom of cereal packets. Even plain, with its slightly burnt top, it's a blessing. When you plunge a spoon into the cooled cup it makes the most delicious sound. Clapping like children every time we hear it. You're hit with the scent of vanilla from the scant drops he loads into the mixture, stoppered from a precious jar he keeps hidden at the bottom of a drawer. All the good stuff is like gold dust, here. It's the warmth and sweetness that we remember most during the day. The last thing we recall before falling asleep. We should recall other things, but we jonesin' for these custards. It's the hunger for more that keeps us returning to the kitchen day after day, to wash plates though the heat, our hands covered with spittle and congealed food waste. Our fingers wrinkled until we resemble newborns. But still we return for our treats. The sacramental wafer nourishes us, but this is life. A little comfort is all that we ask for. That, and a place to lay our heads.

AMERICAN ICONS

1.

We walk museum hallways most days; late afternoon when it becomes quieter; certain passages where the hush has a reverential quality; forgotten chambers where obscure Masters can be laid to rest. No one celebrates our true icons now – those rising from the street who paved the way; not the ones who merely wore good trainers or fucked the right people, but true warriors whose single-mindedness to live their truth came before the desire to be known. We are not dropping hints by spending time in these places, more that the gentility found in certain corridors in obscure museums allows us to gather our thoughts and slowly become ourselves. Walking hallways like we are someplace else; remembering our posture, the flow of steps returning like thawed muscle memory. The clank of our leather heels on parquet flooring feels like love, restorative and brave. Painters came to the balls, but never asked us to sit for their work. Photographed plenty, but never painted. We walk and let the ring of our steps speak to us, upper notes that bounce across the walls in an attempt to engage those immortalised on canvas or bronze; peasants from the street who caught an artist's eye; queens who could only disseminate their message through their hairstyle and clothing. We pass tyrants and martyrs and learn from both. We walk corridors flanked by religious icons feeling unworthy to look at them directly, simply bowing down in the presence of saints. The power is in our walk and dress; the thickness of our wigs, and the dark of our shades. By walking here, we take solace from all that has passed, serving up something we intend to preserve; the summation of our experience, and what jail time has taught us. If not here, then where? Museum hallways are where we regain our equilibrium and presence of mind; the air cool and clean, no longer gagging on the heat and stink of incarceration; free from con brotherhood but also the danger; less revered now we are in the outside, but less expectation, too. We no longer have to hide.

What is sainthood and what is false? Would those icons we glide past rebut their deification had they the choice? Instead, bemused and mocking at their worship. What is deserved and what is opportunism? For whom does deification serve? By whose word is a miracle defined? We are flesh and blood misunderstandings, wishing to challenge what is attributed to us. Our faith is lost but no one can read it. Instead, they follow and attribute meaning into every step and incline of our head. Oh, we still don't speak; that habit is ingrained; silence defines who we are and our contempt for the world. Yet still we are deified.

Word spreads. If we sit with a boy panicking in his cell and stop him from killing himself just by our presence, we are deified. When we have the wigs pulled from our heads without resistance and are thrown down City Hall steps like we are nothing but rubbish to be bundled away, we are deified. When we rip our sheets to tie fabric around Sherry's wrist following a night of depression, when her inward actions are not of her right mind; holding that wrist tight until medical help arrives, our cumulative weight and faith resting on these fragile bones, we are deified. In hiding the blame we feel for the children we have failed – and Teddy for failing us – by holding our heads high we fool everyone but ourselves.

We are of the people, but are aware of our contradictions: how we wish to breathe the rarefied air afforded by our status and the sacrifices we have made, yet remain sleepless from the bravery we lack in seeing things through. How to explain this to those gathering around the museum entrance, as curiosity grows with passing days; that although we had just cause for our fire, knowing always that we would be taken down for acting a certain way, we still chose to go quietly. We reached the point of resistance and did not cross it. For this we are worshipped? For this they make noise? We are humbled but also frightened. We are sour, for sourness is all we have. Snobbish defences to keep us from falling apart.

The museum is where we must express now, bound by the terms of non-disclosure agreements; silence upon silence. We have not been bought; more, funded; using City blood money to fund the children's endeavours, protests at other blocks and in other cities; smaller but noisier; our pictures waved as mascots of wrongful arrest; but only in the far background, their placards taking prominence instead, arguing for justices beyond our neighbourhood. We are old and lack vision in their eyes, needed now only for our banknotes and our image as patron saints of neglected causes. Patron saints of the ballroom; patron saints of the dinner table and lost children; legendary mothers who ascended once they'd walked their last runway. Allow them their noise and leave us to ours; to walk, pose, reflect and fight, for there is still some energy left. We are undimmed.

Acknowledgements

Thank you: Suzanne Azzopardi, Lisa Baker, Gavin James Bower, Stuart Evers, Jenni Fagan, David Hayden, Kerry Hudson, Olivia Laing, Dan Lepard, Sharmaine Lovegrove, Andrew McMillan, Scott Pack, Nikesh Shukla, Chimene Suleyman, Dominic Wakeford.

Bringing a book from manuscript to what you are reading is a team effort.

Dialogue Books would like to thank everyone at Little, Brown who helped to publish *This Brutal House* in the UK.

Editorial
Sharmaine Lovegrove
Simon Osunsade
Dominic Wakeford

Production
Nick Ross
Narges Nojoumi
Mike Young

Contracts
Megan Phillips

Publicity
Millie Seaward

Sales
Sara Talbot
Ben Green
Rachael Hum
Viki Cheung

Marketing
Jonny Keyworth

Copyeditor
Alison Tulett

Design
Helen Bergh
Nico Taylor

Proofreader
Sandra Ferguson